Montgomery Plum is a fantasy fictional writer and is the author of 'The Fantastical Chronicles of Montgomery Plum' series of books. His stories catalogue his adventures through a wish list of the macabre where he fights killer aliens, solves gruesome mysterious murders, grapples with the undead, and experiences the downright silly. But unlike the character in his stories Montgomery Plum is totally scared of heights, absolutely terrified of confined spaces, and petrified of anything that is even slightly dangerous. In truth, he would never be the hero in real life, so he chooses to spend his time on this mortal coil writing about them.

To all the lost souls.

Montgomery Plum

The Fantastical Chronicles of Montgomery Plum

The Last Knightmare of Halloween

LONDON * CAMBRIDGE * NEW YORK * SHARJAH

Copyright © Montgomery Plum 2025

The right of Montgomery Plum to be identified as author of this work has been asserted by the author in accordance with sections 77 and 78 of the Copyright, Designs and Patents Act 1988.

All rights reserved. No part of this publication may be reproduced, stored in a retrieval system, or transmitted in any form or by any means, electronic, mechanical, photocopying, recording, or otherwise, without the prior permission of the publishers.

Any person who commits any unauthorised act in relation to this publication may be liable to criminal prosecution and civil claims for damages.

This is a work of fiction. Names, characters, businesses, places, events, locales, and incidents are either the products of the author's imagination or used in a fictitious manner. Any resemblance to actual persons, living or dead, or actual events is purely coincidental.

A CIP catalogue record for this title is available from the British Library.

ISBN 9781035895861 (Paperback)
ISBN 9781035895878 (ePub e-book)

www.austinmacauley.com

First Published 2025
Austin Macauley Publishers Ltd®
1 Canada Square
Canary Wharf
London
E14 5AA

Preface

Vengeance is a dish best served cold.
But not to Satan.
She likes her vengeance piping hot.

Chapter 1

Have you ever wondered what it would feel like to drill a hole into someone else's head?

No?

Not even slightly curious?

No?

Not even a teeny-weeny bit inquisitive about the whole thing?

No, seriously?

Fair enough, I suppose.

I guess it's not everyone's bag—if that's the saying I'm looking for—to drill holes into someone else's head.

Probably a niche market, I would imagine.

But the question is this: could you do it?

Could you take a drill, press it up against a hard, vein-throbbing skull, count down from three, and then just push it through until it goes no further?

That's the question.

And why?

Well, just for the thrill of it.

Just for the sheer unadulterated enjoyment and excitement of it all.

And don't get me wrong here, I know talking about this stuff feels weird.

It should feel weird.

Because drilling a hole into someone else's head is weird.

It's not quite as weird as drilling a hole into your own head, I grant you, and that's also been done, but it's still weird enough to be getting along with, for now.

But it does sound like fun, though, don't you think?

Uncooked, unrestricted fun, like fun used to be.

And we all know that everyone likes to have a bit of uncooked and unrestricted fun from time to time.

But I do get your anxiety about inflicting harm on others, it just seems rude, does it not?

And improper.

And nobody wants to appear rude and improper.

So, how about a compromise.

How about if you didn't have to drill all the way through to the *squidgy inside stuff* of the head—the brain matter, I believe it's called—but just far enough to unhinge a few cognitive processes?

Still no?

Really?

Wow, how very droll.

How do you get through life?

Well, if you're squeamish about this sort of stuff, then this might be a tough read.

Because this is a story about Halloween.

And not just any old Halloween, but the Halloween when Satan decided that she'd come up to the surface and grace us with her opinion of what a real Halloween should really be about.

And let me warn you, it wasn't the watered-down Halloween for wimps that we've got used to.

No, this Halloween was all about blood and guts and murder.

With plenty of misery and pain thrown in for good measure.

Just for the sheer hell of it.

And you will find it fun, I promise.

Yes, even you.

Even sweet little old you with your *I don't have any cannibalistic tendencies* lie you keep telling yourself—because everyone knows that we all have *that* slightly impish stain of curiosity running through the darkest crevices of our brains to see what it would feel like.

But I digress, so let's get back to the original question in hand.

That is the question of whether you've ever wondered what it would feel like to drill a hole into someone else's head.

Starting to sound attractive now, yes?

And certainly more attractive than watching a chap get eaten alive by his own socks; which also happened and was a sight to see.

But more on that ridiculous story later.

As for now, let's spoil ourselves on a night that'll be celebrated throughout the ages of time.

Where tales will be written of the cruelty and evil that got inflicted upon others.

When drilling holes into unsuspecting skulls, chopping up your fellow neighbour with an axe, and slicing open an occasional abdomen and eating the entrails is perfectly acceptable.

And not just acceptable but thoroughly encouraged.

And when wickedness and depravity ruled supreme.

And now I know that you're definitely interested.

I'll permit myself the indulgence of telling you all about the story of the last ever night of Halloween.

The greatest Halloween night that ever existed.

And the Halloween night when I, Montgomery Plum, came face to face with Satan herself.

So, let's begin at the beginning.

It was the dead of night in the old town of Glint Tae.

A cold and wintery All Hallows Eve, dead of night in the old town of Glint Tae.

Where not even the Beast of Blatherwycke Bill would dare to tread, or the Ogre of the Restless Mountains dares to frighten.

Just thither, with barely a soul in sight and the rain lashing down on its cobbled streets.

Yet, standing outside in the pouring rain, and seemingly oblivious to the torrential downpour, stood Lucy.

Just standing there.

Drenched from head to toe.

Soaked to the core, you might add.

Her gaze was transfixed.

Her eyes were hypnotised.

And there she stood; staring spellbound at a wall where a message had been written in blood.

Yes, written in blood.

Lucy didn't much care for messages written in blood.

And there was a reason for this.

Lucy was a medium, you see, so messages written in blood hit a particular kind of spot with her.

She was funny like that.

In fact, any messages written from a spiritual outlet hit a particular kind of spot with her.

And that was especially the case when the messages were written in blood.

As this one was.

And especially when the messages say things like:

Vengeance is a dish best served cold,
But not to Satan.
She likes her vengeance piping hot,
See you soon.

And as the grammar and spelling were on point, she instantly knew something was up.

Well, you would, wouldn't you?

'Oh, that's how you spell vengeance, is it?' she mumbled. 'I've always wondered that. And as for taking a common phrase and turning it round, well, that's inspired. But Satan saying she'll see us soon…that can only be bad.'

Lucy—as with the rest of us—knew that any visit from Satan, whether planned or unplanned, meant doom and destruction for all concerned.

She is Satan, after all.

And Satan is one bad bitch.

But not only that, but since Lucy had dragged herself from her pit this morning, she'd sensed that the Universe didn't feel as it did yesterday.

It felt like something was different.

And not different in a good way.

And she said as such, 'The Universe feels different today. And not in a good way.'

There, like I said.

'I've got a really bad feeling about all this,' she continued. 'I mean to say, who writes a message in blood these days, that's just eerie.'

She touched the wall.

The blood was still wet.

It was still warm.

It was still slowly moving down the wall as fast as gravity, and the resistance of friction would allow.

And she could feel the soul of the poor victim whose blood was still screaming to get out.

'Urgh, it's still warm,' she muttered alarmingly. 'This wasn't written long ago. Oh God, that's not good. Not good at all. Oh God…Oh God…Oh God.'

You could say, she was all a flutter.

And not the usual calm and in-control Lucy that we've all come to expect these days.

You know, since the change in medications.

But just then, a black crow flew past her head—just missing her rain bonnet by the merest of inches—and Lucy, being the superstitious type of old pudding that she was, got to thinking.

'Perhaps, if the message is gone, then it won't happen. Yes, that's it, out of sight, out of mind, so to speak. I'll just get rid of it, then Satan can't come here and say that she warned us all because she hadn't. And then the Universe will have to step in and tell her to bugger off back to Hell where she belongs and to leave us Dinglewits alone.'

And that was her thought process.

And if I'm being totally fair to Lucy—which I always try to be—I can see her viewpoint here.

Having messages from Satan written in fresh blood could mean nothing but trouble, and if she could remove it, well, that would all be for the good.

But, of course, the Universe doesn't work that way.

And deep down, Lucy knew it.

She'd had interactions with the Universe before, and she'd always found it a vindictive old git at the best of times.

And clearly, this isn't going to be one of those *best of times*.

But still thinking that removal was the more prudent option available to her, she hastily rustled inside her grocery bag for something to wipe the message off with.

'Now what do we have here?' she mumbled.

There was a pomegranate that she was hoping to enjoy later.

An aubergine, which would go nice with the steak she'd got yesterday.

Some mixed fruit, presumably to make a pudding of some sort.

And a turnip.

Nothing she could use to wipe away a threatening message from Satan.

And although she'd considered using the aubergine, she just knew it wouldn't work. Then, not only would she still have the writing on the wall, but then, she'd have nothing to go on the side of her plate tonight.

'Nope, right, that's all gone belly-up, then,' she announced. 'Erm, what now?'

She looked around for help.

But all that was left of the general population in Glint Tae was an elderly old man with an old wooden walking stick and scruffy coat. He was walking straight towards her.

He'd be no use, she thought, *although his scruffy coat might work.*

'Can I ask him that?' she continued mumbling. 'No, of course you can't, he needs that coat to keep him dry. Still, needs must…no, don't be mean, Lucy, you can't take an old man's coat, no matter the situation. Although…no, now leave it. Let him go home and sit by the fire and get warm. You'll be old one day, and how would you like having your coat stolen during a storm by some crazy lady who thinks that Satan is coming to kill us all? You wouldn't, would you? So leave him alone.'

But rather surprisingly, the old man didn't want to be left alone.

In fact, he had something to say.

'She is coming,' he stated. 'She is coming, so you best be ready.'

'Eh?'

'Satan…she is on her way. And when she gets here, all hell will break loose.'

Lucy was astounded.

And she had every right to be astounded.

For here was a decrepit old man who could barely walk from here to there—without the possibility of a coronary artery going pop—offering insights into a potential world-threatening apocalypse.

'Umm, yes, quite,' she answered, thinking it would be impolite not to say something in return for the generous statement. 'Erm, so do you know something then?'

'I know it's going to be quite a night,' he answered. 'It always is when Satan turns up. Plenty of death and blood.'

Lucy had figured that out for herself, she was quick like that.

'Any interaction with Satan ends up with plenty of death and blood,' she responded. 'Tell me something I don't know.'

'Ah, yes. But this will be different. So very…very different. It's going to be a massacre like never before. So you're going to need a plan, Lucy. You're going to need a plan if you're to get through this one.'

'Eh, what? What did you say? How do you know my name? Have we met before? Sorry, I don't remember you, erm, who are you?' she asked, now definitely more fascinated than she was 10 seconds ago. 'Have we met?'

'No, we haven't met,' the old man sniggered. 'Not in this timeline anyway. But I do have a message for you.'

Lucy was agog.

'You have a message? For me! Not in this timeline? What the hell is going on? Speak to me, old man, before I lose my shit. And trust me, you don't wanna be here when I lose my shit.'

'Ha, ha, yes, I suppose I wouldn't,' he chuckled. 'But, well, where do I start with your questions? Erm, yes, okay, you do have a message. It's from, well, let's just say, an admirer whom you don't know. But he *is* from this timeline, although not this dimension if you know what I mean?'

She didn't.

She didn't have a clue what was going on.

But she did like his voice.

A voice that could best be described as croaky.

Like he'd just eaten a spoonful of gravel and was yet to wash it down.

It comes with age, a voice like that.

'An admirer?' quizzed Lucy. 'What do you mean I have an admirer?'

'You have an admirer. Someone who appreciates your work. You have plenty of them, you know. You just don't know it. Anyway, there's no time for all that right now; the world is at stake, and you are needed to save it. But the message is simple. Be at the Old Chapel at Blorkeney Knoll for the Halloween party. It's imperative you are there, apparently. You simply must be there.'

Lucy knew the Old Chapel at Blorkeney Knoll well.

Very well.

And she wasn't that keen to be going through all that again after what happened last time.

'Be at the Old Chapel up on Blorkeney Knoll, whatever for? And who's this mystery admirer, can I ask? I don't like mystery admirers; they freak me out. So, can I ask who it is?'

'You can ask, but I don't really know, I'm afraid. Besides, you haven't met them yet, so it would be fruitless for me to tell you if I did know. Which I don't.'

'What are you on about?' Lucy squealed in a fit of controlled panic. 'And what do you mean I haven't met them yet? Is this some kind of time travel thingy, or something else that is totally creepy that I'm not going to understand? And all this writing on the wall stuff, does this involve me? And if so, why?'

She turned and looked at the message written in blood on the wall.

'Is this message for me?' she gasped. 'God, I hope not because that would be so scary.'

The old man offered little in the way of answers.

'These are very valid questions, my dear. But you see, I'm just the middleman here, no one tells me anything. I just do the work.'

'What do you mean, no one tells you anything, and you just do the work? They told you that the world is at risk and that I need to be at the Old Chapel at Blorkeney Knoll, didn't they? So, they've told you something.'

'Well, yes, okay, they've told me that, but that's just an inconsequential matter. What's important is that you're there, apparently. They stipulated that I must tell you that—'

'Oh they did, did they?' Lucy interrupted. 'Did they indeed? And did they tell you why, or who they were, or where they are…or…or how I'm supposed to sort all this mess out?'

This seemed to stump the old man somewhat.

His brain wasn't as young as it once was, although that particular statement is true for all of us, and it was safe to say that he was sailing three sheets to the wind, what with the lashing rain and all.

But anyway, in the eyes of Lucy, he seemed to know more than he was letting on.

She looked back at the message on the wall written in blood.

'And as for this,' she questioned. 'Is this a generic question for everyone, or just me? Because it looks like a warning that everyone should be aware of.'

But this time, there was no answer forthcoming, for the old man was no longer there.

He'd vanished into thin air.

Without a whoosh of sound or a puff of smoke.

Vanished.

'Hey, what! Where did you go?' Lucy screamed. 'How strange. And rude.'

But Lucy was rather getting used to strange.

Which I suppose you would do, wouldn't you? if you were a channel to the underworld, a so-called centre ground and soundboard for when the dead wished to speak with the living.

But this was something else entirely.

Something much more sinister.

And to be honest, she'd known this all day since the tarot cards that morning had warned her of such.

The Eight of Cups and the Six of Swords. She should've known something was brewing.

The spectacle of them two cards showing themselves at the same time never amounted to anything good.

So I guess some writing on a wall saying that Satan is itching for a fight was probably about right.

But there was nothing she could do just yet.

Not in the dead of a cold and wintery *All Hallows Eve* in the old town of Glint Tae.

A time when absolutely nothing dares themselves to the unknown threat of the darkness, and the only life that taunts the unforgiving nature of the dark will soon regret their recent life choices and shimmer back into the darkness where it can peacefully rest up for the night.

So she picked up her paper bag full of groceries and headed home to prepare herself for whatever was coming at the Old Chapel at Blorkeney Knoll.

And for the rest of the night, she laid out Tarot cards.

Threw bones.

Addressed the spirit world through her Ouija board.

And waited.

Chapter 2

Satan was having a really shit day.

There were no other words to explain it.

It was shit.

Totally shit.

And on today of all days as well.

Halloween…her special day.

Her very own…very special day…that she designed…just for herself.

It was her guarantee of a good night out.

Her only guarantee of a good night out.

Her only guarantee of a good night out, full of plenty of blood and guts and a hatful of gruesome murders.

With perhaps a little bit of torture, if the mood allowed.

Or even a decapitation or two if she got lucky.

But definitely something along those lines.

It was a night when she could carry out all of her vendettas in a civilised and bloodthirsty way that was socially acceptable, no questions asked.

Oh yes, Halloween was definitely a night she enjoyed.

Or at least she used to.

But now…it was shit.

Totally shit.

'Mummy,' asked Satan, as she sat perched on a stool in the kitchen eating breakfast, she preferred to perch, it looked cooler.

'Yes, darling.'

'Have you ever wondered what a brain tastes like?

'Come again?'

'Have you ever wondered what a brain tastes like? You know, all that the gooey stuff that slushes around inside the skulls of the living folk. I think it would taste like strawberries. I like strawberries. They have a little kick. Much better than lemons. Lemons are just sour and horrid. So yes, I think they'd taste of strawberries. I want to try one. What do you think, Mummy? Can you hear me?'

'Yes, I heard what you said. I was merely wondering why you think that's an appropriate question to ask at the breakfast table.'

'Oh, I'm just making conversation, that's all.'

'You don't make conversation, Satan, I know you all too well. You and conversation do not go hand-in-hand. Okay, I'll play along, why do you want to eat a brain?'

'Oh, I don't know. Just for the fun of it, I suppose. Just for the sheer gratification of it all. Yes, that's it, the sheer gratification of it all,' she yelled, as she bobbled up and down on the stool. 'After all, isn't that what life's all about, sheer gratification and pleasure at all cost? You and Daddy always told me it was.'

Mother acridly—if acridly is the word I'm looking for—glanced at Satan and sighed.

'Oh Satan, darling, is this really the conversation to be had over breakfast? Eating brains and gooey stuff and gratifications. Surely you must have better things to fill your tiny, despicable mind. Honestly, I don't know what gets into you these days.'

'Nothing gets into me, Mummy. That's the point. I've not had anything in me for ages. No demons. No spirits. No ghouls or ghosts. No wannabee satanist looking for notoriety. Nothing. I honestly can't remember the last time I was possessed; it's been so long. And as for fun! I haven't had any fun in ages. Not real fun, anyway.

'Not the kind of fun that grabs you by the innards and ties them in knots until you puke. Not that kind of fun. Can you remember the last time I laughed, Mummy? You know, proper belly laughed…a proper belly laugh until I chucked. Because I can't. That's how long it's been.'

'It's not been that long, my little darling. You laughed the other week, don't you remember? When you saw that ship hit a rock and sink to the bottom of the ocean. Everyone on board perished, some quite slowly, as I recall. I've never heard you laugh so much. Do you remember that?'

'Oh yes, that was funny, wasn't it?' Satan acquiesced. 'But apart from that, Mummy, apart from that, there's been nothing. Honestly, death has been such a drag recently. And so has Hell. Honestly, the whole place has become as dull as dishwater. I need some serious fun before I literally explode in a ball of fire.'

'Well, what about that volcano the other week, you enjoyed that, didn't you? It caused total devastation. Everything was ruined and covered in lava. I remember you laughing at all the little stone structures of Dinglewits in their various poses as they went about their daily lives before getting covered in ash. In fact, I've never seen you laugh so much.'

'Oh yeah, that was funny, I have to admit. I think I even did a little wee. Oh, you don't get entertainment like that very often.'

Mother smiled.

It was the sort of smile that you only smile when you're slightly embarrassed to be smiling about something that you shouldn't really be smiling about.

You know, a bit like when you see someone trip over and bash all their front teeth in.

Or when an over-excited jumper misjudges a gap and falls to their death.

That sort of smile.

The sort of smile you try to hide when others are looking.

'And then there was the train wreck,' Mother continued. 'Oh, and the war in the mountains. Honestly Satan, you've had plenty to be happy about. So why all this nonsense about eating brains and being bored? When I was your age, that was all we had. We had to make our own fun. You kids are spoilt these days, that's your problem. You don't know how to make your own fun.'

Satan didn't answer.

Not in words, anyway.

She was feeling too stroppy for words.

Plus, she was all out of sorts.

And, as it turned out, it was not because she hadn't been enjoying some good old-fashioned destruction either; because Mother had debunked that notion.

No, it was because her own very special day had been ruined.

Halloween.

Her day.

Her own, very special, very unique day for a very special girl.

Her.

Satan.

The very reason why Halloween was set up in the first place.

But now it was ruined.

Wrecked.

Kaput.

Taken apart by big corporations and over-commercialisation.

Simply to make money.

And in Satan's defence, she wasn't the only one being grumpy because Halloween had become overly commercialised, either.

For years now, every penny-pinching fun-thief on planet Earth had been giving it the big 'un that the whole darned thing was just another commercial gimmick designed to rid them of their hard-earned crowns, which of course, it was. It was better when it was less governed and allowed to remain underground.

And many would change it if they had the power.

Satan agreed with them.

Only she did have the power to do something about it.

And do something about it, she was.

'It's Halloween, Mummy.'

'What is?'

'The source of my grumpiness. I'm sick to the back teeth of it all. All the jolliness and happiness. It makes me wanna pull my own teeth out. It was supposed to be gruesome and horrible, not happy and jolly. It's like, *oh, I dunno, watching your favourite mortuary burn down*. It's all gone too far. This wasn't what I had in mind.

'And it wasn't the original idea because I remember what it was. This is an abomination of what Halloween was supposed to be all about. So I'm going to knock it on the head, Mummy. Enough is enough. That's it. This whole abhorrent farce must come to an end. And it must come to an end tonight.'

Now, the problem was that ending Halloween on a high wouldn't be as straightforward as one might have thought.

It simply wasn't a case of just unleashing hell and destroying the entire Dinglewit civilisation in one fell blow. The Universe simply wouldn't stand for it.

The Universe, you see, had forged a fondness for Dinglewits.

It thought they were a funny species which was always falling over and walking into stuff.

Hilarious.

And quite possibly one of its favourite inventions.

And at the end of the day, even Satan was at the whim of the Universe; so getting rid of its favourite fad without its permission would almost certainly mean curtains for her.

And as sure as the Universe made little green men with pointy tentacles on their heads, she'd not be getting its permission.

And in this case, asking for forgiveness is definitely not easier than asking for permission.

So she began thinking up ways to end the sordid affair once and for all, and in a way that provided, at least, a small token of entertainment for her troubles.

After all, a bit of laughter was the least she deserved after so many years wasted on second-rate costumes and fake blood, she concluded.

'Yes, that's it! I'm going to end Halloween, Mummy. I'm going to call it a day and cancel the whole thing. This year will be the very last night of Halloween.'

Back at the breakfast table, Mother cut a generous slice of pumpkin pie and passed it over to Satan.

This was always a guaranteed way to cheer up her grumpy bones when she was on a bit of a downer.

And which was normally followed up by agreeing with everything she said.

Mother knew her daughter well.

'Well, if you say so, Petal,' she offered. 'But please cheer up, won't you? I can't bear you moping around the house like this. It's doing my head in. I've got enough on my plate at the moment as it is; what with the discovery of a new vaccine that is undoing all my hard work. Honestly, you'd think that these blighters enjoy living to a ripe old age, wouldn't you? And Gawd knows why, they're just making the place look untidy.'

Satan sighed, realising that her problems probably paled into insignificance compared to the responsibilities of her elders.

And she knew that one day, she too would be answerable for providing a method of mass population control when she acquires the position of *Chief-in-charge of Hell*. Then her whittling on about small matters such as one silly night of the calendar year will have to stop.

And that made her even more gloomy.

'Yeah, okay, soz,' she mumbled, reaching over for a small corner of pie.

'That's okay. It's what I'm here for. Look, I know being a Satan is a difficult gig, we've all struggled from time to time. It's just a cross we must bear. It's about knuckling down and finding solutions. Being proactive. So, this little problem with the Dinglewits enjoying themselves on Halloween is just something you need to find an answer to. So, what are you going to do about it, eh? Just sitting here being all irritable isn't going to solve your problems, is it? Find a solution. That's what you need to do.'

Satan jumped up from the table.

'I'm ending it. That's what I'm going to do. I'm ending it. And I'm ending it tonight. I'm gonna jolly well go up there and give them all a good seeing to.'

'Tonight, Dumpling? Are you sure? You know what you're like in the cold. And you know what happens when you just jump into making decisions like this. You end up regretting it in the morning.'

'Yes, I'm positive. And not only am I ending it, but I'm ending it with a bang. The biggest bang ever to hit the Universe. Well, since the Big Bang, anyway. This is going to be the best last night of Halloween there ever was. It's going to be a bloodbath, just like I did to the humans that year, do you remember? That was a night to remember, eh? It was total carnage. From village to village and as far as the eye could see, there was nothing but a running stream of blood. D'ya remember, Mummy?'

Mother did remember.

The entire universe remembered.

It was hard not to.

The fabric of the entire region of space was disrupted to the point that a mesh field had to be constructed to hold it all together for a while.

And this surprised the humans at the time because they thought they'd discovered all there was to know about the fabric of the Universe until that point.

Little did they know.

But Dinglewits weren't as clever as humans.

And seeing as the humans have now fled Earth and left it to the Dinglewits to bugger up, Satan felt she could let her hair down on this one.

'Actually, I have a brainwave. Wait here a minute, I've been working on something new. Let me know what you think.'

Satan ran out of the kitchen, through the cobbed webs that guarded the spiral staircase, and as fast as she could up to the top.

The house mice, which had made the staircase their home on the grounds that it's rarely used, made an exit for their nearest boltholes.

At the top of the stairs, she made a sharp dart to the right and continued sprinting along the landing; disrupting all the cobwebs as she did.

And at the end of the landing was a cupboard with a red door.

Satan had claimed this cupboard as extra storage space because her room was so pokey and had been slowly filling it with junk ever since.

She flung open the door and rustled through the contents, spilling most of it onto the landing.

'Oh, I'll clean that up later,' she muttered after seeing the mess.

More flinging ensued. And more clutter ended up on the landing.

Until, eventually, Satan found what she was looking for.

'Yes! Here it is.'

Back in the quiet confounds of the kitchen, Mother was enjoying her piece of pie in silence.

BANG, CRASH, WALLOP.
BUMP, BUMP, BUMP.

Then a screech.

And Mother's few moments of solitude with her pie were over.

She looked up and noticed a small spark of enthusiasm had ignited in Satan's eyes.

Like a flame when doused in petrol and given a big waft of oxygen.

Satan looked menacing when flames were in her eyes. It was part of her charm. It was something she'd inherited from her father, along with her flowing red curly hair and freckles.

The rest she got from Mother.

'Close your eyes, Mummy,' Satan instructed. 'I wanna show you something cool I've been planning for ages. I think you'll like it. It's gonna be just like the good old days.'

'Ah, yes, the good old days,' Mother answered. 'I remember them well.'

She didn't, of course, not accurately anyway, because the thing is this: the good old days were never really the good old days as anyone remembers them.

It's more a case of *let's remember the good bits and forget all about the crap bits*. Apparently, this is the thing with every life form, and Satan and Mother, being different in everything else, were no different in this regard.

Satan could remember, with clarity, the screams and the terror of all of her victims as their blood splattered all up the walls and decorated all the dancehalls with the rather fetching colour scheme called *freshly murdered Dinglewit*.

She remembered, in fine detail, a particularly deadly whip that could cut a Dinglewit in half at 30 paces and the noise the dismembered body made as it sloshed to the floor.

And she certainly remembered a contraption made from sharpened bones that she used to chase witch-hunters around the village with, and how much fun it was to win the chase and then enjoy the spoils of victory.

That Halloween game was her particular favourite until all the witch-hunters lost faith in their convictions and rather un-thoughtfully died off.

Which was a shame—she always thought—witch-hunters were her preferred darlings.

They died honourably.

But as for the boring bits, she never remembered them.

Why would she?

The endless waiting for fresh meat to unknowingly wander into one of her many traps.

The conversations of, *it'll all be okay, it's just a bit of mutilation.*

And all the times when her well-organised Halloween bash got cancelled due to poor numbers.

No, she never remembered them.

But tonight was going to be different.

So very different.

And as she entered the kitchen with her, *something cool I've been planning for ages,* face on, she was confronted with—

'Jesus. H. Christ, Satan! What are you planning to do with all that? You can barely close the zip.' Mother shouted who, well, sort of had a point.

'It's all my gubbings for tonight, Mummy.'

'Gubbings?'

'Yeah, gubbings. You know, weapons, accessories, and disguises, and stuff. All the good things that a girl needs to have a jolly good night out. All packed into a suitcase for easy travel.'

'Satan, darling, it's bulging out from the sides.'

True, it could be said that it was a little too honest with its contents, but Satan—you see—was planning a busy night.

And a busy night meant having lots of spare weapons to hurt folk with.

Because, as her father once told her, it's better to have a scythe and not need it than need a scythe and have to use an axe.

Wise words, indeed.

And Satan had been in that situation before.

Although the axe did do the job.

'I need all this stuff, Mummy, I've got big ambitions for tonight. I want to enjoy it. I have it all planned out, see. Biscuit is coming with me and a couple of the girls, and we're going to see out Halloween with a bang.'

'A bang. You'll warp the entire timeline if you're not careful.'

'Oh no, it'll be okay, Mummy. I'm just going to let my hair down for a few hours. A bit of the old slap n' slash. The Universe will never know. I'll make sure I slaughter just under the maximum amount so that it doesn't get audited.'

'But why so many weapons, my little darling? Surely you won't have time to use all that lot, will you? And anyway, wasn't the whole idea to get others to do the killing for you while you watch? I'm sure it was. Yes, I remember it now. You said, "Mummy, I have this idea for a special night. It's a bit like Christmas but without all the tinsel." That's what you said, wasn't it? then you went on to say, "There's going to be lots of death and destruction and with no small amount of blood and guts." That's right, wasn't it? That's what you said. Then you finished by saying, "But the best thing is, I'm not going to be doing the killing myself. They're going to do it for me, and I'm going to watch." That's what you said, Satan, darling. I remember it well. That *is* what you said.'

And it was, so I guess Mother had a valid argument here.

But Satan wasn't interested in valid arguments against the things she wanted to do.

And you could tell this because she had a face like a slapped bottom when Mother mentioned it.

Satan, you see, wasn't very good at hiding her emotions.

'Yes, Mummy. That is what I said, and word for word too. How do you manage it? But things have gone a bit awry recently. They, they don't do it like they should. It's all a bit playful and pretend now.' And a glum expression took root on her face.

'I thought that when the humans left Earth, and the Dinglewits took over, then I might get a more genuine Halloween. You know, just like it was in the beginning, but they've just carried on in the same old manner. It's awful, just rubbish. So no, I can't trust them lot up there to enjoy Halloween like they should be doing. So, I'm taking matters into my own hands.'

Mother gave another provoking look at the suitcase.

'A flamethrower! Honestly, you're going to use a flamethrower, the most dangerous weapon ever invented.'

'Weapons should be dangerous, Mummy. That's the whole point.'

'Yes, just not for the operator, though. That's *what* I'm saying. I swear down, the flamethrower has killed more operators than victims in its time. It's a death trap. Don't you remember what happened to Ogun? Playing around with flamethrowers didn't end well for him, did it?'

'Ogun was a buffoon, Mummy. He deserved to get himself burnt to a crisp. A complete oaf, and I never did have much time for him. He was unpleasant.'

'He wasn't unpleasant, Satan. He was just different to you. And being different doesn't make someone unpleasant.'

'No, he was unpleasant. And really unpleasant at that. He broke my toys and pulled my hair and made fun of me all the time. I was overjoyed when I heard of his fate with the flamethrower. That showed him—'

'Oh it wasn't fate, Satan,' Mother interrupted. 'It definitely wasn't fate. I don't quite know what it was, but it definitely wasn't fate.'

'Why not?'

'Because fate wouldn't be such a cruel mistress like that.'

'Well, the fate I know would.'

'Maybe so, but I liked having Ogun around—'

'Yeah, well, he ain't around no more, is he, eh?' Satan interrupted. 'And that's what you get for breaking my toys; you get burnt into cinders with a flamethrower.'

'Oh Satan, that's just mean-spirited. You should never be mean-spirited. It doesn't become you.'

'I'm Satan, Mummy, mean-spirited is my middle name.'

'No it isn't, it's Mattox. Named after your father. And if he could only see you now, he'd be turning in his firepit. Talking trash of an old friend like Ogun. Honestly, Satan, I thought I'd raised you better than that.'

'Raised me, Mother. You did raise me. And you raised me to do what I do best.'

'Oh yes, and what's that?'

'Raise hell, Mummy,' Satan hollered, with a glee on her face and a new-found sense of elation. 'That's what I do best. I raise hell. It's what I was raised to do. I was born to raise hell. And tonight, hell shall be raised.'

She dragged her suitcase full of her tools of death to the front door.

It was all she could muster; it was heavy.

'Biscuit, give me a hand?' she shouted. 'This case is way too heavy for me. I need it putting in the chariot.'

'Yes, M'lady,' answered Biscuit, unimpressed at being dragged into this façade and knowing full well what the night had in store for him.

He'd always quite enjoyed Halloween up to now.

It was the one night he was guaranteed a bit of rest.

Satan was out busying herself with everyone else's misfortune.

And Mother usually had an early night.

Which, therefore, meant a nice cup of cocoa for old Biscuit and a good night's reading in front of a warm fire.

But not this year, it seemed.

Biscuit, you see, was the long-serving—and some would say long-suffering—butler to the family and was often called upon when heavy lifting was required.

Which was all the time and seemed to be getting even more of *all the time* recently.

Viz, he now has extra-long arms, a stoop, the triceps of a Gigantopithecus, and cracking calf muscles.

Oh, and a grumpy manner about him. Hence, why Mother now refers to him as grumps.

When his time serving the family is over, he always claimed, he'd probably get a job breaking up impossibly extra-hard rocks with a pickaxe or carrying absolutely bloody everything. Absolutely bloody everywhere, for absolutely no bloody obvious reason, ever—which is what he basically does now—as it'd be easier.

'Grumps,' ordered Mother. 'Can you do all the heavy lifting tonight and make sure she gets home safe and sound? You know what she's like when she's got a face on; absolutely no sense in talking to her.'

'Yes, Ma'am.'

'And don't let her get too excited and start destroying the Universe's new pet life-forms. It's taken a lot of time moulding the Dinglewits into an enjoyable pet, and the Universe wouldn't take kindly to Satan slicing 'em all up. I'm still indebted after what she did to the humans all those years ago.'

'Yes, Ma'am.'

'And should the unthinkable happen and some smart Alec pull a fast one, get stuck in and help out, will you? You know what these Dinglewits are like. They'd enjoy nothing more than taking on the underworld and laying us all to waste. Oh, I curse the day the Universe put them on planet Earth. What was it thinking? There was nothing wrong with the humans. Maybe a bit gullible. But at least they were malleable; not like this lot.'

'Yes, Ma'am.'

'And pick up some bread on the way back; we're running short.'

'Yes, Ma'am.'

Then Mother turned her attention to Satan.

'Now, Satan, are we sure this is what you want? I mean, why don't you just not bother? If the whole thing is not worth the effort anymore, then don't put the effort in. Just let 'em get on with it. That's what I'd do.'

'But, Mummy, I can't just leave it. They'd have way too much fun without me. And I don't see why they should have all the fun when I'm not getting any. It's not fair.'

'But wasn't it supposed to be fun, my little treasure? I thought that was the whole idea, wasn't it? Having fun.'

'Yes, for me. Fun for me! Not for them. It wasn't meant to be fun for them. It was supposed to be my day. My very own, very special day—'

'For Mummy's very own, very special girl,' interrupted Mother while pinching Satan's chubby cheeks with both hands.

Satan liked having her chubby cheeks pinched by Mother.

It reminded her that she was still her favourite little child.

And definitely much better than her big brother, of whom she'd just had a blazing argument with because he was being selfish.

And definitely much better than her little sister—who, despite many hours of training—was still more boring than life.

'Ooh, Mummy, I'm excited,' Satan squealed. 'What should I do to end it? I want it to be something I'll remember forever. Something spectacular. Something stupendous. Something rumbustious. Something fun. Real fun. Just like it used to be back when having fun was allowed. Do you remember those days, Mummy? Back when fun was allowed.'

'And encouraged, my little darling. We used to encourage it as well. "Go out and have some fun," we always told you. And you always did. Like the good little girl you are. And I'll tell you what.'

'What?'

'I know just the place for your little Halloween bash to end all Halloween bashes?'

'Where?'

'That Old Chapel at Blorkeney Knoll. Eh? How about that? You always did love a good shindig at the old chapel, as I remember.'

Satan, for the first time today, cracked a mollified smile.

'Hmm, yes, that's a good idea, Mummy. The Old Chapel at Blorkeney Knoll, you say? Yes, that's just the place to have a Halloween party to end all Halloween parties.'

Chapter 3

The first *innocent* victim—if being innocent has any inkling of relevance here—on the last night of Halloween was a young chap going by the name of Wilson.

The name, apparently, was a compromise between his father's choice of Wilbert, whom he'd got from a character in his favourite childhood cartoon. And his mother's preferred option of Samson—her first love from school—although she never mentioned that part when the argument was had.

Yet despite this quarrelsome start to his life, Wilson was a happy young fellow who never said as much as a boo to a ghost.

Tonight, however, it was of no real importance who Wilson was.

He could easily have been a delightful old lady named Gladys, for all intents and purposes. A dear old sweetie pie that was looking for a juicy novel to get her false teeth into later that night.

Or a young travelling whippersnapper going by the tag of Buck (as seems trendy these days), who was an ambitious go-getter who just happened to pop in to buy a short story to read on his lunch break.

It really didn't matter.

They were all just mere flesh and blood in Satan's eyes.

Fresh meat for her own enjoyment, on her own very special day.

But it just so happened that on this occasion…it was Wilson.

A complete nobody.

Wilson the Nobody.

But today, Wilson the Nobody was about to become the first victim of Satan's grand finale of Halloween.

He was on his lunch break, as it so happened, when he popped into the shop to buy a short story to read while eating his lunch. He was there for the week and wanted something juicy to get his teeth into.

After scanning a few isles, he decided that he'd quite like to read a horror story of some nature. His last book, *The Magical Wonky Universe* was such a riveting read he wanted something else along those lines.

So he picked up a book titled *What It Feels Like to be Eaten Alive*. He quickly scanned the first few lines, whizzed through the blurb, and without really understanding the irony of what was about to happen to him. Then, he concluded that was the book for him.

He didn't know why, as stories about being eaten alive weren't something that would normally have grasped his attention. Which, again, only highlights the irony involved here.

But it seemed that on the last night of Halloween, fate was playing mean tricks with poor old Wilson.

He placed the book under his armpit and continued to scan the other bookshelves just in case he found something more worthy of his time while he was eating his lunchtime sandwiches.

You see, reading a book is an investment. As Wilson was a slow reader, that investment needed to be a worthwhile one.

Not that his time was valuable in any way.

Far from it.

Let it be said, Wilson hadn't, wouldn't, and couldn't achieve anything of any note, ever.

For he truly was Wilson the Nobody. The nobody man from nowhere land; doing nothing of any interest to no one.

That was Wilson.

However—and I feel I should stipulate this—when he first walked into the shop, his initial thought wasn't to buy a book on how it would feel to be eaten alive.

Oh no.

He had grander expectations.

For he was actually thinking how nice it would be to read some erotic fantasy fiction for once.

He always quite enjoyed fantasy fiction with all its spaceships and sorcery and wizards and elves.

And he really liked eroticism with all its tits and sex.

Say no more.

So, a combination of the two… result.

But as we now know, that wasn't to be the case.

And for poor old Wilson, his day was about to get a whole lot worse when he felt a sharp bite from under his armpit from where the book had been nonchalantly placed.

'Ooh, ya little git,' he shouted as he quickly grabbed the book and looked to find blood coming from its pages.

His blood.

His armpit blood.

'You've, you've bitten me. What the…how?'

He dropped the book on the floor and attempted to kick it into the corner.

And that was his second mistake.

The book opened up its pages as if it was a gaping, hungry mouth, eating its prey, which, of course, it actually was. Wilson the Nobody found himself having his foot being chewed off right in front of his eyes.

He looked around for help. But surprisingly, the shop had suddenly completely emptied, and all the lights had gone out.

'Hmm, that's strange,' he muttered. 'I could have sworn that the place had life when I came in. I mean, why wouldn't it? No one just opens up a shop and abandons it when a paying customer walks in. And as for this damned book, it's just grown sharp fangs and is trying to eat away at my armpits and feet.'

'YES,' the book responded. 'AND I HAVE A TASTE FOR DINGLEWIT FLESH.'

Wilson grabbed hold of the book by its spine and tried to pull it before it was too late.

But it was already too late.

The book had got a grip on him now and was not about to let go.

He dropped to the floor and gave a scream.

'Get off me, you, foot-eating demonic book! That foot is mine, and I need it!'

The book didn't respond verbally.

It never did like to talk with its mouth full.

And it continued to eat.

And nosh.

And munch.

And chomp.

And as it did, the blood from the foot, and then the leg, spurted out onto the books occupying the shelves of the erotic fantasy fiction section.

Satan watched on.

She found this sort of thing fascinating.

Maybe even arousing.

She'd observed a while ago that the colour of blood in the big arteries is a slightly different colour from the blood in the smaller veins.

She didn't know why this was a thing.

And why the Universe went to such lengths.

She just knew that it *was* a thing.

And that she liked it.

Her preferred colour was the lighter shade found in the big arteries. Not only was it a more pleasant colour and matched her hair, but it would spray way further than the darker stuff in the smaller veins.

So, as Wilson was wriggling on the floor, fighting for his life with a killer book that was consuming him inch by inch, Satan made notes of the different colours of the blood as it decorated the bookshop walls and added them to her colour chart.

Wilson was now in a state of complete denial.

The irony that the book he'd chosen for his night's entertainment had just hit him.

Or I could say, had just consumed him.

Either way, in his final, few, very painful moments of living, he laughed.

And he laughed.

And he laughed.

And as the foot, then the leg, and then the pelvis were slowly being eaten away by the killer book, he laughed uncontrollably.

Then, he passed out due to the pain and the loss of blood.

Satan also took notes of this.

By the end, all that was left was an engorged book full of blood of varying shades in the middle of a bookshop.

And that was the last ever act of Wilson the Nobody; the first innocent Dinglewit to die on the last ever night of Halloween.

Just for buying the wrong book.

The ass.

Chapter 4

So, you've met Satan, a charming little vixen I'm sure you'll all agree. So please, permit me to introduce the second protagonist in today's story.

His name is Barmy. He, by contrast, is a friendly old goof with a fetish for unnecessarily feeling the need to climb out of high-rise windows in order to escape.

Let me explain.

You see, the thing with Barmy was that he'd voluntarily placed himself inside the confined walls of the Glint Tae Mental Asylum on the grounds that he was totally mad and in need of some psychological input.

Don't we all?

And for the whole time that he has been there, he has made it his mission in life to escape the loony bin by means of scaling from his bedroom window on the 10th floor and abseiling his way to freedom.

But like I say, he was only there voluntarily, so there really wasn't any need as he could simply walk out the front door at any time.

You get my point about Barmy being a bit of a goof now, yes?

And a proper goof at that.

But a very likeable one.

You see, I've always viewed the old boy as lacking that general sense of direction in life that we all seek to attain, that certain *detends-toi, tout ira bien,* to quote the French.

And this was probably why he relentlessly insisted on undertaking the rather perilous act of shimmying out of high-rise bedroom windows to make good an escape.

And no matter how much discouragement he received from his cellmate, Baron Cedric Cobbler III—who constantly said what a foolhardy act it was but also thought the whole thing a bit of a laugh—he simply wouldn't relinquish his mission.

'You know you can walk out the front exit, Barmy, they'll just let you out, you know,' said Cedric, while also chuckling under his breath. 'It's a lot less work and a lot less scary.'

'But where's the fun in that?' responded Barmy. 'Not when you can risk life and limb climbing out this window. It's perfect. And what a way to escape, too. Have you ever seen such a thing? It's spectacular. Come, take a look.'

Cedric went through the usual ritual of looking out the window as requested because he knew if he didn't, he'd just end up getting badgered 'til the cows came home until he did.

But that didn't mean he had to like it.

'Yep, the same as last time. And it'll probably end the same way too; with you screaming for help and wetting yourself, and the guards having to get the large ladder out again and turning the air blue. While also laughing, I might add, and taking pictures.'

'Nah, not tonight, my aristocratic friend, not tonight. Tonight is going to be a special one. A night that'll go down in history for everyone to rejoice over. I can see it now; all the best newspapers reporting on the grand escape with their front-page spreads and glossy pictures. And me, 'Ol Barmy, living large from the proceeds of my fame.'

A goof indeed.

But like in, say, a likeable one.

Now, as we all know, the best way to make an escape from a high-rise building is simply to tie bedsheets together with a good sturdy knot—I believe the Zeppelin Bend is the best in this situation—and then make the escape through an unguarded window in the middle of the night.

Preferably when there is a full moon so you can see where you're going, as seeing stuff is always best, I tend to find.

This, Barmy had attempted many times before, and every time gloriously failing.

So why continue to bother? You may ask.

Well, a couple of points here.

A minor side idea is that he is totally bonkers.

Crackers.

Around the bend.

Living in cloud cuckoo land.

However, you want to describe it.

And doing stuff like this makes him feel alive.

And that's fair enough, I guess.

I know for a fact we all have our own little quims in life.

And if Barmy is climbing from windows, then well, let him crack on, say I.

But generally, others might disagree here, but the main reason is that he perceives this as being the most dapper way to spend an evening and is much more fulfilling than listening to the wireless.

So, there you have it.

Now, if by chance you're in Barmy's camp, and you've given thought to this rather silly way of ascending from a high-rise structure, then the big problems with tying bedsheets together to make your escape aren't quite what you might think.

Firstly, after contemplation of specific permeations and outcomes of the whole wretched affair, you could be forgiven that it's the softness of the sheets and the distinct possibility of the fabric tearing down the middle; with the subsequent outcome of falling to your horrific death, is the main downer with such a practice.

As, of course, it would be, as any untimely death has the tendency to lower the tone of any happy plan of escape by scaling down a high-rise building.

Or maybe, and I could say secondly, after even further contemplation of specific permeations, it's the size of the knots required to bind together the appendages of a comfortable night's sleep which could cause the escapee to come a cropper.

For if they fail, then it's beddy-byes forever and, hopefully, a quick death.

Or maybe it's just the daftness of it all. No one, ever, has managed to escape from any high-rise window using such a cartoon method of extraction without the safety blanket of a claque of friends, standing directly underneath with an equally impressive large sheet to catch the falling fugitive.

Any of those three might do.

But the truth—as is always the case—is far more obscure than first thought and may come as a surprise to some readers.

The big bummer to the whole charade is the reality that if the escape plan fails and you're forced to abandon plans and go back to whence you started, then you're in for a long, cold night's sleep without any bedding.

Hence, why it's always better to use someone else's bedding if you are going to attempt this act of foolhardy behaviour.

'Tonight is the night, Cedric,' announced Barmy, as he started taking the pillows from both their cases and tying them together, using a particularly sturdy knot that only ever got used in turbulent winds. 'Tonight, I make my escape to freedom and fulfil my destiny.'

'Destiny,' scoffed Cedric, if scoffed is the right description to imply disquiet. 'You do like to over-dramatize things, don't you? I think you've been watching too many films again.'

And then, he scoffed again.

It's in times like this when scoffing really is the only answer.

You know, in times when you feel disquiet.

In Cedric's case, maybe it was the thought of yet another uncomfortable night's sleep without any bedding just so that Barmy can accomplish an act that can be equally achieved by saying *tally ho* and walking out the front door.

Or maybe it's because he'd heard this tale way too many times before to actually believe that he could pull it off.

Or, more likely, it was the reality of another cold night's sleep without any bedding was starting to wear thin.

Either way, Cedric felt the need to scoff.

As it turned out, it was a heavy night for scoffing because Barmy felt the need to answer the scoff with an equally enthusiastic scoff.

So, with scoffs all around, the conversation continued.

'My dear, Cedric, films are mere make-believe. Stories. Yarns. Not to be taken seriously. One should never live one's life according to films. It would be a disaster. And besides, this isn't a film, it's real. Real life. What I'm doing here is real life. And the voice that I hear, well, that's real life, too.

'A real-life voice in my head. My guiding light. My guiding light through all the noise. My guiding light through all the noise so that I can help save the world from destruction. All plausibly realistic and above board.'

'You're saving the world from destruction?' asked Cedric, with no small hint of scepticism in his voice.

'Yep.'

'And you're doing that soon?'

'Yep.'

'Now look here, old man, I don't mean to be a stick in the mud on the matter, but are you sure? I mean, does it have to be right now, it's cold. And windy. And it's much harder to save the world from destruction when it's cold and windy. You might blow off the building and fall to your death or something.

'Or…or…you could catch your death of cold when you're out in the wilderness. We're miles from anywhere you know, and this clothing won't keep the wind out. So why don't you wait 'til the summer to save the world from destruction? It's much nicer in the summer. They'll be birds singing. And butterflies dancing. And, and, oh, I don't know. But let's just wait until the summer, shall we?'

'Because it needs to be tonight, Cedric. That's why. I can't sit around here and wait for warmer climates. Heroes of the Universe don't just hang fire until the weather picks up, do they? No, that's not how we behave. But also, I have my orders, old boy. So, it must be tonight.'

'You have orders, do you?'

'Oh yes, and they're very precise. It said I was to escape tonight and get over to the Old Chapel at Blorkeney Knoll for a Halloween party. The order was quite adamant on this issue. It's crucial I'm there, you see.'

'Is it indeed?'

'Oh yes, I can't very well save the day stuck in here with you, Cedric, old fruit. My destiny is to be at the Old Chapel at Blorkeney Knoll for the Halloween party. It's written in the stars, you see. Oh, and the voice said so.'

Now, Cedric had shared a room with Barmy for many years. So hearing him speak of being given orders to escape through the window so he could save the world was not a new thing.

It had happened many times before.

Although previously, he'd never been able to ascertain where the orders had come from or, indeed, how Barmy had come about them.

But when you're in a mental asylum, you tend to take some things at face value.

'Well, if that's the case then, and if I were you, I'd be packing for an English summer,' Cedric added. 'It's one thing to be shimmying out the widow and scaling the walls to freedom, but it's another thing entirely not to freeze ya balls off on the other side. It's gibbers out there, and I wouldn't fancy it. I wouldn't fancy it one bit. Oh, and don't think you're using *my* bedsheets again this time. I nearly froze to death on your last attempt. And it's the big match tomorrow, I wanna be in good shape for it.'

'My dear, Cedric. I've no need to pack for any type of summer. Least of all, an English one. All my Earthly needs will be met on the other side. So, my only task is to escape these walls of inhibition and make good my escape.'

'And how, may I enquire, do you know this?'

'Because that's what the voice said.'

'Who?'

'The voice.'

'The voice as in, you've no bloody idea?'

'The voice as in…I don't need to know, my dear friend. The Universe has chosen. It's thrown the dice of fate, and it's landed at my feet with a big, fat, juicy six. That's all I need to know.'

'And you're sure of that, are you? You sure it's not your mind playing tricks on you again?'

Barmy rose from his armchair in a gallant gesture of somethingness.

'Oh, my dear Cedric, you are bound by your own imagination. Let yourself go once in a while. Let your hair down, if you ever grown any, and have faith; there is more out there than you could ever know. Go enjoy yourself. I know life has dealt you normality in the form of blue tablets and group therapy. But don't let all that contaminate that beautiful mind that you once possessed. Remember, I knew you before the pills and compliance. You were a brilliant soul. A soul not restrained to social norms or fashion. So, let your soul be free once more and go run in the liberty of freedom.'

He threw his arms in the air and danced a sort of wiggle, which looked more like mental illness on drugs.

Which it probably was.

'Well, I may be a soul confined by blue pills, as you say. But at least I'll be a soul that'll be warm tonight while you are freezing your nipples off.'

'Ah well, that may well be the case, Cedric. But I'll be living it. I'll be living a…thing…that's what I'll be doing; living a thing while you're sitting here in comfort and warmth.'

'Living a thing?' Cedric laughed. 'And what's living a thing when it's at home?'

'I'll tell you what it is, old boy. It's being given a duty in life that is important to the survival of all Dinglewits. That's what it is.'

'Being given a duty? To save all Dinglewits? Honestly, listen to you.'

'Oh yes. A very important duty. I've been assigned to it specifically. Now let me borrow your duvet cover, I have things to do.'

Cedric grabbed hold of his duvet as if his very existence depended upon it.

'You'll do nothing of the sort, Barmy. Not until you explain who's been giving you these silly orders. I must insist. I must know. In the past, I've overlooked the small details of who's been in your earhole giving you commands, but not tonight. Not seeing as you're about to get me frozen because of your nonsense. Answers would be appreciated. So speak free, old boy, come on, give.'

So Barmy did give.

'A voice, Cedric, I hear a voice. It's as simple as all that, really. And it's telling me what I need to do.'

'A voice? What do you mean you hear a voice?'

'Well, I think the sentence speaks for itself. But erm, well, I'll try and explain further. You see, I hear this voice. It's not in my head. It's real. It's a real voice from another dimension in space. And the voice is telling me what I need to do and when I need to do it. We have conversations on the issue. I've put across my point of view. The voice puts across its point of view. And in the end, we come to a conclusion. That's all.'

'Oh, that's all, is it? It's just telling you what you need to do, and when you need to do it. What is it, some kind of ghost? Are you having midnight chats with a ghost, Barmy?'

'No, not a ghost, a Dinglewit. A chap. A chap that's crossed over to another dimension and is now communicating with me from some different level in the Universe. He's a nice old boy too. He's telling me lots of stuff. Lots of interesting stuff. You wouldn't believe the things he knows, you know, you really wouldn't. He must have a very big lemon on his shoulders, that's all I can say.'

'So, it's a bloke, is it?'

'Yep. A clever one.'

'Oh, that's a shame.'

'Why?'

'Because I always think that girls do this sort of thing better.'

'Really?'

'Yep, they seem to have a knack for it. It must be in their genes. Us chaps, we tend to waffle on and bugger the whole thing up, from my experience.'

'And do you have a lot of experience in talking to folk from other dimensions?'

'Um, well, it depends on what we're talking about here, doesn't it? What…exactly…are we talking about here?'

It was at this point that Barmy felt it high time to come clean on the whole dastardly plan and let Cedric in on the act.

Plus, he hadn't said it out loud up to now, and he wasn't sure whether it would make any sense when said out loud.

Things should always be said out loud to test if they made any sense, shouldn't they?

'You see, Cedric, there was once this old science chappy, very clever too, apparently. And well, not to put too sharp a point on it, he sort of faked his own death.'

'He faked his own death?' screeched Cedric.

'Yes, well, not faked as such. I mean, he did get murdered. But he was the one responsible for his murder. He did it himself, you see, from another dimension. So he didn't actually die in the technical sense, he just changed form, so to speak.'

'Oh, I'm afraid you've lost me now, old friend. Did he die or not?'

'Well yes. But also no.'

'But he was murdered?'

'Again yes. But also no. I can see I might to explain it to you.'

Cedric accepted the charity.

'You see, the big problem with living in a multiverse is that sometimes stuff gets confused.'

'Confused? What do you mean, confused?'

'Not confused. Complicated. Yes, that's it, stuff can get complicated. But I suppose they can get confused as well. I mean, I'm confused already,' he said, and gave an embarrassed laugh. 'But right, okay, back on song. Okay, the thing is this. There was this very clever science chap. A nice fellow, everyone liked him.'

'Would I like him?'

'Oh yes, he's a gentle soul, maybe I'll introduce you sometime. Anyway, he invented some contraption to end all wars, and, well, they were going to kill him because of it. They like wars, you see, these rulers of ours. So they were going to kill him. Or at least they would've killed him had he not beat them to it.'

'So he did kill himself?'

'Yes…But also no. Right, pay attention now, this is the nub of the story. The thing was this: this science chap, actually he was a professor, but I don't think that's important. Well, he found this way of going over to the other side. You know, another dimension, and by doing that he could kill himself in this dimension and then live out the rest of his life in that dimension. And that way, all the baddies will think that he's dead and leave him alone because there's literally no point in killing someone who is already dead, right?'

'Quite, not appropriate one bit.'

'But he isn't dead, you see. Not actually dead. He's just dead in *this* dimension. He lives in another dimension. So he lives.'

'Dimension or Universe?'

'Same thing. I think. I've never asked. Anyway, that's the crux of it, understand?'

Cedric *was* listening, but was listening with suspicion and confusion.

And it wasn't that he didn't believe his friend, insane though the idea was.

Au contraire, he would love to think that Barmy was getting the goods.

He'd actually be relieved that at least someone was.

It was just that he found it hard to believe.

And on a couple of fronts.

One was that he found the whole thing completely impossible to believe in the first place.

I mean, a crazy scientist speaking to him from another dimension.

It's that sort of talk that gets you banged up in here in the first place.

The second, if what he was saying was correct—and he had serious doubts about this—then why would this clever science professor choose to communicate with Barmy—the most unreliable Dinglewit ever—to have their bottom slapped and call someone's mother?

He needed answers.

And he called upon Barmy to give them.

And Barmy was nothing if not consistent.

'Cedric, the answers to all of life's great mysteries are not mine to give,' he answered, as indeed, Cedric did offer the question. 'But what I can give you is this. Something is afoot tonight, something sinister. And if I don't get a wiggle on and escape these confounds of false illusion, then we're all done for. Done for, I say.'

Which, ordinarily, would be enough for anyone.

But not for Cedric, it seems.

'But I say, Barmy. This all sounds a bit gobbledygook if you ask me. All this chatter about reckonings and Halloween parties. What's it all about? I really need to know. What exactly is this chappie telling you? And more to the point, why is he telling you? It simply doesn't stack up,' he asked.

'Well, Cedric, what I hear and what I am told is the way it is and the way it will be. Or, more precisely, the way it will always be. That's all I know.'

Making the next question.

'But what does that mean, Barmy?'

To which Barmy answered, 'It means that there is more to the Universe than you can possibly comprehend. Way more. And not just in the things you can see. Or hear. But many other things besides. You see, Cedric, you are what is known as a flump.'

'A flump.'

'Yes, a flump. I assume you are not aware of what a flump is.'

'No.'

'Then, let me explain. A flump is a word you use to describe someone who only believes in what they can see or can prove. They lack any form of imagination, they've never sung a merry song, and they rarely achieve anything of any importance or worth. So, Cedric, I'm afraid to say—in every sense of the word—you are definitely a flump. And a world-class one at that.'

This only served to further confuse poor Cedric.

So, the next bit went something like this.

'You see, Cedric, old chum, nothing is what it seems like. Take yourself, for example, when someone looks at you from the standpoint of analysing sanity, they always come up with the conclusion that you're a nice bottle of plonk short of a picnic, right?'

'Right.'

'But who's to say that it's not them that are deluded and wacky? Eh? For all we know, it's you who has a grasp on reality and can see through the haze, and they only see the fog that's right in front of their eyes. You should think about that?'

And he did.

But it never helped.

'But all this business with Satan,' Cedric responded. 'And her wanting to kill us all. I just don't understand why. Why would you want to hurt someone so much? We ain't done nothing wrong, have we? So why would she want to do that? And why would the Universe allow that?'

At this point, Barmy would feel obliged to try and educate the poor fellow on the ways of evil.

'Well, she is Satan, Cedric. That is what Satans do. Always have. Always will. It's in their genes, you see. They like to cause harm and suffering. I remember the old man. Ruthless. He would kill a dude at a thousand paces just for laughs. No warning shots. And no rationale. Just for badness. At least, the daughter has her ulterior motives other than just being a douchebag. At least she wants to enjoy the whole affair rather than just do it for the hell of it.'

'Oh, so you like quite this one then?'

'I wouldn't go as far as to say I like this one. But the point is I understand her. There is a reason for what she's doing. That I can work with. Also, she has a weakness.'

'A weakness?'

'Yep, a weakness. And it's a weakness we can manipulate. And if I wanna be a bit cocky on the matter, I'm mildly confident it will bring her downfall.'

'That is a bold statement, Barmy. Mildly confident of bringing down Satan. Now, that's a claim.'

'Not just a claim…it's inside knowledge, old badger. The voice told me.'

'The voice from the other dimension?'

'Yep, he's been filling me in with all kinds of useful hints to get one over Satan. It's like he has a personal vendetta against her. And he knows stuff too.'

'Like what?'

'Like she doesn't like being mocked. She can't bear it. It drives her crazy. Even crazier than you. He claims that all you have to do is come up with some rib-punching taunts, and she'll be done for. She'll have no comeback. No witty riposte. Done for.'

'Surely, you're not serious. Please, don't tell me that your only solution to fighting Satan is to throw insults in her general direction.'

'How do you mean, old boy?'

'Barmy, that isn't going to work. She'll pulverise you. And probably pulverise you even more because you called her names. Get a grip, man.'

'Ahh, but that's where you're wrong, Cedric. And very wrong at that. You see—Satan—she hates having the mickey taken out of her. Hates it. It's her kryptonite. I tell you, a few choice words from the Barmster, and she'll be running for the hills, blubbing like a little baby.'

'Oh God, you are serious, aren't you?'

'Deadly, old chum. This is how I go down in history. This is how I make my mark on the fabric of the Universe. This is what folk will be saying all over the galaxy when they hear the name of Ol' Barmy. They'll say—'

'What, that you defeated Satan by calling her names?'

'You got it in one, old crumb. Now, tonight, I make my escape to get to the last night of Halloween, and I don't wanna miss it. So, pass me your bed sheets, I've some tying to do.'

Chapter 5

Meanwhile, down in the depths of Hell, which, rather surprisingly, was a particularly chilly morning, word had got around of Satan's plans.

Hell was well-known for being a hotbed for gossip, and anything of any significance tended to spread through the smoking fires and molten lava quicker than a red-hot poker through an unsuspecting eyeball.

And sometimes, considerably more painful.

And as with every other rumour doing the rounds that morning, it wasn't long before the news reached the ears of a devilishly beautiful vampire going by the name of Blood.

'I say, Wolfie,' asked Blood. 'Have you heard the rumours? It's exciting.'

Wolfie, a werewolf sentenced to hell for doing what werewolves do, was never one for gossip, but she did have a bit of a soft spot for Blood.

There was just something about a vampire that moistened her right in the middle of the thighs.

Even female vampires.

Especially, female vampires.

'No, what rumours? And how do you mean, exciting?' she responded.

'You've not heard?'

'No, I've not heard. What are you on about, you silly vampire? Come on, spill the beans, I'm all ears.'

And Blood was only too happy to spill the so-called beans.

'Well, the word is Satan is having a big shindig up at the surface tonight. And that means we might all be going up on a day out or a night out, seeing as we're her best friends and all. How cool would that be? And hey, less of all this *silly vampire* business, I'm a vampire of the highest order.'

Now, Wolfie and Blood did consider themselves best friends with Satan, if that was ever such a thing. But in reality, they were merely playthings.

Playthings at the mercy of Satan.

Which, most of the time, was a pretty uncomfortable place to be.

Even more uncomfortable than hell itself.

But the perks were pretty good because they occasionally got to go up to the surface for some fun. Also, they were—by and large—left alone by the guards when down in the depths of Hell.

So, they were willing to put up with a few things.

And they did have to put up with them.

Satan wasn't easy to work with.

But the two girls, God bless their souls, made the best of it. No matter how chilled their bones got, they never lost their zest for life, which was more than can be said for their victims.

'You've heard that Satan is planning on making an entrance in the upper place, have you? Are you sure, you're certain it's not all hot air, you know what Hell's like this time of year. Rumours quickly run amok among the inmates and get everyone's blood boiling up to fever pitch. Are you sure this isn't all just tittle-tattle because Halloween is coming up?'

'Nope, all true.'

'Really?'

'Yep.'

'Woohoo, Blood, you fine-looking vampire, you warm my heart. Or probably just make it less cool. But I hope this isn't just another red herring. You know what happened the last time Satan went to the surface; all hell broke loose, and safeguards were put in place to stop it from happening again. Her mother was livid.'

'Well that may well be the case, but the rumour to which I refer is that Satan is about to make an entrance into the upper place for a night of mischief, and we, being as we are her best friends, will accompany her. Me, you, all the girls, it's gonna be a girl's night out. I mean, it's only right she invites us along otherwise what's the point in being her friend?'

Wolfie put down a freshly severed leg that she'd been roasting over a fire for the last hour and gave Blood her full attention.

Going to the upper surface was a biggie and a rare treat not to be missed.

'Are you sure? Have you asked her? Because I've not seen her in days, and I know the others haven't either.'

'Oh yes,' Blood responded. 'I'm one hundred percent sure. You hear me right, sister, the word is that she's planning a big bash—and that big bash includes all of us being let loose up to the surface for some Halloween carnage.'

'Oh, I do hope you're right. I'm just not sure Mother would allow it, not after last time. And you know what a mummy's girl she is, she wouldn't do anything Mother doesn't want, it's sickening really.'

Blood sniggered because, despite all the grime and the unpleasantness, she found it hilarious that the master of evil was a bit of a mummy's girl at heart.

As did the rest of the occupants of Hell.

'Well, Mother hasn't got anything to do with it,' Blood responded. 'Apparently, she's so sick to the back teeth of her moping around the place, lowering the mood, that she'd let her do anything to cheer herself up.'

'Even unleash the depths of hell onto the upper place?'

'Well, not just everyone from the depths of hell, Wolfie. But definitely her posse. That's all of us. Every single rotten soul of us. All at once, yippee.'

Wolfie jumped up and down on the spot like the excitable schoolgirl that she once used to be before she got the lurgy and turned into a flesh-eating maniac when there was a full moon.

'But why?' she asked. 'She's never done that before. Not even hinted at it. Not even when Viktor got all mashed up that time. Do you remember that? Satan was grumpy for weeks after. And even then, she wasn't allowed to go the upper surface.'

'Aye, I remember it well as we all do. I couldn't bear the taste of lava for months after the smothering we all got. I still don't know why she chose to pour that all over us, it wasn't our fault, was it?'

'Because she doesn't like losing, Blood, that's why. So, to lose to a living Dinglewit was more than she could bear. But even then, she didn't unleash us all. And we offered, didn't we? We said to her, "Satan, let us all out of here and we'll get the buggers that killed Viktor." But she refused. She wouldn't entertain the idea. One of her most favourite pets had been killed, and even then, she refused to let us all out to the upper surface for some fun. So why now, that's what I want to know?'

'Well it doesn't matter because she is now. Or that's the rumour anyway. Something to do with Halloween becoming too commercial or something, and no fun anymore. So she's planning one last hurrah before she knocks the whole damned thing on the head.'

'Say what! She is planning to stop Halloween?'

'Yep. And for good too. And from what I've heard, she's deadly serious.'

'Is there any other kind of serious?'

'Nope, deadly is the only form.'

'And you say that she's planning on not doing Halloween anymore, at all, forever. Wow, I've never heard of such a thing.'

'Well, now you have.'

Overhearing the conversation, and getting a gist of the general tone, was a blue-haired cannibal going by the name Blue. For obvious reasons—for it appears—like here on the upper surface, that those living below also have a propensity for using the obvious.

Her real name was Barbara before she made the big move to a cannibalistic diet. Although she wasn't classically the sort of Dinglewit that many would regard as outstandingly beautiful, she was interesting enough to be getting on with.

An acquired taste is how she was often described.

But Blood thought her magnificent.

The most divine and splendid-looking cannibal in all of Hell.

Or at least the lower depths of it, there were a few closer to the surface.

'Did you say we're getting out of here?' Blue asked. 'Oh I do hope so. All this darkness and brimstone is so bad for my complexion. It brings me out in scabs.'

Wolfie grimaced at the sheer thought of it.

And with no small hint of jealousy, seeing as it was Blue who got the affection from Blood and not her.

'Oh lovely,' she muttered. 'That's just what we need…cannibals with scabs.'

'It's alright for you,' Blue snapped back. 'You only have to worry about your appearance once in a full moon. And even then, you're too concerned with filling ya belly with raw flesh. But this is something I have to live with on a daily basis. It really brings a girl down, you know.'

And then pretended to look upset.

Blood walked over and put her arms around her to offer friendly solace.

'Oh behave yourself, Blue,' jumped in Wolfie. 'You're not upset. And honestly, this whole diva routine might fool a sweetheart like Blood, but it doesn't fool me. I'm on to you. And anyway, who's ever heard of a vain cannibal? That goes against everything you all stand for, isn't it? You're supposed to have dripping flesh and blood hanging from every orifice, aren't you? Otherwise, what's the point in being a cannibal?'

Blood chastised Wolfie for being so insensitive and continued with her slime.

'My beautiful Blue,' she mused. 'Ignore her, she's being a big meany. No matter how many scabs you have, or no matter what the state of the flesh left on your magnificent bones, to me, you are the most splendid ghoul that ever set foot in Hell.'

Wolfie attempted to vomit.

'Get a room, you two. This is no place for mush. And this certainly isn't the time. It's Halloween. Satan's night for misery and wretchedness. If she hears you two going at it like a couple of love birds, she'll have you back on the rack. "The most splendid ghoul that ever set foot in Hell?" Honestly, you'll be for it if she hears that kind of talk.'

On this, Blue agreed, 'I suppose you're right. But I'm not a ghoul. I'm a cannibal. And a dedicated one at that. But there's no harm in wanting to look good when I'm eating, is there? That's all I'm saying.'

And clutching her head with both hands, presumably to stop anything from falling off, she turned and ran away like the spoilt flesh-eater she was.

'Arhh, you still pining over her, are you, Blood? Eh? You poor little loved-up blood-sucking parasite. Well, I'd say you'll need to make your move on her real soon because that flesh won't be sticking to her bones for too much longer. It's starting to smell. And then what will you have left? Just a skeleton with blue hair. Ughh, the very thought of it.'

'Even her skeleton with blue hair would be divine,' Blood answered. 'She is an angel that walks among us. That's what she is.'

'No, she's a cannibal that walks among us. *That's* what she is. And one that's beginning to go past her sell-by date. So I'd get in quick if I were you. Especially as Gnasher has his eyes on her.'

Blood looked over and saw Gnasher drooling from the mouth.

'If he takes one bite from her magnificent bosom, there'll be war,' she muttered.

Gnasher was also a cannibal who had been banished to the depths of hell for—let's just say—over-indulgence in the culinary department.

And when he finally swung from the rope of the hangman, he rightfully took her place along with the rest of nature's most sordid creatures.

'You hear that, Gnasher?' shouted Blood. 'Don't you bloody dare, you depraved flesh-eater. You stay well away. You hear me?'

Gnasher laughed.

Nobody took Blood seriously.

Not anymore.

But the conversation of their impending entrance up onto the upper place had still to be concluded.

And Wolfie was hoping for some cooperation on the matter.

'Well, I say that when the time comes we should work together and make light work of 'em. What do you reckon? That way, Satan can enjoy her night and maybe invite us to the next one.'

'No chance,' answered Blood. 'I intend to split up from you lot and hang out with Blue. So, you lot can do what you like as long as you stay well clear of me. Especially that thing—' she said, pointing at Gnasher.

'Oh, he'll not be coming. From what I hear, it's a girl's night only. Just us girls. And nobody wants an over-sexed bloke tagging on to a girl's night like some horny third wheel. God no. I can't think of anything worse.

'And to be honest, I don't think Satan likes him very much. I'm surprised he hasn't been banished to some other region out of the way. Maybe you should have a pop at him rather than Blue. At least he'd be well up for it.'

Blood was slightly insulted by the insinuation that she would find a man-cannibal attractive. And especially one that smells of man germs and has slept with the whole of lower hell, regardless of their genera.

'My dear Wolfie, I wouldn't be seen dead with something with a mane of hair as hairy as that. Magnificent though it is. I prefer my play friends with a little less mileage on the clock, thank you very much.'

Wolfie was impressed with Blood's laudable intentions in that department.

She, on the other hand, was not quite so stoic.

She summoned Gnasher over and gave him the eyes.

But just then, a beam of light illuminated their little soiree, and in walked Satan.

She was dressed up to the nines with broaches and things hanging from other things and was followed, quite warily—I must state—by her faithful servant, Biscuit.

'Ladies!' she announced, as if nobody was paying attention anyway. 'We're out on a jolly tonight, up at the surface. Who's up for it?'

Biscuit dropped to his knees from the weight of all the weapons.

Satan looked round in bemusement.

'Oh ignore him. Weak. So very weak. So, who's in? What about you, blue hair, you up for it?'

Blue was quite honoured to have been the first one chosen, even though it was evidently obvious that she didn't really know her name.

'Hell yeah!' she answered. 'I'm well up for a night out. Especially up at the surface.'

'Good. And what about you, erm, vampire?'

'Blood, Satan.'

'What?'

'My name is Blood.'

'Yes, of course it is. How silly of me to forget. So are you coming up to the surface for some blood and thunder.'

'Blood and thunder,' responded Blood. 'Sounds right up my street. When do we leave?'

'Excellent. We leave in a bit. I've organised a Halloween party at some old chapel in the middle of some little hick town in the middle of absolutely bloody nowhere. We should be left alone to enjoy ourselves. And what about you, the hairy one, don't we hang out from time to time?'

'Yes, Satan, I'm Wolfie, you obviously don't remember.'

'I'm not good with names. And anyway, I can't be expected to remember everyone who traipses through Hell, can I? There's been so many over the years. Hard to keep up. And none of you last long down here, you can't stand the heat. Weaklings. Just like Biscuit over there. I'm just surprised that no one has learnt their lesson yet and decided not to do evil stuff and have an enjoyable afterlife. Baffles me, it does. But then, if everyone was a goody two shoes, what a boring place the Universe would be. Plus, I'd have no one to play with. So easy come, easy go, I say. So that's settled then, us four, oh and Biscuit, are off to the upper surface for a Halloween party that I'll never forget.'

'Can I come?' chirped up Gnasher, thinking that if it was just him with four girls, it would be a guarantee of some action.

And Gnasher was nothing if not a man of action.

'You?' snorted Satan. 'You're a bloke. And this is a girl's night out. And I don't like you. You make me feel uneasy. In fact, I banish you to the boiling pot of eternity.'

She pointed her finger at Gnasher, and he immediately flew over to a cauldron of boiling fat, landing headfirst.

'There, that's the end of him. Right girls, we've got two hours before we need to get off. I've got a bag full of weapons that are here for all of us to use, can you think of anything else?'

Blue looked over at Biscuit and then at the bag of weapons he'd been lugging around all day.

'Is that a flamethrower?' she asked.

Satan gave a wry smile.

'Hell yeah, ain't it magnificent?'

'Erm, well, yeah, it is, but—'

'But what?'

'Well, aren't they meant to be dangerous?'

'Of course they are, that's the whole point of them. You point them in the general direction of whom you want to be burnt to a crisp and then squeeze. And before you know it, they're rolling around in agony before turning to dust. Loads of fun.'

'Yeah, I mean dangerous to the operator,' added Blue. 'There's been loads of stories of them going wrong and blowing up. Some say they're more dangerous to the operator than the potential victim.'

'Oh, you sound like Mummy. So dull. Look, if you don't want to use my flamethrower, then don't use it. In fact, no one can use my flamethrower except me, got it?'

'YES, SATAN,' they answered in unison.

'Good, right. Then get yourselves ready. It's gonna be a hot time in the cold town tonight.'

Chapter 6

The second victim on the last night of Halloween was a dear old lady going by the name of Ethel.

Ethel was the very definition of the word lovely.

The kindest and dearest old lady one could ever hope to imagine.

She hadn't harmed a single soul in all her long and delightful life, never made a single enemy. She had not said a single slight against anyone and had no intentions of ever doing so.

On the morning of Halloween, she dithered around the marketplace, speaking with traders and examining their products. Generally, she was being a decent and kind soul, totally unaware that this would be her last act on this pleasant and wonderful existence of hers.

Today, she was on the hunt for fruit.

'Hello, my dear,' she'd say, as she passed each stall and squeezed the pears looking for freshness.

'Ooh, they're lovely,' she'd mutter, as she scoured a critical eye at the strawberries, looking for any sign of mould.

'Ethel, my darling,' would cry a marketeer. 'Any two for a crown. But for you, you can have an extra one, seeing as you are so nice.'

The pleasantries would continue as Ethel slowly meandered her way along the cobbled market streets, looking for a bargain.

But if Ethel was to have one weakness—and she did—it was berries.

Ethel loved berries.

It was an addiction for her.

Her crutch.

Her guilty pleasure.

Her irrational obsession.

Red berries, green berries, white berries (oh, how she loved white berries), round berries, square berries, and even those rancid-smelling sour types of berries that nothing should go near.

And the market at Glint Tae was awash with berries this time of the year.

Ethel wobbled around the stalls seeking out the rarest berries that only ever seem to find their way to the market stall owners at Glint Tae Market.

And today, she was in luck.

Lucian, a somewhat untrustworthy seller of all things berry, had just received a new stock of berries grown from the dark side of Saturn's moon, Lapetus.

And being so close as Lapetus was, it was somewhat of a mystery as to why she'd never tried them before.

She has heard that they taste like cheese but with an afterburn that singes the larynx.

And she'd always been on the lookout for them, but to date, no joy.

But there they were.

A whole box full.

A whole box full of yellow Lapetus berries.

Freshly picked two weeks ago.

And frozen so as to maintain, at least, a small amount of their goodness.

And only a crown, a bag.

'I'll take three bags, please, Lucian, if you don't mind?'

'Mind, Ethel, mind? I don't mind at all. It would be a pleasure. Three bags, you say. Wow, you must really like 'em. If I'm honest, we can't ever get hold of 'em. This is the first lot I've ever seen. Very rare, Ethel, very rare.'

'And how did you get hold of them, Lucian, if you don't mind me asking?'

'Oh, I don't mind you asking, Ethel. Oh no, I don't mind at all. Well, these, they sort of…fell off the back of a spaceship, if you will. Fell off the back of a spaceship and onto my market stall.'

He then leant into Ethel's ear and whispered, 'And, erm, if you don't mind, I'd prefer it if you didn't tell anyone, if you know what I mean.'

Ethel did know what he meant.

But if that was the price to pay to finally feast upon the yellow Lapetus berry, then she was more than happy to pay.

That, and a crown a bag, of course.

She quickly scuttled home wasting no more time looking through any of the other frivolous berry stalls.

She had what she wanted.

She entered her little cottage and placed the basket full of berries down on the kitchen table.

Poured herself a glass of fresh water.

And grabbed one of her best plates from the cabinet.

Slowly and gently, she emptied the bags of berries onto the plate, carefully examining each one for imperfections.

She didn't want imperfections, not on her first time.

The first time was always the most special.

She remembered the first time she tasted an Olcocian melon, oh, it was divine.

But, and for a reason unknown to Dinglewit nor beast, things never taste the same the second time.

Ethel believes it's because the taste buds recognise the unique flavour and no longer release adrenaline or any of the other lovely sensational releasing hormones; so that kick is purely a one-time thing.

Therefore, the first time is the best time.

She closed the curtains and lit a candle.

There was no need for cutlery either, as Ethel always said that eating berries with your fingers is the best way to enjoy them.

None of these spoon and knife techniques seem to be popular these days.

It was fingers or nothing for Ethel.

She examined the plate, and a bunch of four perfectly formed and perfectly ripe berries were eager to be eaten.

And with a big sigh of excitement, she placed them onto her tongue and crunched.

'Mmmm,' she mumbled, groaning with pleasure. Surely a lady of her years shouldn't be enjoying something as much as this. 'Oh, the flavour,' she continued.

And then grabbed a handful more and slumped back into her chair with a satisfied desire.

If only for a few seconds.

Because then came pain in her stomach.

And then a bigger pain.

It was as if something was inside her, eating away at her innards.

She looked over at the plate of yellow Lapetus berries and noticed that a few were starting to grow faces.

And teeth.

Really sharp teeth.

And then more did the same.

And as they did, the pain in her stomach increased.

And it continued to increase until the pain was so bad that she slumped to the floor in abject agony.

She screamed.

But there was no one who would hear her agonising screams.

There was no one around to help dear old Ethel.

And even if there was, it was already too late as deep inside the body of poor old Ethel, the few yellow Lapetus berries—that had escaped the mastication process were now fully formed eating machines and—had set about devouring Ethel from the inside.

They chewed, and they swallowed.

They drank, and they digested.

And as they chewed and they swallowed and drank and digested, they grew bigger and bigger.

And as they grew bigger and bigger, their appetite grew greater and greater.

Until, after only a few short minutes, there was nothing left of the late, great, lovely Ethel, who hadn't harmed a single soul in all her long and delightful life. Also, she had never made a single enemy or said a single slight against anyone, ever.

Nothing left.

Not a single morsel of flesh.

Or a single drop of blood.

Nothing.

Except her slippers that sat neatly at the side of her chair.

Chapter 7

After making the mind-numbingly banal task of climbing down tied-up bedsheets look both clumsy *and* mind-numbingly banal, Barmy eventually felt the grass of freedom between his toes.

He'd forgotten how the feel of *real grass* allows just enough of the breeze to travel between your toes, and those soft bits in between to send you all giddy, and how it magically lifts your heart to places that no potion is ever able to do.

'Nothing, I repeat, nothing can lift the heart quite like real grass,' he muffled as he felt the sensation between his scrunched-up toes. 'Better than anything ever invented. Or created. Or grown in Cleese's garden shed, come to that. Amazing.'

Then he grunted because he'd also forgotten how wet it gets after a day of heavy rainfall. Then grunted again when he realised that if he'd brought some shoes along with him, the walk up to the old chapel would be much more enjoyable.

But now was not the time for practicalities as he was way beyond the point of no return, and he wasn't about to let the flesh tearing from his feet deter him from making good his escape.

He'd got his orders, you see.

And his orders said he simply must escape tonight and be at the Halloween party without fail.

And not just any old Halloween party, but it had to be this particular Halloween party at Blorkeney Knoll.

And not just any old night, but it had to be tonight.

It was of the utmost importance.

So squelching his feet around in the grass and mud, he set off.

'Tweedle dee, tweedle dum, tweedle dee, tweedle dum. What a glorious day to have some fun,' he hummed, as he waded through the trees and set his massive feet on the cobbles for the long walk ahead.

He liked humming songs when he was on his daily walks, he said that it broke the monotony of putting one foot in front of the other all the time and that it would be much better if another way of walking was invented.

I don't think it ever will, but Barmy wasn't ruling it out.

Anyway, there he was, Tweedle dee, tweedle dum-ing.

Not a great song I think you'll agree, but it was the best he could come up with on such short notice.

Also, he didn't have a dance to this new song he'd just made up just yet, just a second verse.

Which was equally dreadful.

'Tumble tee, tumble tum, tumble tee, tumble tum. One should never be afraid to scratch one's bum.'

Utterly terrible. He knew that much.

And it certainly wouldn't be winning any prizes or topping the pop charts any time soon.

He knew that much too.

But if a song was designed to represent an emotion, which apparently they are, then it was perfect.

Or perfect for Barmy, at least.

For he was what can easily be described as, feeling in high jinks and fine fettle.

Which, in itself, couldn't really be regarded as a total surprise considering he'd just high-raised a building.

But even with that in mind, he was feeling above average in spirit for the time of year.

And as daylight broke, and the sun shone brightly on his big pointy ears and muddy feet, Barmy was feeling pleased with himself.

He was out of the loony bin for the day and eager to fulfil his destiny.

His calling.

His *voyage de la vie*.

His mission to save the Earth.

So bounding along the road he went.

And singing a merry song he sang.

Until he came upon a peddler who seemingly needed a helping hand.

'I say, squire. What seems to be the issue?' asked Barmy, in a particularly posh-sounding voice for this hour of the day. 'From here it looks as though a wheel has come off your wagon.'

The peddler looked around in despair.

'Oh, you noticed, did you? How very perceptive. What gave it away?'

'Well,' answered Barmy, who never did get the joy of sarcasm. 'That wagon you are in possession of should have two wheels attached to it. One at each end, you see. But it only has one, the other being in your hands and absolutely not attached to the wagon. And this is making it all skew whiff and totally not suitable for the purpose for which it was intended, I would imagine.'

The peddler gazed aimlessly, wondering how much worse his day was going to get.

Little did he know.

'Very good,' he answered. 'Did you work that out all by yourself? Because I was all a fluster until you mentioned it,' still persevering with the sarcasm.

'It's the old bean, you see, it still functions, despite all the medication. And I am on some serious medications. Red pills, blue pills, uppers, downers, pills to make me sleep, pills to wake me up, you name it, I'm on it. It's a miracle I still function, to be honest.' And then he shimmered head to toe and made a quacking sound. 'But not just that. The voices told me…well, okay, a single voice. A nice chap, actually, he lives in another dimension. And he tells me things. And he told me to be at the Old Chapel at Blorkeney Knoll tonight for some good old-fashioned fireworks. And I'm not actually talking about fireworks. I simply have to get there. It's vital. But he also said that you might be able to help me if I help to fix your wheel, so that's how I knew your wheel was off.'

The peddler was not amused.

'Look, I can see you've escaped from somewhere for the day, but I'm busy here. I'm heading up to the chapel for the big bash myself. And on this cart is the food. So if I don't get it there on time, they will have my guts for garters. So, please, let me get on with it, will you?'

'Guts for garters,' repeated Barmy. 'Hmm, that's the second phrase of the day I've heard. I wonder where that came from. Guts for garters, I like it.'

'Second phrase of the day?'

'Yes. I think today will be a day of phrases. I can tell. Now, I see you've got yourself in a bit of a quandary there, can I help in some way?'

The peddler leant the wheel that he'd been struggling with for the last 20 minutes up against the cart and mopped his forehead with the back of his hand.

'I don't know,' he responded. 'Can you help? Are you a carpenter by any chance?'

'A carpenter? Me. No. I don't even know what a carpenter is. Or what they're supposed to do. I think it's something to do with wood, isn't it? Or at least, I presume it is. But that's all I can say. But you never know these days, do you? It's a strange old world.'

The peddler looked to the sky and prayed for a quick death.

'You're right there,' he answered. 'And none stranger than right now. Anyway, thanks for that, I'll just struggle on here then, if you don't mind?'

'Oh, I don't mind. I don't mind at all. But I don't see how that helps your situation. You see—'

And then Barmy appeared to freeze on the spot.

The peddler closed his eyes in incredulity at what was happening to him.

'Oh right,' Barmy said, as if answering someone. 'Okay, right, got it. Okay, Mr Peddler, apparently, what you need to do is mend your broken linchpin. The voice reckons it's no good putting that wheel back on without it, or it'll just come off again. And then you might end up with a damaged bogie frame, whatever that means, and—'

Barmy froze on the spot again for a few seconds before completing his sentence.

'Okay, right, got it. Okay, what you need to do is use that screwdriver that's under that old blanket in the back of your cart and thread it through the hole. The voice didn't say which hole. But it's probably not important. Just pick any hole, I suppose. And then it's fixed. According to the voice anyway.'

'According to who?'

'To whom.'

'Eh?'

'It's according to whom, not who. You could say what. But *according to what* sounds abrasive, don't you think?'

The peddler was now temporarily speechless.

But with a shake of the head to loosen a few neurons, he was back on track. 'Yes, of course, abrasive.'

'So, the screwdriver,' re-iterated Barmy, as he pointed to the back of the cart. 'The voice says it's under some old blankets.'

Now defeated but with nothing to lose, the peddler scurried under the old blanket that he hadn't moved in donkey's years and found an old rusty screwdriver.

'What!' he hollered. 'How? Erm, how could you know that was there? I didn't even know it was there.'

He looked around but found, the only Dinglewits that were there were just him and this crazy escapee who likes talking to the air but who evidently seems to know stuff.

'I mean. What is going on here?'

Barmy shrugged the old shoulders, both of them, it was a double-shoulder shrugging moment, you see.

'Oh, don't ask me,' he answered. 'I just work here.' And then smiled.

'You work here?'

'No, it was just a phrase. But it sounded good, didn't it? That's the third phrase of the day. I just wanted to get one in of my own.'

The peddler held out a hand of welcome. 'The name's Biffin, and I would be very grateful for a helping hand if you wouldn't mind. This wheel is the weight of two of me, so unless you can help, I'll be walking myself. And if I'm walking, then I'm having to carry all this stuff on my back, and, well, that ain't going to happen. So if you don't mind giving me a hand fixing the wheel, I'd be most grateful to you.'

Barmy accepted his hand.

'Well, everyone calls me Barmy. Ol' Barmy. And, erm, well, if I may be pushy also, but if I give you a hand fixing your wheel, would you mind rubbing some ointment into my sore feet? No shoes, you see. Starting to sting a tad, what with all this walking. I'd be most grateful back at ya.'

The peddler looked down at Barmy's feet with astonishment.

'Oh, goodness me, yes. Of course. Wait, hold on, I might have a spare pair of clogs in here somewhere.'

He rustled about the back of his cart.

'Yes, here you are. I guess you are 16. Just like me.'

And he got out a brand-new pair of bamboo clogs from some boxes he was hoping to sell at the Halloween party tonight.

'And don't worry about the price, Barmy. Let's call it the cost of you helping me. In fact, I could give you a lift too, if you like.'

'To where?'

'Blorkeney Knoll. I'm going to the old chapel too, remember? I could give you a lift, save you the effort of walking.'

'Oh, no thanks, Biffin, but that's mighty kind of you. But I'd prefer to walk. I'm thinking it will be more of an adventure if I walk.'

'It's miles away.'

'I know.'

'You sure?'

'Oh yes, quite sure.'

'Right, well, if you insist.'

'I do.'

'Here, have the clogs. You can have them for giving me a hand.'

'Like a trade?'

'Yes, like a trade. Your labour for the price of the clogs. That sounds a fair trade, don't you think?'

'Yes, it does. But I can do better.'

'How so?'

'I can offer some inside knowledge to you as a form of tip.'

'Inside knowledge?' asked Biffin the Peddler.

'Yes, inside knowledge.'

'On what?'

'On tonight.'

'Tonight? You mean at the Halloween party.'

'Yes, the very same. You see, and try to keep this to yourself, but tonight is going to be a blood bath. A full-on blood bath. So, if I were you, I'd be dropping off your delivery and getting the hell out. No, wait—'

And Barmy looked once more into the air as, presumably, the voice gave him another piece of fine advice. 'Right, got it. Apparently, you have choices. Either you can drop off your delivery and make a run for it, or you can stick around and make some money selling weapons.'

Biffin the Peddler was again astounded.

'Now, how did you know I do that?' he asked in amazement. 'I hadn't told a soul. That's amazing.'

'Oh, my friend seems to know it all.'

'Yes, he does. Yes, he does indeed. A blood bath, you say?' Now starting to look interested.

'Yep. Lots of death and murder. That's what he tells me.'

'Who, the voice?'

'Yep, the voice. And the voice is never wrong. Or as far as I know he's never wrong. I guess I'll find out later. So if I were you, I'd be well away from the shenanigans tonight in Glint Tae. Or, of course, grab a weapon and fight. You know, if that's what you want to do.'

Biffin the Peddler inserted the screwdriver into the hole that held the wheel in place and climbed into the back of his cart.

'They're in here somewhere,' he muttered, as he rambled through some packages at the bottom end of his stock.

'What are?' asked Barmy.

'Weapons. Lots and lots of deadly weapons. And if there is going to be a blood bath, then that means a bull market is about to take place. And a killing can be made if you pardon the pun. Yep, here they are.'

'And another phrase.'

'Is that number—'

'Four,' interrupted Barmy. 'That's phrase number four. But wait. You, you're actually planning on sticking around and selling weapons?'

'Hell yeah. I'm a peddler, that's what I do. I sell stuff. I've got everything here. Everything you'd need for a battle on Halloween night. Look! I've got a nice range of swords, here. That's a crossbow. Some hammers, but I wish I'd brought more now, you know. But you never know how the day will go, do you? Look here, this is a fork. You can really do some damage with that. This is a skewer-type device; apparently, you stick it in and turn it around, and the intestines just fall out. These are baseball bats, famous for clubbing folk on the head. See…everything you need. And it's nearly all profit because I picked these up at rock-bottom prices. Yep, I'll tell you one thing, Barmy, old fella, if what you say is right, then there's some serious crowns to be made tonight, that's for sure.'

'And you have no conscience about selling deadly weapons?'

'Weapons don't kill anyone, it's us who kill. And there's no profit in peace.'

'Evidently not. But what a coincidence, don't you think?'

'What is?' asked Biffin the Peddler.

'You. You being here with a cart full of weapons. That's a coincidence, don't you think?'

'Coincidence? Maybe I suppose. But a nice coincidence. Especially for me because I'll be making loads of lolly.'

'If you survive, Biffin. You'll be making loads of lolly—as you say—if you survive. But there's no guarantee of that. Not tonight. Because it's going to be a blood bath.'

'So, you've already said, old boy. But you can't be an arms dealer without a blood bath, Barmy, my friend. Not a successful one, anyway. That's what I've come to learn. Besides, I've never been killed yet. And I've no intention of starting tonight.'

'Yeah, well, no one ever does. But as sure as the Universe made little green lizards with poisonous tongues, someone always dies. I'm afraid that's what a blood bath implies. So if I were you, I'd be trading carefully.'

'Nah, no one kills little ol' Biffin. Why would they? I'm neutral. I'm nice—'

'You're an inconsequential part of the story; that is what you are.'

'Eh? What do you mean?'

'Like I say, you play a small and inconsequential part of the story. And they always end up dead.'

'What story?'

'The story of tonight. This—the Halloween story. The one that we're all about to take part in. I've no doubt the Universe has it all planned out. It always does. It's assembled some major players in one place, apparently. And I've no doubt it will want blood too. So like I said earlier, I'd be treading carefully.'

Biffin shrugged off Barmy's words as he'd already made his mind up, and it didn't support the narrative he wanted, and then put the finishing touches to his wagon.

He would be going to the Old Chapel at Blorkeney Knoll tonight to drop off the food.

He would be sticking around and selling his weapons for a massive profit.

And he would be taking his chances with the Universe's plans for the last night of Halloween.

Now, for those ignorant of the geography of Glint Tae—which would be most of the Dinglewits that lived there as it turned out—the psychiatric hospital is perched out on the outskirts on one side of the town, and the Old Chapel at Blorkeney Knoll is as far on the other side as is theoretically possible.

This was good because it meant that the two institutions of hellion would never find themselves in touching distance of each other.

As heaven help us if they ever did.

So in a sense, Glint Tae acts like a sort of rose surrounded by two thorns and thistles and all things dark and miserable.

In fact, there couldn't be more distance between them, and a greater difference in mood, if they'd planned it that way.

Which maybe they had.

But with a favourable wind and a good stern rambling pace, the journey between the two would take an ordinary Dinglewit about three hours to four hours to walk.

But for Barmy, you can double it.

Maybe even triple it, he gets easily distracted, you see.

Just the mere sight of a moth or a butterfly—minding its own business chopping around in the flowers—would amuse him to such an extent that he'd spend hours glaring at it without a thought for the outside world.

Or maybe the twirl of a tree branch swaying back and forth to the rhythm of the wind, that would need looking at for a while too.

Or an ant, clambering through the grass looking for something gigantic to carry to impress its friends, a period of observation would be required there also.

All in all, a three-hour hike from one side of town to the other could easily take nine, and quite possibly longer.

And that's before he meets yet another fellow traveller with whom he may wish to engage in another uncomfortable conversation.

Like this one.

'Good day to you, fine madam. It's a lovely day, what?'

'Is it?' came the answer, as the female traveller made it abundantly obvious by her stance that she was ready to punch him in the throat should he try any funny business.

Heaven forbid.

'Oh yes. A very fine day. And upon further analysis I can conclude that this is turning out to be a most enjoyable experience to boot. I've met a peddler who has given me all kinds of insight into his trade. And now I'm off to save the world.'

'Right…well…good for you. I'm glad someone is enjoying an early morning shufty around this dump. Me? I've had enough of this day already. Have you just got out of the hospital by any chance?'

'Very good!' Barmy gasped. 'You have an eye for investigation. Are you a sleuth? Or a detective? Or maybe one of those genius types that I've heard all about. You know, the ones, really good at patterns and numbers and stuff, but not very good with sudden loud noises and large crowds. Are you one of those?'

'Nope, it's because you're wearing a hospital gown. That was the big giveaway for me. So no, not a sleuth, just observant.'

Oh yes, I forgot to mention that Barmy lived and breathed entirely in his hospital gown while at the psychiatric hospital.

He didn't need to however, he had his own clothes there.

They all had.

He could wear whatever he liked.

But Barmy liked the look.

He couldn't get enough of those faded green stripes and lack of buttons.

He thought he looked like *Beau Brummel of Loonyville.*

Sometimes, he accompanied his look with an old straw hat, boater style.

Other times, he'd be donning a yellow rose in his lapel.

That was for special occasions like funerals or chess nights.

But he always wore a hospital gown.

He insisted upon it.

It was his *go-to.*

He said that he liked the way that his bum was partially on show at the back.

And he never took the time to tie it up properly, and most days he didn't bother tying it up at all.

He used to get sanctioned for it all the time.

But after the guards realised that they were just wasting their time trying to put some order into his wardrobe selection, they just let him get on with it.

They even sometimes referred to him as Bare-Bum-Barmy because of it.

'Oh yes, the gown,' Barmy replied. 'Do you like it? I do. It's rather fetching, yes. I like the stripes, they make me look slim. Especially the green stripey ones. And the string instead of buttons. And that I can—'

'Let your bum be free?' came the interruption, while she squinted her eyes at the sight of a bare bum, and then muttering that she wished she'd been born without eyes at all.

'Well, no, but that is another plus point,' laughed Barmy. 'I like the breeze whistling through the cheeks, you see. Ya know, if I'm being honest.'

'A little too honest, I'd say.' But now she was intrigued. 'So, have you just been medically discharged then?' she asked.

'Medical? Oh no, Flower. There's nothing medically wrong with me. I'm as fit as a butcher's dog, I am. Not a bone out of place or a hormone out of sorts. I'm what you might call, as fit as a fiddle. Strange saying that, isn't it? As fit as a fiddle. Why did the humans use that term, then, do you think? As fit as a fiddle. I'm sure fiddles aren't fit. They're just bits of wood glued together, aren't they? I don't know, I get so confused these days, I find it hard to keep up. Probably the tablets.'

'Probably,' answered the female traveller. 'But if there's nothing wrong with you, then why were you in hospital? And why are you wearing that silly gown out here? There's nothing to it, you'll catch your death.'

Barmy looked dissatisfied.

She was obviously one of those practical types.

The type that makes plans and draws up lists, so nothing gets forgotten.

One of those types.

'Because I wasn't in *that* hospital, my dear,' he responded. 'I was in the one on the other side of the road.'

'Oh… the, erm, the, the.'

'The loony bin, that's right,' Barmy intervened, sensing some social awkwardness from his new-found friend. 'I'm from the happy home, the nut house, a fully paid-up member of the happy club, that's me. I'm not embarrassed by it, why should I be? I'm enlightened, you see. My mind is free. Barmy is the name, and being barmy is the game. I do prefer to be called Barmy, if that's okay with you. It is a nickname, but I like nicknames. You only give nicknames to those you like, don't you think?'

'Er, yes. I suppose you do.'

'And how may I address you?'

Somehow the honesty had eased her mind somewhat, and she was feeling a lot more comfortable about meeting a stranger in a hospital gown with his bum on show and wearing a straw hat.

And that's a state of affairs that many don't enjoy every day.

'My name's Lucy,' she replied. 'And everyone calls me Lucy. It's very nice to meet you, Barmy, I'm sure.'

'Why, hello Lucy. What a beautiful name. I think I'll call you…Lucy. Yes, Lucy, that's what I'll call you. Lucy. No need for nicknames here, I think. Not just yet anyway. Maybe later. And what brings you along this particular road to nowhere at this ungodly hour of the morning?'

Lucy wasn't sure whether he was speaking metaphorically, or he was simply pointing out the geographical nature that all hospitals are built in hard-to-reach areas where the traffic is bad these days.

It was hard to say.

He wasn't the easiest chap to judge.

So, she presumed the latter, for now.

'I'm going to call on a friend. I have urgent business to talk with him about. And it's most urgent I get there as quick as possible.'

'Oh, well if you have to get there as quick as possible, then it must be important business,' Barmy replied, clearly not taking a hint that Lucy was trying to get away from this weirdo she'd just met with his bum out on show. 'That's how it works, you see. The inner workings of universal administration, or temporal action, as it's called back at HQ. If something is important, then it must be done straight away. They insist on it, you know. But, erm, there's nothing down here except those two buildings of ill repute that we call hospitals, oh, and the mountains of course. This friend of yours, he isn't a mountain dweller, is he? Or is he one of us?' Barmy felt the urge to enquire.

Lucy was confused.

'I'm not sure what a mountain dweller is. What do you mean by a mountain dweller?'

Barmy was stumped.

Even he wasn't sure what a mountain dweller was, and he'd just used the term.

But this was a common thing for the old boy, he often opened his mouth before engaging the brain.

And usually what came out was complete piffle.

Like just now.

'Do you know, Lucy, I really don't know. I honestly don't. But if I ever see one, I'll let you know,' he answered.

Up until now, Lucy had been enjoying her chat with what was obviously a completely screaming lunatic.

And as much as she found him fascinating, I mean, who wouldn't find a strange fellow in a hospital gown and a straw hat fascinating, it's not something you come across every day, she simply had to call upon me as a matter of urgency.

Yes, me.

I'm finally in the story.

But more of me later.

'Look, Barmy, I really don't mean to be rude, but I must get on and visit my friend. It is a matter of the utmost urgency. Otherwise, I would love to stand here and chew the fat with you about…whatever it is we've been talking about. But I must get to Mr P as soon as I can. The entire world may depend on it.'

Barmy's eyes lit up.

'Mr P, you say. *The* Mr P? As in Montgomery Plum?'

'You heard of him?'

'Heard of him! I know him. I know him very well. Very well indeed.'

'Oh, right, really?'

'Oh yes, we've shared a few adventures together. He's a pheasant enough plucker, if a bit frayed around the edges, shall we say. Oh yes, I like him a lot. A good egg, if a bit, you know, doolally.'

Which I have to say set me back a little bit when I heard how I'd been described.

'Yep, that sounds like him, alright. I'll tell him that I met you. I'm sure he'll be pleased to know that you're okay, and, erm, walking the streets unaccompanied.'

'Well, you can, my dear. But he won't know who I am. Not yet anyway.'

'Eh? I thought you said you two knew each other.'

'We do know each other. We just haven't met yet, you see.'

'But you said—'

'Aye. And we have. Or we do. We have some terrific adventures together.

Or had. But not yet, you see. They're all in a future timeline. You know, in the future from…now. But not yet. If you know what I mean?'

Lucy didn't.

And furthermore, she felt this a good time to bid her farewells and get on with the job at hand.

Barmy agreed.

After all, he always said there is only so much flannel you can throw at a funnel.

But the chat had cheered him up.

He'd forgotten all about his troubles back at the psychiatric hospital and was looking forward to getting to grips with Satan at Blorkeney Knoll.

And he wouldn't want to be late.

Not tonight.

Chapter 8

Time for another victim on this—the last ever night of Halloween, me thinks.

He went by the name of Melancholy.

And if we're being honest here, Melancholy was always destined to be a victim.

He was that sort of chap.

Doomed in life, I think they say.

A tragic case.

Well, today he stumbled from the public inn and made his way down by Boris's Butcher Shop to the alleyway to empty a bladder, or two.

This was a regular exercise for old Melancholy after leaving the pub following an all-day session on the ale.

That and crashing out on the sofa until the toxins wore off.

No hassle.

No one giving him grief.

Just old Melancholy and the sofa and nothing else.

He was a loner, you see. He didn't have many friends outside the drinking establishments, and that's just the way he liked it.

Friends took too much time away from drinking.

And drinking was his life.

And he enjoyed his life.

You could tell this because his beaming red face always possessed a smile.

Not many teeth.

And a lot of wrinkles.

But always a smile, hence the name Melancholy, because he was always so happy.

So back down the alleyway he reached out an over-stretched arm and leant up against the wall, the other hand attempting to undo his trousers.

He was going to enjoy this.

He'd broken the seal earlier that day, and was, what was commonly known as, *busting*.

Now, if there was one thing about Melancholy's habit of urinating in his favourite alleyway after a few bevvies, it was that he likes to do it alone.

He considered it a solo sport.

It's not the sort of thing that an audience should be appreciating.

He could never urinate in front of other Dinglewits anyway.

So, as you would expect, when Melancholy heard the giggling of mini-imps while he was in mid-flow—so to speak—it put him off his game somewhat.

He he, he he. Giggle giggle, giggle giggle.

'Go away!' he shouted. 'I can't do it when I'm being watched.'

He he, he he. Giggle, giggle, giggle, giggle. Scurry scurry.

The crashing of bin lids, and a cat screeching.

'Go away. You're putting me off, I say. This isn't for spectators, you know. Can't a chap do his business in peace these days?'

But that was to be the least of his worries.

'Owwwww! Why you miserable little imp. You've bitten me!' he shouted, as he quickly turned around and booted the mini-imp over to the other side of the alleyway.

He then looked around for more.

They always hung out in numbers.

But he couldn't see any.

The mini-imp he'd just booted, dusted itself down, giggled, and scampered off.

'Good, right, now, back to the job at hand.'

And he turned back around to the wall for some unfinished business.

But he was right to be suspicious.

For mini-imps do hunt in packs.

They always hunted in packs.

It was the only way they got a decent meal.

And today, Melancholy, was that decent meal.

A mini-imp dived from above and landed plum centre of his head, and with a giggle and a beaming grin, rammed a finger in each ear.

This was followed by another flying mini-imp who took refuge in old Melancholy's bum crack.

It gripped in tight with its sharp nails and took a generous bite, after all, they'd be enough to go around.

'Ooooooohhhhhh! You little bugger,' Melancholy shouted.

And while he was aimlessly flapping around to unhook the savage little bum-eater, another ran from the shadows and jumped directly at his face.

He hit the floor and rolled around in pain.

But his pain wouldn't last long.

As within a few more seconds, the rest of the pack made themselves available for a spot of lunch and tucked right in for their first dish of the day—Melancholy Surprise.

Devoured.

Chapter 9

I guess it's high time in our little story to introduce the hero of the show, me, Montgomery Plum—the man of the hour, for heaven knows we've been talking about killer imps and poisonous berries for far too long already.

Well, I awoke early on that Halloween morning at a disgustingly obscene hour.

I didn't even know such a time existed, not abstemious anyway.

And if it did, why would anybody in their right mind choose to engage in such a practice like getting out of bed at this dirty, unconscionable hour?

Normally, my extra-large ears would refuse—point blank—to leave the pillow until at least the stench of breakfast had displayed the good manners to disperse itself into a mid-morning snack, and the morning mist had congregated into a cloud formation.

But it takes all sorts, I suppose, and where would we be if everyone was the same?

So, there I was, wide awake, the old blood trickling through the muscles, and about to start the day.

And with so many extra hours to use up, I was all at sea thinking how on Earth I would be able to fill it.

But Montgomery Plum is nothing if not resolute.

And so, with a shake of the head and a finger wiggled in the ear socket, I roused myself from the old slumber, climbed out from my pit—still confused as to why my head had woken me up so early—and made my way to greet the world.

But then it struck me, Lucy was at the door, and it was her heavy-fisted approach at door-knocking that had kicked me into life in the first place.

This was a relief as I didn't much wish to make this sort of thing a habit.

It simply isn't what gentlemen do.

And by the time I was finally able to get my act together to clamber down the stairs, Gertie had answered the door and let her in, and they were, both sitting comfortably on the sofa, schmoozing girly talk and generally being—well—female.

Now I'm normally the placid kind of chap in these sorts of situations.

To each their own, as the saying goes, but today I'd decided that urgent action was required, or else this sort of might carry on and become convention, and then all and sundry may feel the urge to call upon me whenever the mood overtook them, and then I'd be out of bed at this ungodly hour every day and would be at sixes and sevens as to how I would occupy all those extra hours that I'd unwantedly inherited.

Words were needed.

'Lucy, old bean. You know me,' I began. 'I'm normally the easy-going and fancy-free type of chap, wouldn't you say? Let everyone live by their own rules, say I. And far be it from me to tell anyone how to live their life, I wouldn't have thought I'm qualified even if I wanted to. And, of course, you have every right to squeeze every hour out of the day like some orange that's about to go out-of-date. But even so, old girl, this is a brutal start to any day, don't you think? I mean, why so early, old sponge?'

Lucy and Gertie both laughed.

'It's nearly lunchtime, you lazy arse,' Gertie responded. 'And look at the state of you. You look a fright. Most normal folk have completed half of their day by this time, and here you are, whingeing that you've been dragged from your pit before the sun's hit zenith. Honestly, I'm embarrassed for you.'

Lucy agreed and stated that she would be embarrassed too if I were her lesser half of a double act.

To which I totally ignored because, well, I wanted to.

And I was hungry, as they say, I could eat a horse and its jockey, or words to that effect.

So on this occasion, I overlooked the obvious slight on my character and made for the kitchen.

'It's nearly noon, you say. Does that mean I've missed breakfast?'

'Yep, you've missed breakfast and your mid-morning snack. You must be starving. Your stomach will think that your throat's been cut. How will you ever cope?' responded Gertie, still laughing with Lucy.

Who then responded with her own jibe.

'Oh God, you look emaciated. Your skin is practically falling from your bones. I can see your skeleton and everything.'

And the pair continued to snigger like they were enjoying this far too much for my liking.

But again, I ignored them because, as Gertie was polite enough to highlight, I'd missed two meals already today and was absolutely famished.

'Right, where's the food,' I moaned, and then tripped over a chair.

Which only caused more merriment with the two girls.

'Have you heard about the party tonight?' Gertie shouted. 'Lucy's been doing some bone-throwing and tarot reading and thinks that something smells fishy. And we're not talking about your feet.'

I grunted, through the clattering of bowls and silver cutlery, 'My feet do not smell of fish, they smell of cheese. A nice and mature cheese.'

So she was wrong on that one.

One nil to old Monty.

But I felt it best not to give running commentary on the scores until the end of the day, otherwise Gertie would start doing underhand things to win, as she always did when there was a game to be won.

She didn't much like losing.

But I was still hungry.

So hungry.

In fact, it would be safe to say I'd never been so hungry in all my life.

So, while the insults kept coming, I scavenged around the fridge looking for food.

And having not got the response she wanted, Gertie continued, 'And I agree with Lucy on this one, *I* also think something's fishy. The bones and cards don't lie. There is definitely something afoot. And we think it involves the dark arts of the Universe. And if it involves the dark arts of the Universe, then invariably, it will involve you at some point. What do you make of that?'

I remarked that she was always *with* Lucy whenever she came up with something spooky, and that I think she only does it to get at me.

Which was so plainly true.

And after this observation was battered away with a very sensible question of, "And why would I do that?" I conceded that it was, as they say, fishy, and that once I find my head at this god-awful hour of the day, I'll be right on it.

And I then staggered into the larder for a drink.

'And I'll tell you another thing as well,' Gertie continued. 'If there's going to be some sort of party where bad stuff happens, then we're definitely going. Me and you. We're going together. Because if something is kicking off at this party, then I'm going to be right next to you so you can't get into any trouble. You got it?'

I took a big slurp of fresh juice and immediately sprang to life.

'A party! I love parties. Where?' I shouted.

Then took another big slurp of juice.

'Blorkeney Knoll. The Old Chapel. Lucy has hired it out for the evening and organised a Halloween party so she can get some money in doing tarot readings and the like. But now she suspects that it's been hijacked, and something is about to kick off. Don't you Lucy?'

'Definitely.'

'So we were chatting, and we think that in order for us to have some semblance of control over what is about to happen, then it's better to have it on familiar territory. And I have to say, I've never agreed with anything so much in my life. If this is going to happen, then at the very least we should choose the battlefield. And I can't think of a better place than the Old Chapel at Blorkeney Knoll to do battle. Do you remember, she hired it out before?'

I sprung my head from around the larder.

'Of course I blooming remember it. Who doesn't? That was where you unleashed the demon of the undead onto this unsuspecting planet and nearly got us all killed.'

'Unwittingly,' Lucy responded. 'It was an accident.'

'Be that as it may, but if it wasn't for my magic coin and me being magnificent, then the whole world would now be under the control of an evil warlord from hell.'

'Yeah.' Giggled Lucy. 'Fun, wasn't it? I'm hoping for more of the same tonight.'

'Fun?' I interrupted, 'Fun? I would hardly call bringing old *what's-his-face* back from the dead—fun.'

'Viktor,' answered Lucy. 'King Viktor.'

'That's the badger, King Viktor, what a douche ball he was. A real psycho, and not the sort of chap you want running the joint, I'd say. Also, didn't you end up having a thing with him? Yes, I think you did. You definitely did. You had a thing with him, didn't you?'

'I don't want to talk about it,' muttered Lucy.

'I bet you don't. Talk about embarrassing exes. Not many can lay claim to an undead king of the underworld. How's that for an embarrassing ex?'

And I revelled in the fact that the shoe was on the other foot for once.

'But it was fun while it lasted, though,' responded Lucy. 'And besides, you chopped him up and sent him back to oblivion, so at least I'll not be having him pester me forever as my other exes do. So, in fact, I'm all good.'

'True dat, Lucy, true dat. I did open a can of whoop-ass on his…Erm, ass. But I'd hardly have called it fun.'

'Really? You don't think it was a laugh. Fighting zombies and getting into duels with fire-breathing dragons. I bet you loved it.'

'Yeah, okay, you've got me there,' I replied. 'I guess it was a little bit fun.'

'It was more than a little bit fun. It was a *lot* of *bit* fun,' Lucy responded. 'It was the sort of fun that writers write books about. So although I'm cautious of what might happen tonight, at least it will be fun.'

Not wishing to be left out of the conversation in fear of becoming irrelevant to tonight's proceedings, Gertie jumped in on the side of Lucy.

'Agreed, we need some fun around here. It's all been as dull as dishwater recently. And you know you've not been yourself. You never are when you're just sat around the house with no one to kill. You need the action. You thrive on it. So perhaps a splash of paranormal horseplay will put some lead back into your pencil…Figuratively speaking, of course.'

I looked sternly at Gertie.

Then looked awkwardly at Lucy.

I mean to say, I was okay with the Universe unleashing murderous demons onto the unsuspecting Dinglewits of planet Earth.

And I was okay with having to risk my life to kill them.

That's my job, after all.

But questioning the lead in my pencil, well, that was a step too far.

'There's nothing wrong with my lead, Gertie old sparrow, is there? Or my pencil. My lead and my pencil are still as sharp as granite, yes?'

And I gazed expectantly at Gertie looking for support on this matter; I didn't want word getting around that there was something wrong with the old pencil, so to speak.

That would do my, already low, street cred' no good at all.

But the support didn't come.

Just more insults.

'I wouldn't say granite. More like limestone. But still worthy of the cause,' Gertie acceded, and as had been the habit so far this morning, they both laughed again. 'But you don't need to worry, darling, with enough stimulation, it'll do the job.'

'If only for a few minutes,' laughed Lucy.

And has had also been the habit this morning, Gertie agreed.

But all this talk of stimulation had, somewhat, stimulated old Montgomery.

'Blorkeney Knoll, you say?' I asked.

'Yep.'

'And the Old Chapel.'

'Indeed.'

'The very same Old Chapel that you summoned old, erm, who was he again?'

'Viktor,' Lucy answered. 'We've already established this. I think you're losing your marbles.'

'Yes, that's it. Viktor. Well, well, well. The Old Chapel at Blorkeney Knoll. Yes, this does propose a fun night ahead. And you think that the Universe has something planned for us too? Cool, this could be splendid. I'm in, I'll clean down Excalibur and tell Cleese. He'll be well up for this.'

And it was at this point Gertie's mood changed from laughing and playful, to a woman enraged.

This wasn't new for Gertie.

She had a tendency to switch from being nice and happy to as mean as mustard at the drop of a hat.

She said it kept me on my toes, but I know it's just because she can be a grouchy old so-and-so at times.

And especially when Cleese is mentioned.

'You can go flush your head down the toilet if you think that's happening,' she yelled. 'Whenever you two get together, it spells nothing but trouble. And if Lucy is right about tonight, I think we'll be having enough trouble to deal with without Cleese's special brand of nonsense going on. So, I don't want Cleese anywhere near us, got it?'

'But pudding, I was just thinking—'

'Well unthink it. Because it ain't happening. Now, if you wish, I'll flush your head down the toilet, then you'll have to spend the whole day drying out your beard. And remember, this might be your last day on Earth. Or, if I find out you've arranged to meet Cleese at Blorkeney Knoll, I'll flush your head down the toilet then. And then you'd be spending the whole night with a wet beard and smelling of toilet. Either way, Cleese is not coming anywhere near us tonight, not while I have a hole in my backside.'

'Oh, right,' I grumbled, like one would when they've just been told that they can't go out and play with their best friend. 'So apparently I can go flush my head down the toilet then, can I? But wait, hold on a cotton-picking minute; isn't tonight supposed to be trouble? Isn't that the whole point of Halloween? That's what I heard, anyway. So if that's the case, then Cleese is just what the doctor ordered, right? Because nothing means trouble more than Cleese does. That's practically his middle name.'

It isn't, by the way.

'Well, yes, but there's trouble…and there's *trouble*. And if we're doing this thing at the Old Chapel, then I'd say we'll be having enough trouble to be getting along with, don't you?'

She had a point.

'Yes, that may be true, but if you think about it, whatever is about to do their worst tonight won't be expecting us to be aware of it. They might have a plan, you see. And if they have a plan, then we'll need to destroy it. And you know Cleese, he's an absolute dog when it comes to destroying plans.'

'Yes, but he'll destroy our plans and get us all killed. Please, no Cleese, Montgomery, just for once, eh? Just think about it, for me.'

'Think? Oh, I haven't thought for ages, my little pumpkin. You know that. It's bad for the old ticker. I'm more of an all-action hero—me. I'd rather just do than think. That's where I shine.'

'Well tonight you can do what you like, just not with Cleese. He'll balls the whole thing up and get us slaughtered.'

There was no denying this was true.

Even I could see that Gertie had spotted the apparently obvious nail and hit it on the head.

But dash it, I thought, *what was the point in having a friend that enjoyed fingering with death as much as I did, if I can't invite him along for some guaranteed fingering on Halloween?*

Sad times.

But some things, as they say, are simply out of your control.

'Got it, but erm, we should at least let him know though, yeah? We should at least give him the heads up, don't you think? He'd be most put out if we went there without a mutter in his shell-like. You know what he's like when these sorts of things come along. He'd be devastated to miss out.'

Gertie was not impressed.

'Well, it's up to Cleese what he does. But he ain't coming with us. So if he wants to go, then he'll have to find another play friend because I'll be keeping tabs on you. So tonight, it's either me or your best friend…decide?'

Of course, I knew it was a trick question and that I didn't really have the option of deciding between Gertie and Cleese.

That was all a rouse to get the old testicles squeezed if I got the answer wrong.

And the two options that I'd just been served weren't really options at all, they were just statements disguised as options.

And I was way too smart to fall for all that.

Even at this hour.

Although I was no longer sure if Gertie knew this fact.

For her part, she just wanted me to fall into line and do as I was told.

Which, of course, I did.

Most of the time.

It was safest that way.

At least, on the outside.

So opting for the self-preservation of the old cojones, I quickly changed the subject.

'So, what have the bones been telling you, Lucy?' I asked. 'Or was it the tarot cards? Sorry, I can't remember now. It's tricky all this. Hard to keep up.'

Lucy shuffled uncomfortably in her seat.

She knew that what she was about to say was going to sound extraordinary.

Talking about the occult always did.

But then she *was* speaking with me, Montgomery Plum, and Gertie, probably the only two Dinglewits on planet Earth that would dare to believe in something this amazing, so onwards she began.

'Not bones or the tarot, both,' she answered. 'They both say the same thing. Exactly the same. And I've tried it a few times, and every time, the same.'

'Which is?'

'A reckoning. That's what. A reckoning is coming. And it's coming tonight. That's what they say. No doubt about it. A reckoning is coming.'

Gertie sighed. 'Oh God, here we go again. And what sort of reckoning are we talking about here? Another demon from the past? Or is it a demon from the future this time?'

Lucy shuffled even more uncomfortably in her chair.

There was no reason to be shuffling so much; the cushions were divine, but I could see that this whole thing was making her feel uneasy.

'I think it's Satan herself,' she declared. 'Or whatever she's calling herself these days. But it's definitely her. I can feel it. And she's got something up her sleeve for tonight too. Something special.'

'Well, yeah,' I answered. 'Today's Halloween. She always does something special on Halloween. It's her day. Her special day. I'd be disappointed if she didn't do something special, if I'm honest.'

'But not like this. Something's wrong. Very wrong. I can feel it. The bones have felt it too. And the cards. So that double proves it. This isn't going to be like any Halloween that we've ever known.'

'I bloody hope not,' I interrupted. 'It's all been so overly commercialised beyond belief recently that it's no fun anymore. Absolute gibberish, my dear child. So, personally, I'll be glad if the old girl livens things up a tad.'

Lucy shuffled even more, even more uncomfortably, in her chair.

'I think it's going to be worse than that. The bones, the bones tell me a reckoning is coming. And it's coming tonight. And I don't think it's going to be just a few unpleasantries, either. This could get nasty.'

I was curious, for I do like a good reckoning.

And if it involves unpleasantries and nastiness, well, I'm all in.

'Yeah, you've mentioned this reckoning thing before,' I said. 'But what, exactly, do you mean by a reckoning? Because I've heard lots of threats of reckonings before, and they've all turned out to be damp squibs. Remember that time of the headless horse thing, Gertie? That turned out to be boloney, didn't it?'

'Do you mean the headless horseman?' Gertie answered.

'No, no, no. The headless horse. The headless horseman was actually great. I loved that night. How often do you get the chance to fight a headless horseman of the apocalypse? But a headless horse, well, that was a damp squib. Right Lucy? Total crap.'

'Yes,' came Lucy's response.

'And the curse of the Blue-Bottomed rabbit. Damp squib, yes?'

'Well, there was some amusement in that initially. But, as it turned out, it petered out with nothing more than some minor collaterals.'

'So a damp squib then?'

'Yes, okay, a damp squib.'

'And the Giant Turtle?'

'Yes.'

'And the apparent return of Vlad the Impaler. Turned out to be some nutter with an axe, yes?'

'Yes again.'

'So about tonight then. This, so called reckoning. Am I to get excited and dampen my britches with enthusiasm in anticipation of something worthwhile? Or is it just another damp squib that'll barely moisten them?'

Lucy eyed me square plum in the face.

'Well, you can keep your damp squib in your damp britches. Because this time we should be worried. Very worried. Gertie, tell him.'

'Yes, dry out ya britches, mud for brains. I think Lucy is right, things might get a bit sticky tonight. And I don't know what to do about it yet. A part of me says we should just stay well away, while another part says that there isn't a way in hell that it won't affect us and that we should concoct a plan and stay one step ahead of the game. I'll tell you what, Montgomery, you put the kettle on and get some tea on the go, and me and Lucy will brainstorm a few ideas and see if we can get a plan together to defeat the hounds from hell, how does that sound?'

It sounded good to me.

I rather like a cup of tea first thing in the day. Orion nettles being my favourite, they offer that tangy aftertaste that one finds thrilling.

At one point Gertie thought me addicted to the stuff.

But when I pointed out that you "Can't really get addicted to fresh-tasting citrus products," she felt silly.

That was a good day.

Chapter 10

So Lucy had thrown the bones, read the tarot cards, and concluded that tonight was going to be a bit of a blood bath.

And that's all well and good, but why should anyone believe her?

Well, because she knows stuff, you see.

She'd spent years of her life honing her skills to such precision, that her in-depth knowledge of the dark Universe was unquestionably spot on.

She is the type of girl who craves the darkness as if it were the very elixir of life itself, and yearns for nothing more than to witness the blackness of the soul rising up and causing carnage, just for the hell of it, if you pardon the pun.

But more importantly, because she was dark herself.

As dark as it came.

Her inner soul was as naturally drawn to the darkness of the Universe as a moth is to a flame.

And you need to be dark to understand it all.

For it's the dark spirits that grips her soul.

As they always had.

She's what most would call, other-worldly.

Eerie.

Spooky.

Probably slightly disturbed.

But definitely special.

And tarot is her main thing.

It used to be her only thing.

Maybe a touch of palm reading, if the mood took.

And every now and then she would look up at the stars for a sign, or two, about how the future would present itself.

But mainly tarot.

She lived her life by it.

She never did anything, not even leave the house, without checking the cards for advice.

'What are you doing, Lucy?' her mum would ask.

'Just checking tarot, Mum. Down in a bit.'

'But we're just popping to the shops, Lucy.'

'Yes, I know. I'm just checking tarot before I leave.'

You get the idea.

It must be draining.

On the odd occasion, usually when there was a paying customer, then a good séance pleased her soul as much as anything else.

But a séance can't be an everyday thing.

It just takes too long and requires too much effort.

And more recently, she'd started exploring the power of throwing bones.

Throwing bones felt as natural as the cards to Lucy, and she seemed to have this knack of being able to interpret them, as if they were talking in a pure dialect.

A simpler language.

And she liked to keep things simple.

Life, she always said, was much happier the simpler it was.

But there's a snag.

And that's whenever Lucy speaks about it to other folk, she has a bit of a tendency to overdo things a touch.

Exaggerate, you could say.

And not in a small way.

Lucy didn't do small.

She didn't see the point.

And that's probably because she normally has to juice everything up to satisfy the paying customer.

And you should always give the customer what they want, shouldn't you?

So when she warned of impending doom, it was always a catastrophic impending doom.

As if there was any other kind.

And if something was coming up from Hell, then it was a cataclysmic coming up from Hell.

I knew this.

And Gertie certainly knew this.

We were both well aware of Lucy's propensity for over-exaggeration—all except that time when she accidentally unleashed some demons of the undead during a séance, which then tried to kill everyone and take over Earth—she didn't overdo it then.

If anything, she under-did it.

But otherwise, the statement stands.

So, for Lucy to come to the conclusion that, according to her tried and tested methods of bone-throwing and card reading, we're about to face an existential crisis, it was all in a good day's work for the young sparrow.

But, and I can't stress this point enough, she was quite anxious about the whole thing.

And acting weird.

More than usual.

And although Lucy is a connoisseur of anxiety and weirdness.

Her anxiety and weirdness were at levels that prompted me to consider paying more attention than I currently was.

Or as much as I was able to pay at this unseemly hour.

But here is the snag, you see, exactly *how much* attention should I pay to Lucy's prophecy of doom?

I mean, should I totally believe everything she muttered as the unhindered truth and draw up extensive plans to save the Earth on the risk that, if what Lucy was suggesting was all a load of old nonsense, then I'd look very silly.

Or should I just go along to the Halloween bash, check out the vibes, see if the entire existence on planet Earth is at stake, and if it is, then concoct some scheming and devilish plan to save everyone, right there, on the spot, so to speak.

Decisions, decisions.

And all of which were a bit murky, to say the least.

I mean, I didn't wish to appear rash and turn up at a party armed to the teeth with magic coins and medieval swords if the mood of the place was one of fun and frolic.

That would definitely destroy the party vibe.

However, I also didn't wish to turn up to an uprising from the deep depths of Hell with a pee shooter and a toffee apple.

I'd look a total goof.

Oh decisions, decisions.

'So, erm, Lucy,' I said. 'If I may say, old Pidgeon, but tell me again how you know all this bumph about catastrophes and dooms?'

'It's simple, you fat head,' interrupted Gertie. 'She's been throwing bones and reading tarot cards.'

'Correct,' added Lucy.

'Cool, and let me get this right,' I added. 'But what they've been saying is that something bad is about to happen. Tonight. On Halloween. At the Old Chapel at Blorkeney Knoll?'

'That's right,' interrupted Gertie again. 'So open your big fat hairy ears and listen to what Lucy has to say. This is important. The world is at stake.'

I smirked; I like it when Gertie talks trash to me.

And she knew that I liked it when she talked trash to me too, that's half the reason she did it.

The other half is a story for another day.

'Oh Gertie, the world is always at stake,' I replied. 'Don't you know that by now? But you must have no fear because Montgomery is here. The chap for all occasions. But I just wanna know how you can be so sure, old sponge. I mean, it's quite a big deal, all this talk of destruction and doom.'

Lucy reached into her pocket and grabbed a handful of bones.

'It's the bones,' she stated. 'The bones…they're landing consistently now. Look, all the time, they're the same. Look.'

She stood up and walked over to Gertie's new coffee table made from slate excavated from the Restless Mountains and threw the bones once more.

They spread evenly across the table.

I looked at Gertie in befuddlement.

Gertie looked back at me with menace.

Neither of us looked at Lucy.

And there was a reason for that.

For it was fair to say that—although we would quite happily announce that we weren't experts in any sense to the ways of bone-throwing—but even we could only conclude that they landed in no discernible order.

'See,' Lucy continued. 'Do you see that?'

'Erm, well, yes. I do see that. How…bizarre,' I answered. 'What does it mean?'

'It means danger is coming. That's what it means.'

'And you can tell that because…?'

'Because of the formation they've landed in.'

Lucy picked up the bones and threw them once more.

'Look, it's the same every time.'

Now, I have this unfortunate trait of not being able to hide my facial expressions in situations where it would be best if I did.

I was sort of famous for it.

And with hindsight, this was probably one of those situations where a little facial insincerity might have oiled the old cogs somewhat.

But like I said, I wasn't known for hiding my facial expressions in situations where it would be best I did.

I grimaced, trying to find the appropriate wording. 'Erm, Lucy, old thing,' I stuttered, while looking for help from Gertie, which didn't come. 'I, well, I don't wish to be an old stick in the mud here, but, well, the thing is. They've landed differently than before.'

Lucy was bemused.

'Of course they've landed differently, you oaf. They're not going to land the same, are they? That would be impossible. Be like a million to one.'

'Oh right.'

'It's how you interpret the stones, you see. It's how you feel them. It's their energy. Their aura. If you know how to understand them, you'll know what they're saying. And they've been saying the same thing every time. Look, every time.' Then she threw the bones again. 'And tarot is saying the same too. Every time. It's conclusive. No doubt about it, something is about to kick off.'

I grimaced again.

You see, I've always considered myself a fair enough type of fellow.

You know, seen a few things.

But even I find throwing bits of old bones around a coffee table to predict the future something of a stretch.

I mean, if that's the case, then every abattoir worker should have divine knowledge of everything and be stacked to the teeth with money in lieu of knowing the lottery numbers, I hypothesise.

But Lucy was well into it.

And I knew this much to be true.

So I approached with apprehension. 'And you can tell all this from the bones, can you?' I asked.

'Yes.'

'And are these special bones or something?'

'How do you mean?'

'Well, are they magic bones…or bones from a sacred cow…or animal bones, or—'

'Yes, they're animal bones.'

'Animal bones?'

'Yes, animal bones. As in bones from animals. I assume you've heard of animals?'

'Oh yes, quite, I love 'em. Wouldn't want a Universe without 'em, old sport. But, well, if you don't mind me asking. But are these bones from specific special animals? Special animals. You know, a certain type of animal with mystical powers or something. Maybe a griffin or a dragon of some sort. Do you know where I'm coming from here? Because, surely, they must be special animals for this sort of gig, I would imagine. I can't think that just any old animal will do. Would it?'

'All animals are special,' Lucy replied. 'They all contain the secrets to the Universe. That's because they all live on instinct. Not diluted with material matters, like us. Just pure natural instinct the way the Universe had intended. And if we Dinglewits had anything about us, we'd be more receptive in that matter.'

'Even Marshwarblers?' I asked.

'Especially Marshwarblers.'

'Really? Marshwarblers?'

'Yes.'

'Oh, okay, well that's all rather splendid then. So these bones, they've been telling you what, exactly?'

Lucy could sense that an explanation of bone-throwing was in order.

She didn't specifically mind explaining the art of bone-throwing.

If truth be told, it gave her a warm and fuzzy feeling whenever she was able to converse with another on the lost art.

It was like she was a pilgrim, educating the new world on the benefits of some God or other.

Or a schoolteacher explaining calculus to a bunch of young scholars for the first time and watching their faces when the light hits them.

But conversing with me about bone-throwing, well, I sensed this might be a challenge too far, even for Lucy.

However, she was a damsel in distress, and she was where she was.

And in times of distress, she knew making a path to old Montgomery's front door was the order of the day.

So here we are, Lucy in distress, and me, the prancing knight in shining armour.

But a question you might be asking yourself at this juncture is this, why does she always come to me?

And that, my intrepid reader, is a question I can easily answer.

Firstly, the old Montgomery lemon is of the finest order when it comes to sorting out issues of devils and demons.

Nothing better.

In fact, if I didn't know me, which of course I do, but if I didn't, I'd be seeking me out whenever a ghoul was on the loose and trying to kill everyone.

And secondly, and probably the most pertinent in this situation, is that I have a tendency to believe in her fantastical stories.

I hang on to her every word as she spits lyrical theories of the spirit world.

I love it.

Quite why is anyone's guess.

But one guess would be that I quite like fantastical stories. And seeing as I was basing my life on as many fantastical stories as I possibly could, then I would, wouldn't I?

And not only would I believe them, but I'd try my dandiest to become a part of them.

So, if, for example, she was to tell me that she had a feeling that all hell was about to let loose and every Dinglewit on planet Earth was in the soup, then more than likely than not, I'd have her back and take her at her word.

Why wouldn't I? I'd fought in way too many fights to the death with spirits of the underworld for me not to believe in this sort of stuff; although I was starting to suspect that the Universe had it in for me, or at the very least was using me for its own enjoyment.

But if it wanted some entertainment in the form of me giving it to the establishment in bloodthirsty battles to the death, who was I to complain?

I do like a bit of the old rough and tumble, and would be deeply annoyed if I was left out of such shenanigans.

'Look, I can't very well teach you the art of reading *bone-throwing* this morning, can I?' Lucy responded. 'And I don't have either the inclination or an organised teaching program sorted out to highlight all the essential and non-essential learning outcomes for such a topic. And, if you don't mind me being honest, seeing as you've just risen from your grave, you wouldn't have the mental acuity to take it all in, anyway. So you might just have to take my word for it on this one.'

Which I resolved was a fair enough point.

'True, my dear, very, very true. And I've no objections to taking your word for it. I'd prefer it that way. But don't you just feel like the bones are doing a lot of heavy lifting on this one? You know, all things considered.'

'And the cards, don't forget the cards.'

'And that chap you saw on the way here,' added Gertie.

'Yes, the old chappie from the loony bin. Let's not forget him, he seemed to know some stuff about tonight too. Oh, and the other one too.'

'What other one? And what chap from the loony bin?' I enquired, now thinking that, however nice my late arrival to the day was, maybe I'd missed out on a few important aspects of it.

'Oh, I forgot to tell you, didn't I?'

'Yes you did.'

'Okay then, let me fill you in. Are you comfy?'

I wasn't, but I was letting that one go, as well.

'Well, this morning I thought I'd take a walk into town and have a wander through the marketplace to see what veg they had in stock. I do like fresh veg, you see, it still has that crisp that you lose with time. You know what I mean, don't you? But anyway, the weather was lousy so there wasn't much about, but on the way back I saw some writing on a wall; it was by the old bank on the corner, you know, the one that closed last year due to it being constantly turned over. Well, the thing was this: I saw this writing, so I thought I'd go over and take a closer look, just out of curiosity. Well, as it turned out the message was written in blood, and—'

'Whoa, whoa, whoa,' I interrupted. 'Just slow down there, tiger. Did you say written in blood?'

'Yes, written in actual blood. Scary, eh?'

'I'd say.'

But Lucy continued undeterred, 'Now, while I was reading the message, this really old geezer walked past and said something like "she's coming," Or some other such nonsense to similar effect. But, well, to cut a long story short, he seemed convincing to me. And my day has gone from that to worse.'

It was one of those instances where you'd actually prefer the long story and had no practical need for the shorter version.

The longer, the better.

'What did the message say?'

'Oh I can't really remember now, but it was something like, Satan likes her vengeance cold, and that she's on her way. Or words just as scary and twice as menacing.'

'Just as scary! We're talking about Armageddon here. Didn't you write it down?'

'Nah, couldn't be bothered. But I'd got the general gist of it. It was something like *the world's about to end and Satan's on her way.* And let me reiterate: it was written in blood, so I'm not sticking around to take notes, am I? Not when a wall is dripping in blood telling warnings of impending doom.'

'Evidently not.'

'And then,' she continued. 'As I was coming here, I bumped into this oddball who'd just got out the loony bin, and he knows you, or will get to know you in the future, and he said the same thing. And not only that, but he's on his way to the chapel too because he's under orders from some voice that he hears in his head. So there you go—evidence.'

This was all a bit much to take in.

Especially at this ungodly hour that it was.

'Slow down a smidgen here, Lucy, old sport. You say that this voice-hearing character knows me from the future?'

'Yes, but that's not the point.'

'Hang on, hang on. And you also say that he's also on his way to the Old Chapel for this so-called, bust up with Satan?'

'Yes, but the point is—'

'Hang on, hang on, I've other questions. What I want to know is, how come I didn't know about it? I'm obviously lined up to be involved in it all. So you'd think I'd have been informed, wouldn't you?'

'You are being informed,' added Gertie. 'Lucy is informing you now.'

'Yes, yes, yes, but the Universe couldn't have known that, could it? And then the whole thing would have gone off without me being there.'

'So what are you saying?' asked Lucy.

'All I'm saying is this; if there is something afoot within the Universe, I normally pick up on these things; I have a sensitive bladder which keeps me informed. And I've not felt a thing. And my urine output is normal. So if the Universe wanted me there, it would have told me, surely.'

'It has, Lucy has told you.'

'Yes, but it can't rely on Lucy to belay all the facts, can it? Well, not accurately, anyway.'

'Are you calling me a liar?' said Lucy.

'Oh no, heaven forbid, Lucy, old flower. All I'm saying is that you can sometimes massage the truth a tad, that's all I'm saying.'

'And what's wrong with that?'

'Oh nothing, nothing at all. I like the truth massaged, keeps it nice and tender. No one wants the truth to set, do they? But these sorts of things need to be properly addressed. It's no good just passing messages around willy-nilly, hoping for an appropriate outcome. There's a system. A way of doing things. A structure, if you will.'

'Then maybe it doesn't affect you,' Gertie said mischievously, knowing full well that it did.

I mean, why wouldn't it?

I'm Montgomery Plum.

The Universe's plaything.

But I was wise to her little game.

'Now there's no need for flippancy, Gertie, of course it involves me, we both know that. Tonight is going to be—as they say on the streets—*balls awesome*, so why wouldn't it involve me? It's just a question of how, that's all. I just have to figure out *how* it affects me, or should I say us, both of us, Gertie, yes, that's it, both of us.'

Styled that one out.

But me believing that the Universe evolves around me was something that Gertie had got used to.

And she was well past the stage of trying to convince me otherwise.

It still grates on her though, that much is true.

It also gives her the hump; that much is also true.

It also humps on Lucy, and actually really annoys her for some unknown reason.

Which was something I found strangely satisfying.

'Look, the point is this,' Lucy moaned. 'There seems to be a convergence of the spirits, and not nice spirits either. And it's all happening over at the Old Chapel at Blorkeney Knoll. And it looks like we're all invited. That has to be it. There's no other way of looking at it. That has to be what's going on. And when you put it together with the bones and the tarot, it all adds up to something big. So I suggest we stop quibbling about the whys and the whos and get ourselves prepared. Because if Satan is going to make an appearance, then we'll be needing all our guile and gut instincts to survive this one.'

'Amen to that,' added Gertie.

'Never mind, "Amen to that,"' I mumbled. 'Look, I have a magic coin and a magic sword, so if any demons, whether it's Satan herself or any other swinging dick from Hell, want to volunteer themselves to come a cropper tonight, then they know where I am and where I'll be. That's all I'm saying.'

Fighting talk.

My favourite kind.

'And all this talk of plans and guile, well, I've never heard the likes,' I added. 'And now, it appears that we've exhausted everything there is to say on the matter, if it's okay with you two, I'm off back to bed to rest for the big night ahead. I got me a Satan to kill.'

And without a goodbye or a tinkety-tonk, I was gone.

Back to my pit.

My favourite place.

For some well-deserved rest.

Chapter 11

Satan was starting to enjoy herself as the victims of the final night of Halloween were beginning to nicely pile up, preparatory to the big night ahead of course, where they would pile up even more nicely, and she was particularly enjoying the hilarious and novel ways that they'd all been dispatched.

There'd been a killer book that ate from the armpit down.

Genius.

Yellow Lapetus berries that relish the taste of Dinglewit innards and like to eat their way out.

Sublime.

And mini-imps with their little sharp teeth and fun-loving attitude to murder.

Inspirational.

And it was still only early afternoon, plenty of time to get some more in before the big party tonight.

All was going well.

But although it was a good start, it still wasn't quite indulgent enough for the last ever night of Halloween, which would need something on a much grander scale.

Something imitating the gothique and fanstastique would be nice.

Something that would make the storybooks at the local bookshop bleed at the spine.

Something that would waggle the lacerated tongues of the fabled storytellers of history into a quimmer of excitement.

Something like unleashing the Bog Monster of Wokey Hole, for example, known locally as Wokey.

'Yes!' screamed Satan. 'Let's do that. Let's release the Wokey. That will be so much fun. They'll be no more jolly jolly rumpy pumpy when the Wokey gets its mits on 'em, that's for certain. Biscuit, make it so.'

'M'lady?'

'I said release the Wokey, will you?'

'The Wokey, M'lady.'

'Yes, you cretin, release the Bog Monster of Wokey Hole. Didn't you hear me? Do you need me to clean your ears out with acid again? Is that what you want?'

'No, M'lady.'

'Good, then release it now before I decide to let you be its first meal of the day.'

Biscuit sighed. 'Yes, M'lady.'

Now, it may come as no surprise, but bog monsters come in all sorts of shapes and sizes of structure and nature.

Take Wokey, for example.

On the surface, and with a fair mind, the tales of Wokey could all be mistaken as merely an old myth passed down through the ages of time by teenagers sitting around a campfire as they circumnavigate the rite of passage into adulthood.

I believe the common saying used in such circumstances is, "And as the night approaches midnight, and if you still haven't found someone to make out with, then Wokey will appear from the bog and eat your hearts out."

And, I would imagine, sometimes the threat of having your heart eaten out would have been substituted for something even more sinister as the night grew on and ancient ritual was still being evaded.

But if one were to hazard a guess, and I like nothing more than hazarding guesses, that not even in their wildest dreams did any teenager ever actually think that the bog monster would really make an appearance and indulge in the very practices that they'd been threatening all this time.

And if one were to hazard another guess that after the event when the victim was laid bare on the floor with a big hole in their chest, there may be a sense of *did we tempt fate* lingering in the backs of their minds.

But little did they know that, tonight anyway, it wouldn't have mattered, as Satan had decided it was time for Wokey—the Bog Monster of Wokey Hole—to make an appearance.

And it was time for yet another victim.

Barbara Bullwinkle disliked but two things.

Anything and everything.

She just couldn't bear anything.

If it crawled, she disliked it.

If it walked, she disliked it.
If it ran, she disliked it.
Or if it swam, she disliked it.
If it talked, it annoyed her.
If it muttered, she wanted to batter it.
If it sang, she'd want its vocal cords removed.

And if it hummed, then she'd be spending all her spare time praying for its death, and not a nice death at that.

She disliked everything.

And everything disliked her.

If one had to put Barbara Bullwinkle into simple words, those words would be:

She had a cold hard heart, and her eyes could frost a man out at a thousand paces.

Apart from that, she was a delight.

However, in regard to her looks, well, that's another story because Barbara Bullwinkle was strangely beautiful.

As in absolutely beautiful, but in a rather strange kind of way.

She had this long blue-hair look, you see, which flowed and danced in the wind, even when there wasn't any wind.

She had these short, stumpy legs with the appearance of being six feet long and going all the way up.

She had eyes that looked right into your soul and out the other side just for good measure.

And when she laughed, well, it was often said, Hell laughed with her.

In short, she was a sight to behold.

Or a sight to be scared of.

It had never been decided.

But she still disliked everything.

And everything disliked her.

So quite how or why Barbara Bullwinkle ended up organising a Halloween party at her own home is quite beyond the scope of rational thinking.

But there it was, the very definition of Glint Tae in a single sentence, beyond the scope of rational thinking.

The idea of a Halloween party had never occurred to Barbara Bullwinkle before.

In truth, she had very little time for it.

She always saw Halloween as a form of children's party that should be enjoyed in the privacy of one's own home, and not something that a social circle should indulge in.

But for some unfathomable reason, tonight, she'd got the urge to invite a few folks over to her place for some Halloween drinks.

Which also seemed to spark a flame of vigour into her bones.

'Bunting!' she shouted. 'We need bunting. And flags. Plenty of flags. We can't have a party without flags. And where are the vol-au-vents? I specifically told them to be here early so I could inspect them. Oh, heavens above, this will be a disaster.'

'Calm down, Barbara, you'll give yourself a heart attack. It will explode and jump out your chest and make a mess of the trifle if you're not careful.'

'Yes, yes, trifle. Where's the trifle I ordered? And the jelly. I need flavoured cattle bones for this party.'

And she continued to spend the rest of the afternoon scurrying around organising everything and anything she possibly could to make the event a success.

But she needn't have bothered.

Because all the important stuff had already been taken care of.

Like her eventual demise.

Wokey watched on from the bog as Barbara Bullwinkle left the chaos and ventured into the downstairs pantry to defrost some winkles.

Its plan was simple.

Find someone with a nice fresh heart and eat it.

And today, Barbara Bullwinkle was on the menu.

'They're bloody in here somewhere,' she moaned, while tossing frozen foodstuffs around the freezer. 'I'm sure they're in here bloody somewhere. I wouldn't have eaten them already. And nobody else in this godforsaken house will have been bothered to defrost them. So where are they.'

'What ya lookin' for?' asked a voice.

'Winkles.'

'What type?'

'The type you buy from the market. And please stop asking questions, whoever you are. Wait, who are you?' she asked, as she popped an enterprising face from the top of the freezer.

'I'm Wokey. I'm from the bog.'

'Hah ha ha, that's very good. Where did you buy that?'

'What?'

'Your costume. It's very realistic, if a bit too realistic. And you're dripping all over my pantry floor. I've just had it painted. Go outside and dry yourself off with an old towel before going into the house, will you? I don't want your slavering chops all over my new carpets.'

Wokey looked down at its hands and legs as they slimed ooze all over the pantry floor.

'I drip. It's what I do.'

'Not in my house, you don't. Now be gone with you. If you wanna play those sorts of games, there's a Halloween party up at the Old Chapel over the hill. I'm sure they'll accommodate you dripping everywhere. But not here. I've only just bought the carpets, and I intend to keep them in pristine order.'

'Oh, I'll be heading over to the Old Chapel later. Right after I've eaten.'

'You won't be eating anything if I can't find these bloody winkles, you won't,' Barbara Bullwinkle rattled, still searching through the seemingly bottomless freezer.

'What about heart? Do you have a heart going spare?'

Barbara Bullwinkle paused from her hunt and looked Wokey clean in the eyeballs.

'Look, you strange little bog monster, if you want to play hooey, go play hooey elsewhere, I'm busy here, and I've no time for strange. Lord knows we're overstocked with that already. Now please, shift some ass and dry yourself down before I ram this thermometer up your rear end.'

And those words, along with the screams of pain, were the last sounds that came out the mouth of the late, unforgiving, but strangely beautiful Barbara Bullwinkle, the latest victim of the last night of Halloween.

And who'd suddenly acquired a hole in her chest courtesy of a hungry bog monster named Wokey saying.

'Yum, yum, I do enjoy a cold heart. Now, where's that old chapel again?'

Chapter 12

To describe the Old Chapel at Blorkeney Knoll as a place of beauty would be somewhat of an exaggeration of the truth.

A vocabulary fib, if you will.

It would definitely be doing a dis-service to the word's, beauty, place, a, and of; words normally associated with splendour and various other pleasantries.

In fact, it's a fright of a place and one that very few would wish to spend an evening frolicking in, let alone their last evening of frolic; should they have been aware that was the case, of course.

Which they weren't.

However, and in all truthfulness, it's not such a gloomy old place considering it's made up of all the unknown unpleasant entities of existence within the Universe; mashed up into a pulp, and served up to cause a nasty aftertaste in the mouth.

Something you may wish to describe Satan as, as indeed many have.

But behind her back, of course.

You wouldn't dare say it to her face.

That would be silly.

And we wouldn't want to appear silly now, would we?

'Well, from the outside, it certainly looks like the right sort of place for a massacre, Biscuit,' Satan sought to mention. She was good at that, mentioning the obvious. 'We wouldn't want to let standards slip now, would we?'

'No, M'lady.'

'Not on the last ever Halloween.'

'No, M'lady.'

'And I do like the prospect that it sits upon. Reminds me of that other place that we used to use back when the humans were around. Do you remember, Biscuit? It stank of greed and villainy. The sort of place you would only attend when you were really desperate and at your lowest ebb in life.'

'Yes, M'lady. It was the old council building.'

'That's right. Proper dreary, was it not? I always had a sense of hopelessness whenever I entered the place.'

'As do most, M'lady.'

'Yes, quite. Well, this place is much more like it, me thinks. I'd say that this is the perfect place for our last ever night of Halloween. Come, Biscuit, and bring those weapons with you. We have a slaughter to undertake.'

'Yes, M'lady.'

The Old Chapel at Blorkeney Knoll is situated along the muddy banks of the River Bog, where, in a peculiar sort of fashion, it lives quite happily acting as a vortex between the underworld and the upper surface (what *we* know of as the living) and forming a line of communication between the living and the dead.

Or in other words, it's a gateway to Hell.

But let's not get bogged down and let that small anomaly get in the way of a good story, for the Old Chapel at Blorkeney Knoll is the perfect venue to host a slaughter on Halloween night.

The last ever Halloween night.

And Satan was getting excited.

'I don't know about you, Biscuit. But I always get a little tickle in my belly whenever I do something that I know will be amazing. Do you get that little tickle, Biscuit?'

'No, M'lady.'

'No, well, you wouldn't. You're not like me, Biscuit. You're what we call a hog-carrier. Do you know what a hog-carrier is, Biscuit?'

'Yes, M'lady.'

'Well, that's what you are. A hog-carrier. A very intelligent hog-carrier, I grant you, but a hog-carrier nevertheless. You should exert yourself more, Biscuit. You'll find you'll have more fun that way.'

'Yes, M'lady.'

'Quite, well, those Dinglewits won't be killing themselves tonight, and I'm sure there isn't a bishop watching over them, so let's put one foot in front of the other and make tracks.'

And on the subject of bishops, she was correct; there hadn't been a bishop at the Old Chapel for ages.

The last bishop to consider the place as a worthy venue for spiritual solace was a certain rotten apple going by the name of Bishop Aloysius.

A squeeze of a chap who'd never seen the light of day without a hangover.

And even that was a very long time ago.

A very, very long time ago.

And even then, he wasn't exactly feeling his best.

But Aloysius thought the place spectacular.

Especially for midnight sermons.

The old bish' would speak for hours on end; jabbering on about some burning tree or other, or a lake of wine situated someplace no one had ever seen. He wouldn't stop with his readings until the sun rose a merry head and kissed the new day with sunlight.

And when it eventually did, he'd take the sunrise as a sign of mission accomplished and deduce that Satan must have been content with his work and would look forward to more twaddle again tonight.

And not without good reason.

Because, as the story goes, the last bishop to fluff their lines at the Old Chapel was mysteriously struck down by lightning, and ended up as being nothing more than an ectoplasm stain on the main door that was impossible to wash away.

There are a few such mysterious stains scattered about the place.

Thus, being assigned as bishop at the Old Chapel was considered nothing less than a death sentence.

Challenge accepted, thought Aloysius.

Now whether Satan was responsible for this *act of God* was anyone's guess.

It was certainly doing the rounds in the underworld that it was possible, it was certainly her M.O.

And she'd never demur from the implication when challenged on the matter.

Why would she?

She liked nothing more than an act of God.

Even if she, personally, had nothing to do with it.

It all added to the mystique, you see.

Her mystique.

And she was rather fond of mystique.

But Bishop Aloysius didn't seem too concerned by the pressure of certain death in the event he ever crossed words with the devil because, in all honesty, Aloysius was way too self-absorbed to consider that such a thing could ever happen to him.

And for a few decades, all seemed to be going swimmingly.

Bishop Aloysius would give his sermon.

Finish off the wine that was left over.

Head off into the vaults for more wine.

Wake up with a hangover.

And repeat.

And as the decades flew by, Aloysius's self-absorption in his own ability grew to out n' about hubris.

But all that changed on one—nothing out of the ordinary—Halloween night, when the bishop had just finished a perfectly decent sermon when…boom…splash…gust of smoke…a disappearing bishop…and a new stain now occupied the wall right near to the main door.

And there hasn't been a bishop there since.

Or a congregation.

Much to everyone's relief.

So now it sits as a chapel for hire.

Available for births, deaths, christenings, bar mitzvah, knitting clubs, and yoga nights.

And anything else that takes your fancy.

So for a party to be held at the Old Chapel was nothing of a surprise to the general populous.

Even if it was a Halloween party, which could almost be quantified as tempting fate.

And with the big question being, who would dare tempt fate in this way and organise a Halloween party at the Old Chapel?

If, indeed, it had been organised at all.

This is often the case, don't you find? That something just tends to happen out of the ether, without any warning or prior advance.

A mere coincidence that a group should happen upon a place and things take off from there.

As was the case here.

And it seemed that no one had been bothered to ask why a party was happening here at all.

At the gateway to hell.

After all, a party is a party.

And if it's free entry and the scram is good, then why would you question anything?

But even so, holding a Halloween party at the Old Chapel at Blorkeney Knoll was still regarded as a strange thing to do.

A situation not lost on Satan.

'But don't you find it rather peculiar, Biscuit, that they're coming to a Halloween party organised here of all places? A place that is so synonymous with cruelty and horror. I mean, I think it's great and certainly *my* first choice, but why would the living choose to come here? It's like they're asking for death.'

'It does seem particularly foreboding, M'lady.'

'Foreboding, eh?'

'Yes, M'lady.'

'And suspicious too, I dare say. But then, it is a Halloween bash. So where else would you have it, I suppose? But even so, we should keep our wits about us, Biscuit, dark forces may be afoot, and we wouldn't want to get caught with our britches pulled down, now would we?'

'Quite right, M'lady.'

'Yes, quite right. Good. Well, I'm glad we're on the same page. I'm good at these sorts of things, you know, Biscuit.'

'What's that, M'lady?'

'Noticing things. Sensing when danger lies ahead. Picking up on the finest of little details that others miss. I'm good at it.'

'Yes, M'lady.'

'Yes, I always have been too. It's a natural talent for me, you see. I just seem to be able to look at a situation and figure out if something is untoward, so to speak, and then take the appropriate course of action. It's like a natural gift.'

'Yes. M'lady.'

'Yes, quite.'

And Satan mused in her self-proclaimed genius as they continued with their slow meander up to the main door of the chapel.

And all the time, Biscuit, fully aware that all was not as it seemed.

Inside the chapel, Lucy had been busying herself setting up for the big night ahead.

She'd got there early and took ownership of a side room just off the main hall where she placed all manner of accessories on her cherished antique table.

She was wearing her favourite gown; the one with the purple edging.

And had spent hours with her make-up, not that she needed it, she was scary enough as it was.

Her plan was to sting as many as she could for a quick tarot card read tonight: A crown is a piece.

Hopefully a touch of palm reading on the side at half a crown.

And if she was lucky, maybe the odd bit of Ouija board chucked in for good measure.

Two crowns.

And who knows? Maybe drum up some follow-up trade and make the whole venture a profitable and worthwhile one.

It was Halloween after all, and if you can't sell this sort of stuff at Halloween, then, well, where are we?

And as for the growing doubts that she was beginning to have—which was understandable knowing what she knew—well, they would have to be put to one side, she'd been running a little low on funds recently, and needs must, as they say.

'Okay, okay, listen up,' she barked, to absolutely anyone who would listen. 'This is possibly going to be the craziest Halloween party ever held, so I want nothing but the outstandingly impressive. That's right, I want no excuses and no expense spared. Only the best will do tonight, understand? This has to dazzle. This has to amaze. Are all the giant candles lit?'

No response.

So, she shouted again, 'Are all the giant candles lit, I say? It's imperative all the giant candles are lit. Fire is absolutely essential for a good Halloween party, and the more fire, the better, everyone knows that. I want fire and brimstone tonight. Nothing else will do. You! Over there. Yes, you, would you be a delight and check if all the giant candles are lit, no one else is listening, and I just need to make sure everything is perfect.'

But they weren't listening either.

But luckily enough, all the giant candles *were* lit, and all looked rather splendid as well.

But unbeknown to Lucy, the amount of fire would have a secondary effect, a secondary undesired effect, a secondary undesired effect of epic proportions.

Satan liked fire as well.

It reminded her of home.

It reminded her of all the best bits of home.

The heat.

The smell.

The fear.

She loved it all.

So making lots of fire tonight may not have been exactly prudent.

But there you go, you can't have it both ways, I guess.

'Okay, what about wall art? Is that all sorted?' Lucy continued to yell. 'Is the décor up to scratch? It needs to be exquisite, not the usual poxy shoddy workmanship that normally accompanies Halloween night. I don't want flimsy paper signs and plastic heads with cheap lights in their eyes. I want quality. I want proper skulls and signs made from cotton. And none of this fake blood crap, either. We need real blood for tonight. Real blood from real animals. Do we have that?'

Again, no response.

But she needn't have worried. The entire chapel was awash with hanging sheets of black satin and red tassels.

There were skulls of real animals hanging from walls.

And dangerous animals too.

And as for the blood, well, who knows where that came from, but let's just say there was a lot of it.

'Impressive,' said Lucy. 'I must find out who'd done all this later. It would look great at my next séance.'

If she survives, that is.

But the décor of giant candles and flowing satin curtains wasn't the only ornamentation on show within the Old Chapel tonight.

Hanging in all four corners were the naked skeletons of the Four Headless Horsemen of the Apocalypse.

A nice touch everyone agreed upon.

And a touch not lost on Satan as she poked her head around the front door.

'Oh wow,' she said, with a renewed sense of pleasure in her voice. 'This is splendid. They've done an outstanding job. A fitting place to end Halloween for good. And there are plenty of the right type of Dinglewits here for the big slaughter too. How delightful. And as for the four skeletons, well, sublime is all I can say.'

'What do you mean, *the right type of Dinglewits*?' asked Biscuit, her long-suffering servant.

'Plump, Biscuit. That's what I mean by the right type of Dinglewit. Plump and willing to die for my amusement. Like all Halloweens should be. And used to be before all this slushy nonsense we now get. Oh, the very cheek of it. Enjoying Halloween, who'd ever have thought of it?'

'Certainly not you, M'lady,' answered Biscuit. 'That's not your cup of tea at all.'

'It certainly isn't. There's no fun in cups of tea, Biscuit. Now, what do *you* think of all this then?'

'Think of all what?'

'The setting and the décor, you philistine. Look at what they've done. They've got candles and long drapes covering all the walls. It looks divine, don't you think? It's like they're excited to be getting slaughtered tonight. I love it. The attention to detail needs to be applauded. Whoever did all this should be commended for their work, Biscuit. For never let it be said that Satan doesn't admire true dedication and commitment to the cause. Plus, an eye for detail. Truly divine.'

'Divine?' asked Biscuit. 'Are we sure that's the right look we're going for here? I mean, we certainly don't want any divine intervention tonight, do we? That could scupper the whole thing, and not in a good way.'

'It's a look, Biscuit. A look, that's all, you chump. I'm not implying that we'd welcome any divinity in tonight's proceedings. Heaven forbid. But you know what, if it does, it does. I'm not afraid of some holy deity gallivanting at my Halloween bash if that's what they want to do. In fact, bring it on. They can have some as well.'

'It might even add to the fun, M'lady.'

'It might, Biscuit, it might. It would certainly add to my fun. I haven't smashed a God in years. Not since—'

'Hermes, I believe.'

'Yes, that's right. It was Hermes, wasn't it? The little trickster thought he could scam me. But I showed him, eh?'

'Yeah, you showed him all right, M'lady.'

'Yes, I did.'

Now, Biscuit, being long-suffering as he was, found that sarcasm was a very good way to cope with Satan's constant nonsense.

He'd use it all the time.

It kept his little spark just bright enough to function on a daily basis.

She knew this, of course, and although she would pull him up on it from time to time, she tended to let the odd snide remark tiptoe past.

Because she was—if nothing else—self-aware that she needed Biscuit for her own means as well.

And if this meant having to let some things slip from time to time, then so be it.

But she was keeping score.

Keeping score for when the day came.

Biscuit knew that as well.

'But you know what, Biscuit, it always astounds me that they embrace Halloween in such a forthright manner. I have to say, it's like they have no idea what the whole thing is about.'

'Well, Dinglewits were never the brightest of sparks, M'lady. I believe that's why the Universe put them on Earth in the first place. Because they weren't very smart. From what I heard, the humans were too smart for their own good and destroyed the place. The Universe didn't want any more of that, so it put the Dinglewits there instead. That's what I heard.'

'Oh, drivel, Biscuit. Where've you heard that? Down at the servant's quarters, I suppose. Where all the other rumours come from. Honestly, you lot, I don't know where you get it all from, I really don't. Utter gibberish, but I presume it helps you pass the time of day while in service, I suppose.'

'M'lady?'

'All this talk of replacing humans. The Universe didn't replace the humans. They left. All by themselves. No one forced 'em to go. They did it all by themselves, the slackers. One day, they just upped sticks and buggered off. And it put me right out it did. I had 'em all trained up just how I like them. I had to start again when the Dinglewit lot turned up. It took me ages because they're so clueless. It would have been easier to have trained the chimps.'

'And yet here we are, M'lady.'

'Here we are what?'

'Slaughtering them all because they don't do as they're told.'

'Yes, well, perhaps you're right, Biscuit. But it won't be the first time. It's just the nature of things, you know. Those with the power, killing those that don't do as they're told, it's a yarn as old as time. Every civilisation, everywhere, always the same. So, if the peasants don't want to get themselves skewered, then they should just do as they're told.'

'Oh, I see.'

'Yes, so let's just relax, shall we, and enjoy ourselves for once?'

'Yes, M'lady, but if you don't mind me asking.'

'What?'

'But who else is taking part? Or is it just us? The only reason I ask is that word has got around in the furnaces of Hell and, well, not to beat around the bush'

'Which you are.'

'Yes, well, not to beat around the bush, but…well…the word is that you've invited a few of 'em to help out a bit.'

'I have, Biscuit, I have. But just my friends, that's all. My close friends. After all, there's no point in having a party all by yourself, is there? That's no fun. No, I've just invited along a few of my faves. Should be a giggle.'

'And if I may be as bold as to ask whom, M'lady.'

'Oh, just the old gang, Biscuit. The brood, if you will. Or the gaggle, if one was to be slightly more accurate. I'm going to use it as a reason to catch up. Gnasher's coming. So is Blood, and Siren, and Wolfie. You know, just the cool crew. I want it to be a little evening soiree just for us. The gang. That's all, Biscuit. Oh, but I did unleash a few of the ghouls earlier. Just as a bit of a livener.'

'Wolfie! And Blood, and Gnasher. They're psychos—'

'Of course they're psychos,' interrupted Satan. 'That's why they're in Hell. They wouldn't be there if they weren't psychos, would they? You silly oaf. And by the way, they're my friends, so I'd prefer a bit more warmth towards them, if you will. You know what they're like, one false word out of turn and they'll be dragging the whole night down with their cranky intentions of putting you in the boiling pot. Then I'd have to get involved and sort the whole thing out in case Mummy tells me off for letting you get boiled, and the whole thing will get out of hand. And I don't want things getting out of hand just because you've wound them up the wrong way, understand?'

'Yes, M'lady.'

'Good, because I've been looking forward to tonight, and I want tonight to go according to plan. My plan.'

Chapter 13

So I entered the old chapel and saw Lucy putting the final touches to her *spectacle*, as she so eloquently described it.

'Well this all looks rather splendid, old girl,' I said, always wanting to start an interaction with a compliment whenever possible. 'In fact, I'd go as far as to say you've done us all proud. I don't know how you think it all up, I really don't,'

'How do you mean?'

'The room, old puffin, the room, the…ambience, is that what you call it—ambience? It looks superb. The candles and the blood. And those skeleton things hanging in the corners, it all looks marvellous.'

Lucy knew that I was easily pleased at the best of times, everyone knew that, it's one of my things, but even by my excruciatingly low threshold of being spellbound, I'd obviously seemed to be very impressed.

'Yes, you can call it ambience, if you wish. But it's nothing to do with me,' she answered. 'And do stop looking so awestruck, you're starting to dribble.'

'Eh, I don't follow. What do you mean it's nothing to do with you?'

'I said it's nothing to do with me.'

'What? None of it.'

'Well, I assume you're chatting purely about the drapes and the candles and the blood and all the other stuff.'

'Yes.'

'Well they're nothing to do with me. I mean, this is what I would've done, and I did vocalise the need for giant black candles, but as for who organised all of this, I've no idea. None whatsoever.'

'A big mystery then?'

'Yep, a big ol' massive mystery. So I'm just gonna set up my Ouija board and let all things be as they must.'

'Good idea, old girl,' I agreed. 'I'm going to do the same. I mean, I'm not setting up a Ouija board and all that sort of stuff. But I am going to let all things be as they must, as you say. Anything I can help with?'

'Do you know anything about Ouija boards?'

'Nope.'

'Then no.'

I took her point, there's no point in an outsider delving into the underworld, it never ends well.

But on the subject of Ouija boards, there is an interesting nugget here to be had, that being the whole thing gives Satan the goolies.

The absolute lowest of all goolies that one could think of.

In fact, it's safe to say she disliked them.

No, worse than that, she loathed them.

The sheer sight of the Ouija board was enough to send her into the most dreadful of rages.

The sort of rage that takes days to come out of.

And why?

Simple. Ouija boards reveal all her secrets.

All of her top-secret secrets.

And without her saying so too.

And there was nothing she could do about it.

And believe me, she'd tried.

On quite a few occasions.

She'd even petitioned the Universe itself.

But the Universe was adamant that Ouija boards should remain because they afforded it a small amount of titillation, and the Universe does like titillation.

And it wasn't to be turned on the matter either.

No matter how much she begged.

And she did beg.

To a point that made her feel uneasy.

But no sweat, she thought.

Because today was Halloween.

The last ever day of Halloween.

Her special day.

Her very own special day.

Her very own…very special day…that she designed…just for herself.

So, surely the Universe wouldn't be as vindictive as to let the Ouija board in on the gig and ruin her whole day, would it?

Well, it had.

As Satan was about to discover when the killing began.

But more on that later, for now, back to Lucy and her Ouija board.

So, to get away from the hustle and bustle of everyone tripping over themselves on their last night alive, Lucy had set up in a side room. I believe I've already mentioned this.

The room was cramped, and I'd spent the last two minutes whingeing about such.

'How are you gonna cram 'em all in?' I asked. 'There's barely room to swing a cat in here. Do you still swing cats?'

'I've never a cat swung. Nobody has.'

'Oh, I wonder where that phrase came from then? Never mind, I was just saying there doesn't seem to be much room to spread one's elbows, if you don't mind me saying. Surely there's only room for—what—one at a time, two at a squeeze.'

'It's bijou, Montgomery. Compact. And there's nothing wrong with one at a time; it gives it that personal touch. Like I'm giving everyone my undivided attention. Plus, it's better to do one at a time, it's what most clients ask for. And anyway, it's all that was available. And beggars can't be choosers.'

'True dat, Lucy old sparrow, true dat. Still, I'm sure you'll make a pretty crown once the punters get wind of your talents. They'll be queueing round the block.'

As you can see, in spite of the cramped conditions that Lucy had to work in, I was still doing my best to encourage the old girl.

But for myself, it would be safe to have described me as being in low spirits.

This was unusual for me. Normally, I'm the chirpy, enthusiastic sort of chap that can't be broken.

Especially on Halloween.

I mentioned this to Lucy, hoping to get some inside information on my gloominess. But all she could conclude was that, perhaps, the thought of a fight to the death had probably lowered my disposition somewhat.

I opted not to challenge her on the issue.

I love a fight to the death, this is true.

But she did have a revelation, of sorts, that she'd forgotten about, and thought this a good time to bring it up in an attempt to lift my morale.

'Oh, there's something I forgot to mention,' she mumbled, while innocuously scratching around, looking busy.

It was a terrible habit she'd formed as a consequence of being bad at confrontations.

'Say what?'

'There's something I forgot to mention earlier.'

'Is it important? I mean, I only ask, Old Crumb. Because if we're about to take on redemption, then perhaps we should keep the trifles elsewhere for now, don't you think?'

She didn't.

'Well, it's like this,' she started. 'As I was walking to yours and Gertie's this morning, I met a friend of yours. Well, not a friend. Well, not exactly a friend anyway. At least not a friend yet. But he is a friend. Or he will be. He's a friend from the future, you see. And I don't know how, but he said he knows you. Like now—even though you meet in the future. And you're his friend too—just not yet. But in the future. Anyway, he'd escaped from the mental asylum on the other side of town, you see, and he's on his way here tonight because he's been hearing voices. Sort of like…instructions, if you will. And they've been telling him to get here and save the Earth from annihilation. Or something like that.'

I sniggered.

'Oh dear Lucy. I'm afraid your wiring has gone all doolally, my little splodger. You've burnt yourself out, old bird, with all this talk of redemption and bones, you've blown a fuse or two. Right, let's go back to the top.'

'Eh?'

'Back to the top.'

'Back to the top?'

'Yeah, back to the top. Okay, so you met this random geezer that had just made a bolt from the Glint Tae loony bin, right?'

'Right.'

'And he claims to be my future friend at some point in the future?'

'Correct. Do you have a problem with that?'

'Not at all, sounds perfectly reasonable to me.' And it did. 'But you also say that this loco absconder has been getting signals from another dimension telling him to get a wiggle on over to this Halloween bash to save us all, right? That is what you're saying, yes?'

'Yes.'

'Now that's the bit I don't believe.'

'*That's* the bit you don't believe?'

'Yep.'

'And why wouldn't you believe *that* bit? You do know your life, yeah? This is nothing compared to what you've been getting up to. Gertie, don't you agree?'

'Oh, absolutely. One hundred percent,' answered Gertie.

'Thanks, Gert.'

'Anytime.'

'Hang on, hang on,' I defended. 'Let's get it straight here. You are speaking with the original inter-dimensional time-travelling adventurer here. So it's not that I don't believe that there isn't another dimension. Because I know there is. And it's not that I don't believe there isn't some good Samaritan wishing us well from that other dimension. That sounds plausible also. No, the bit I don't believe is that they went to some oddity in some raving cuckoo nest and didn't come to me. I should be the first port of call for these sorts of jobs. Especially, if they know who I am.'

'Oh God.' Sighed Gertie.

'Exactly. And if he does know me, then, he would definitely have to come to me first if he wanted all of the world saved from evil. So that's the bit I don't get.'

This seemed to jar Lucy a tad.

'Whoa, whoa, whoa,' she bit back. 'Just you hang on in there for just a second, will you? Are you seriously trying to tell me that you think you're the only one that can save the Earth from evil, are you?'

'Well—'

'And while we're on the matter, don't you—of all superhero half-wits—lecture me on doolally wiring. Have you seen what you're wearing tonight?'

And, along with Gertie—whom Lucy always looked upon for sisterly support—took a second to cognise the choice of garments that I thought appropriate for tonight's festivities.

I, on the other hand, didn't have a clue what they were on about and thought I looked swish and would be the beau Brummel of Halloween.

It appeared I was in the minority of one on this issue.

But I did rather like being called a superhero. So again, I let it go. I was letting a lot go today.

'Look, the point I'm making is that if this chap knows who I am—whether from the future or not—then he would definitely have come to me first. We obviously have a history with stuff like this.'

'Why doesn't that surprise me,' responded Lucy. 'I think only you would have a history with weirdos from other dimensions in the future and consider it an insult that you're not front and centre of all this total insanity.'

'It's the burden I carry, Lucy, old sponge. My cross to bear. My lot in life. But I don't complain. It gets you nowhere, I've learnt.'

'Not that you don't try,' Gertie said and smirked. 'And boy, do you try.'

And then the sisterhood joined together in some more laughter at old Montgomery Plum's expense.

'Yes, yes, yes, you're both very funny. Now, what are you gonna do with that Ouija board? It looks like it needs some action. Bung it over here, I'll give it a good once over and see if I can't have a chat with my future friend.'

Lucy looked mortified.

Which to those that know Lucy wouldn't be a surprise.

Everything mortified her.

But as well as that, the way she wore her make-up always seemed to offer the opinion that she was mortified even when she wasn't.

'You'll do nothing of the sort?' Lucy hollered. 'This isn't a toy; I'll have you know. This is an instrument to communicate with the other side. A very serious instrument. A powerful instrument. A powerful instrument when in the wrong hands can do great damage.'

'But it won't be in the wrong hands, it'll be in mine,' I argued, even though I didn't believe me.

But this sharpened Lucy back to the task at hand—saving the world.

Which she deemed quite an important task to do. Certainly, too important to be letting me handle the power of Ouija, apparently.

So, after a quick rebuttal of my generous offer, she beckoned us all to sit down and form a circle.

This I was happy to do; once I'd removed my top hat and placed it on a nearby chair for safekeeping.

'Right, everyone finally ready, are we?' spluttered Lucy. 'You sure you don't want to groom your beard a bit more or put some more shine on your shoes before we start, eh?'

'Oh, sarcasm,' I commented. 'It's an old friend I know well.'

And gave an obvious look at Gertie.

'Just sit down and do as you're told,' Gertie ordered. 'Lucy's gone to a lot of time and effort to save the world tonight, and the least you can do is give it your whole, undivided attention.'

I answered in the affirmative and sat like a rose between two thorns at the table—doing as I was told.

Then Lucy began.

Outside our temporary little squat, the party had begun in earnest.

The cold night seemed to have dragged in a good crowd from the dark and dank streets of Glint Tae, and the Old Chapel had filled up rather nicely.

Some chap had brought along an old wooden fiddle and was doing his best with it; even though he only appeared to know four chords.

There was a bongo drum quartet made up of three maidens and what looked like their grandmother; but at least they could string a rhythm together.

And Chompy, the local drunkard, was dancing as best he could, considering he'd lost one and a half legs.

But that aside, the place was rocking, and a good time was being had by all.

Barmy, now finally having completed his journey from the loony bin a few minutes prior, was slowly making his way through the vol-au-vents and was eyeing up the cheese and crackers.

'Well,' he smirked. 'I'd say if the end of the world is coming, then it's best to end it on a full stomach, what ya reckon?'

He glanced over at a random stranger who'd had the unfortunate outcome of ending up next to the self-proclaimed saviour of the Earth.

'Oh, are you talking to me?'

'Absolutely, old chap, you're the one. You seem to have been allocated a spot next to me, so you must be part of the plan, eh? It's a strange old business all this, don't you think? Still, if that's what the Universe wants, then who are we to argue? The name's Barmy, I've just escaped from the asylum for the night so that I can save the world. Do you have any updates?'

'Up…updates?'

'Yes, you know, any new additions to the plan, or is it still *just as you were chaps and jolly-ho, and all that*. I have to say, the Universe is a clever old bugger, don't you think? Arranging all this just to give everyone a good night out. You'd think it'd have better things to do with its energy, wouldn't you? But there you go, you never can tell, can you?'

'No…no, you can't.'

'Yeees, this'll be a good one tonight. We got some big hitters on our side, and they've got some big hitters on theirs too. Yep, this'll be a good one, no doubt. One for the ages. Sorry, I didn't catch your name.'

'Erm, Bonzo. They call me Bonzo.'

'Well, it's nice to meet you, Bonzo. Like I said, I'm Barmy, Ol' Barmy to my friends—saviour of the world. I normally reside on the other side of town, but I've managed to sneak out for the night. Tied bedding sheets together, I did and scaled the walls. Cedric wasn't best pleased, but then he lacks vision on these sorts of things. Besides, he can always get some more from the night guards. They're pretty generous, are the night guards. Better than the day guards. Lack of sunshine, I put it down to.'

And he stuffed another vol au vent into his already engorged schnozzle.

Bonzo, it was fair to assume, was confused, and desperately searched for an excuse to leave.

But as yet, I couldn't think of one.

'Erm, nice gown.' He muttered, along with some other mumblings about how come his life had come to this.

'Thanks, it's standard dress. I mean, I don't have to wear it, I can wear my own clothes if I want. But I like the stripes, they bring out my curves, don't you think?'

Bonzo didn't want to think about Barmy's curves, or anything else for that matter, and scorned himself for not being able to think of a reason to leave.

'And…nice hat.'

'Made it myself, old boy. It's lined with tin foil so they can't read my brain activities. It's the only way. I've tried everything: lead, aluminium, salt, but nothing beats tin foil. It's light and manoeuvrable, and it doesn't cost much. Genius invention. I'd like to meet the fellow that invented it and shake his hand.'

Bonzo had a brainwave.

'Yes, me too. Anyway, I need to take a squat. Do you know where the toilets are?'

'That'll be the vol-au-vents, you poor pickled fish. You may wish to take some reading material with you, if my experience is anything to go by. If nothing else, it'll keep the flies away. But yes, the latrines are right over there.'

'Perfect, works every time,' Bonzo muttered.

'And I'd get a move on if I were you, Bonzo, not much friction with vol-au-vents. Oh, and good luck for tonight. I'll keep my eye out for you. Make sure you get out alive. You're just my sort of Dinglewit, Bonzo. Not many of us left.'

'I am?' came the response, not knowing if that was supposed to be a compliment or not. 'Erm, thanks. Yeah, I'll look out for you too.'

Back in the side room, Lucy was doing her thing with the Ouija board.

'Okay, let's join hands and form a circle,' she announced.

'But if we're joining hands, who's moving the planchette?' I asked.

Lucy, for the sake of a better word, was affronted.

'What do you mean, who's moving the planchette?'

'Well, okay, maybe not the planchette then. But that's just what I thought it was called.'

'What was called what?'

'The wooden thingy in the middle.'

'That *is* a bloody planchette.'

'Then what you on about then?'

'What do you mean, what am I on about?'

'Well you said we should join hands.'

'Yes.'

'Well if we join hands, who's going to move the planchette? That is what it's called, right?'

'Yes, I've just told you this.'

'Well?'

'I'll tell you who's going to move the planchette…the spirit is going to move the planchette, you heathen. This isn't a parlour trick. We form the circle and ask questions, and the spirit answers by moving the planchette. It's a simple system and has worked for centuries.'

'What…all by itself?'

'Well, yes. That's sort of how it works.'

'Wow, that is clever, I have to say.'

'Not really, Montgomery. It's just how the Universe works.'

'Well, I think it's clever anyway. Don't you Gertie, old crumpet?'

'I think we should let Lucy get on with it, darling,' Gertie answered, as she gently stroked my hand.

And I knew exactly what that meant.

'Okay, let's start again. Join hands and close your eyes. Try and relax and empty your mind.'

'That was quick,' quipped Gertie in my general direction.

To which I simpered, for I do like a sharp quip.

'Please, children,' snapped Lucy. 'This is serious.'

'Sorry, Luce.'

'Yeah, sorry, old bean.'

'Good, right, Okay, now then, right, let's crack on. Now empty your minds,' and she looked around again for any sign of exuberance. And after being satisfied she had their full attention, she continued. 'Oh, and if you must think of something, think only of positive thoughts as we try and connect to another dimension. The spirits can pick up on negative thoughts and it can apparently cause bad juju. And we wouldn't want any bad juju, would we?'

'Nope.'

'Oh, hell no.'

'Good,' and she grasped tightly to mine and Gertie's hand.

A little too tightly, to be frank.

Especially, as her hands were all clammy and cold.

'Is there anybody out there? Is there anybody out there?' came the melodic chant. 'We hear you. We hear you. Come to us, come to us.'

'And if it's you, Granddad, stop arsing about and talk to me,' I said, thinking the whole thing a tad repetitious and in need of some intervention.

Lucy wasn't impressed.

But it did the trick.

The planchette moved rigorously.

H.E.L.L.O. P.L.U.M. H.O.W. Y.O.U. D.O.I.N.G?

There was a moment of stunned silence.

'Oh, he called me Plum from time to time,' I reassured the audience. 'Something to do with public school, he always said.'

But they didn't seem interested.

They just sat in stunned silence.

The sort of stunned silence you only get when everyone is stunned.

Like when something untoward has just happened that no one thought possible.

That sort of stunned silence.

So I broke it.

'How are you, you old rogue you? How's life on the other side?' I asked.

The planchette moved assuredly once more.

A.L.L. T.H.E. B.E.T.T.E.R. F.O.R. N.O.T. S.E.E.I.N.G. Y.O.U.

'Well, ain't that charming. I save your reputation from rack and ruin, and this is all the thanks I get. Well, I'm not biting, Granddad. And if I must say, I'm rather disappointed you haven't been in touch. You never ring, you never drop me a message. Not even a prank. For all I knew, you'd forgotten all about me.'

I.M. N.O.T. Y.O.U.R. G.R.A.N.D.D.A.D.

'Oh, right, sorry, and all that. I had you for someone else. Erm, yeah, sorry. So, who are you then?'

M.Y. N.A.M.E. I.S. C.R.U.M.P.

'Well, how you doing Crump? It's nice to make your acquaintance. Now if you don't mind, old chap, would you mind telling us what all this all about, eh? You know, all this nonsense. All this Halloween massacre stuff. Surely, you don't believe the Universe is going to get rid of its favourite toy, do you? The Universe loves us Dinglewits. We're fun. We're entertaining. We're its favourite invention since the Wallyjollops. And you know how it felt when they came a cropper. It destroyed a black hole. So, come on, spill the beans. And while we're on the matter…how come you didn't come to me first?'

C.O.M.E. T.O. Y.O.U? I. C.O.U.L.D.N.T.

'Why not?'

Y.O.U. H.A.V.E. T.O.O. M.A.N.Y. H.A.I.R.S. I.N. Y.O.U.R. E.A.R.S.

'Too many hairs in my ears!'

Y.E.S. I.T. W.A.S. I.M.P.O.S.S.I.B.L.E.

'I told you about your ear hair,' Gertie responded. 'Now look what's happened, you've been left out of a good old tear-up with the devil.'

'But they keep my ears warm,' I answered. 'It's like a warm and loving glow at the side of my head. I like it. And every time I have 'em cut, there's this uncompromising breeze that shoots right through the old lug holes and into the encephalon region. It's horrible. I don't know how you put up with it.'

'Guys, guys,' interrupted Lucy. 'Can we discuss excessive ear hair and horrible draughts later, we've more pressing matters at hand, I think. Like the destruction of everyone on Halloween night.'

'Oh, yes, quite. Sorry, Lucy, old bird. I got a bit carried away there. Yes, you carry on. Unless you want me to ask the old crooner the questions.'

'It might be best,' concluded Lucy, as it had become clear to all concerned that she was now just a spare wheel in the conversation. 'You ask him the questions, you're obviously on the same sheet of existence. I'll just make sure the connection isn't lost.'

I didn't know what she meant by that, but—

'Well, if you're sure.'

'Just get on with it.'

And so I did.

And that's pretty much how the next five minutes went.

Crump explaining Satan's plan, and me replying with questions and repeating the answers.

Such as:

'You mean to tell me that Satan is planning a massacre just because she thinks Halloween has become too commercial?'

Y.E.S.

'And you say that she's planning to unleash a dearth of un-friendly rotters from the depths of hell to help her?'

Y.E.S.

'And that unless she's stopped, then we're all for the chop?'

Y.E.S.

You get the drift.

So like I said.

Crump telling me what was going to happen, and me replicating the answer with a question.

Crump having to answer the question to the answer that he'd just presented.

And me going *'gosh,'* and *'well I never,'* after every interaction.

But at the end of the chat, it was quite clear that tonight's Halloween was going to be something quite special.

Something that wouldn't be forgotten in a long time.

For once.

Chapter 14

I can honestly say, hand on heart, there's nothing more impressive than watching Gertie hop up and down in pain after she has walked into something solid.

On this occasion, it was the wooden leg from the séance table.

Even the table leg yelled out in pain from the contact.

Of course, I can't comment out loud, even if it comes in the form of a compliment or a funny anecdote—as from past experience—I know that it ends in gratuitous profanity and something heavy being thrown in my general direction.

But luckily, Gertie is not a good aim.

It's also not a good idea to laugh either, as this only secures the same outcome, and the same level of disappointment when she misses.

So that leaves only two options.

The first option is to ask her if she's okay.

But as with laughing and making general remarks about her impeccable balance and seemingly limitless ability to walk into the most unfathomable object and hurt herself—that option only tends to end in passive-aggressive remarks about my testicles, and with me still having no idea why she always focuses on my testicles whenever she's angry with me.

And if I'm being blunt, I think she needs therapy on the matter.

And the second option is to say nothing, which usually has a mixed response.

Sometimes she will pick on me anyway, just because, and then I refer back to the previous outcome for the consequences.

But sometimes, and only sometimes—mind—the outcome is favourable, and the direction of the blue language and thrown articles remains firmly focussed on the Universe; for whose fault it was that she'd stubbed her toe in the first place, and not in the general direction of old Montgomery Plum, who is always faultless in these matters.

Either way, Gertie needs to stop walking into things if she's to make old bones with some of them still intact.

'Shit…shit bugger…bugger, shit…shit,' she shouted, while holding her right foot in what could only be described as a very advanced and complicated yoga position. 'That bloody table leg. I told you I shouldn't have sat here. I wanted to sit where you did. This is all your fault, you buffoon.'

And it was at this point, I sensed that this was to be one of those occasions where I wouldn't be escaping with my testicles intact.

So, I braced myself for further scapegoating and possible scrotal damage.

'All you seem to be bothered about these days is trying to save the Earth from demons and ghosts and everything else besides. Meanwhile,' she continued, 'I'm bashing my toes on table legs and probably breaking every bone in my foot.'

Now, most sensible Dinglewits would be able to sense that a bit of the old sympathy would be the best course of action in this situation, especially when knowing the possible consequences to future parenting.

And indeed, past experience and learnt behaviour should also have pointed this out. However, I was never one to learn from my past mistakes, so as such, I leapt in with the response that was guaranteed to get my plums kicked.

'Never mind, old puffin. Your bones will mend. They're probably not even broken. If anything, they'd be just slightly fractured. Or even just bruised. And besides, if we don't save the Earth tonight, there'll be nothing for you to bump your toes on come the morning.'

A good point well made, I construed.

And certainly, one that would stand up to scrutiny.

'Fine by me. The whole place can do one, as far as I'm concerned. All it seems to offer these days are fights with demons, plenty of blood and guts, and painful toes.'

'Oh, come now, Gertie, old squirt. It's not as if you're new to a bit of the old toe-bashing, is it? You're practically the world champion at it. I'd say if there was ever a league table of world-class toe-bashers, then you'd be winning it by miles. You're practically a pro. Tales of your toe-bashing are known far and wide and throughout the land. And as for blood and guts, well, it is Halloween.'

Gertie ceased with her excruciating pain-hopping and sat on the sofa, vigorously rubbing her toes so as to stimulate her beta fibres.

'Is there a point to what you're saying?' she asked sarcastically, and if I may mention, rather nefariously.

'Well, yes, actually there is. And the point is this. If Crump is right—and I've no reason to believe he isn't—then we need to crack on with some crucial, top-level planning; a bit like what a war cabinet would do. Proper planning. We need to make an inventory of what we have on our side, ya know: guns, bullets, bombs, swords, and any other form of weaponry, and then figure out what we'll need to get the job done. Then we need to draw up a plan of attack with a plan A should everything go swimmingly, and a Plan B should it not. And perhaps, even a plan C should it all go proper tits up, which sounds highly possible. Satan is one tough cookie, you know, she knows how to slash up a few Dinglewits for pleasure. And not only that, but it sounds as though she's got herself a posse of hounds from Hell coming to party with her tonight, and that means double-trouble, or even triple-trouble. So we don't have time to be breaking toes or busting Montgomery's plums. It's all hands to the pump, say I.'

'What on Earth are you on about?' interrupted Gertie. 'A blooming war cabinet. Inventory. Plan A, B, and C. All hands to the pump. Where have you got those words from? And anyway, if you wanna know what weapons we have, I can answer that: guns zero, bullets zero, bombs zero, any other weapons zero. All we have is you and that silly magic coin, and if Cleese turns up, then we'll have his ability to get beaten up and still remain exasperating. And as for busting your plums…they'll be plenty of time for that later.'

Gertie was right.

I knew it.

So did Lucy.

We didn't really have much to fight with.

It was true that I did have a magic coin, and it was true that Cleese had a remarkable ability to get beaten up and still function.

But apart from that…well, there was nothing.

Apart from optimistic ignorance, of course.

'You're always worrying about this and that, Gertie, old thing,' I said. 'You never take the time to enjoy the chaos. It's a tragic waste of anarchy. Look, let's take off our gloomy pants and go join the party. I always find that these things have a way of sorting themselves out, don't you?'

She didn't.

'Also, if we're going to die, then let's die having a good old-fashioned knees up. I'm not going out feeling all gloomy. I'm just not.' Then I poked my head into the main hall. 'Hey, look, it's Bonzo! I've not seen him in years.'

'Bonzo!'

'Yep, Bonzo.'

Gertie was not so pleased to be hearing *that* news.

For her, she'd be happy never to hear the name of Bonzo ever again.

But as with everything else tonight, this is how it was going.

'Oh God, now we are in trouble if that goof is here. Montgomery, I don't want him anywhere near this stuff, do ya hear me? No where near it. We've enough on our plates as it is without that dimwit poking his extra-large eyeballs into it and making it worse.'

'Who is Bonzo?' asked Lucy.

'Bonzo, my dear Lucy, is a legend in his own time,' I responded. 'A gunslinger. A vagabond. An all-rounder when it comes to a back-to-the-wall fight for your life type situation. And he's the sort of chap that will have your back when Satan crashes your Halloween party and tries and slaughter everyone. So if he's made an appearance, then the odds have swung quite considerably in our favour. Gertie, old pudding, stick him on the inventory list as a valuable weapon.'

'I'll put him down as a tool. Will that do?'

'A valuable and very deadly tool.'

'I'll just put him down as a tool.'

'I take it you're not his biggest fan then, Gertie?' asked Lucy.

'No, Lucy, I am not. He's a creep of epic proportions, that's what he is. He's a slime ball. A gunk punk. A complete low-life. And he gives me the willies.'

'Gertie, my sweet little viper, there comes a time in everyone's life when you must let bygones be bygones. Now, I don't know what Bonzo has done to warrant your scorn, and, as you know, I'm always on your side regardless of the crime. But in this case, I must insist that you welcome Bonzo into your heart in order that he can heroically get killed saving the Earth.'

'Is that a promise?'

'What?'

'That he gets himself killed.'

'Heroically! Gertie, heroically.'

'I don't care how it happens: heroically, wimpingly, or by friendly fire; just as long as it does. So do you promise?'

'Well, I can't make any promises on this, as you well know. For Satan may decide not to chop him up into small pieces for her evening's skewers. But if I was a betting Dinglewit—which I am—I would say that the odds that he'll be a tasty morsel on her dinner table tonight mooch somewhat into the odds-on certainty category.'

Gertie paused for thought.

Something I never did.

'Okay, then, if you're sure. Tonight, I shall be the hostess with the mostest. But let it be known if that skuzz-ball survives tonight and goes around bragging that he and Gertrude are now bosom buddies and together they saved all Dinglewits…you will pay the price.'

'Gertie, that is a chance I am willing to take.'

And with that, we entered the fray.

The tables were laid out in columns.

And it appeared—in true Dinglewit fashion—that the male half of the sketch sat on the right-hand side of the room, and the female section on the left.

No one actually knows how, or where this silly tradition was born, and what purpose it serves.

It certainly isn't written in any book form or tablet.

And definitely isn't something that either sex would choose to do, even though we do.

It just appears to be a natural phenomenon that we just do because we do.

Me and Gertie plumped ourselves near the bottom end of the table nearest to the door.

That way we could see, first hand, who came and left the Old Chapel and keep tabs on any sign of trouble.

But there was one small detail that we did find puzzling though.

And that was that. There were name badges of all the guests placed neatly on a table at the rear wall.

This was puzzling for two reasons.

First, this wasn't an invitation party.

Anybody can turn up.

So, how did they know whose name to write on the name badges?

And second, the names were spelt correctly.

I thought this very odd, for no Dinglewit in the history of—well—ever, has ever prided themselves, or taken the time, to spell things correctly.

We don't see the point.

I was starting to get suspicious of the whole propitious festivity.

Perhaps this wasn't some random gathering after all, and greater forces are amongst us.

I grabbed Gertie's badge.

'There you go, Gertie, my little fruit pudding, your name badge.'

And I handed over the correctly spelt appendage.

'What's this?' she asked.

'It's some sort of insignia.'

'Oh, and why do we have these?'

'I've no idea, but what do you notice?'

She looked quizzically at the shiny, and if I may say, professionally made name badge.

'Nothing.'

'Nothing?'

'No, well, apart from the name being spelt correctly.'

'Exactly, and don't you think that's a bit suspicious? I mean, who goes around getting letters in the right order? What a waste of time and effort. No, I say this is the work of the devil herself.'

'You, you think Satan wrote these. Actually wrote them herself?'

'Yep, who else? Maybe the Universe, perhaps, that's a possibility. But not likely. But that's not all. If you look around, everyone has a name badge on.'

'So?'

'So who knew who'd be here? It's an open-door kind-o-do. This is all very tantalising, I must say. And very, very suspect. An investigation is in order.'

'You think everything is a suspect tonight, and what exactly are you going to investigate? And anyway, what's the point?'

'Eh?'

'Well it doesn't matter, does it? It doesn't matter if Satan wrote the name badges herself or if someone else did. And it doesn't matter who's here either. They're all just sport for the big event, aren't they? The only important thing is that when Satan does show her pretty little mug, you bash it in and save the Earth. That's how I see it.'

Gertie always did have a pragmatic opinion on life.

And on this one, she had a point.

There is no real point in how folk got here.

Or who is here—to be honest.

All that matters is that I'm here, and when Satan makes her appearance, I chop her head off at the neck.

Simple.

'Ok, a fair point made, I concede. Tell you what, you stay here and keep our spot at the table, I'll go and chew the fat with Bonzo and see what *his* game is.'

'His game will be a low-down and devious one,' Gertie replied.

But by this time, I was already pacing the chapel floor and re-acquainting myself with Gertie's old nemesis, whom I greeted in the usual way.

'Bonzo, you deviant of the third kind, how's it hanging?'

'To the left, Mr Plum, always to the left. You?'

'Oh, straight down the middle, Sir. Always straight down the middle. Always have, always will. Hey, it's been a while. What have you been up to? Nothing too ill-disciplined, I hope.'

'Just hanging out, Mr P, just hanging out. You know how it is, the life of a bachelor; you're here one minute, there the next, and no two minutes are ever the same. A rolling stone gathers no moss, my friend. None whatsoever. And I don't intend it to either.'

I couldn't deny that a rolling stone doesn't gather moss.

How could it? Friction would put pay to that.

But I also couldn't deny that Gertie had probably got him right too.

Bonzo does possess this uncanny ability to blow his own trumpet a little too loud for everyone's liking.

But all that will have to wait tonight, because I needed Bonzo's muscles if I am to defeat Satan.

An appreciation of decorum was required.

'And you have a name badge too, I see. Strange, eh? What do you think is going there then?' I asked.

'How do you mean?'

'Well, it has Bonzo on it.'

'Why wouldn't it? That's my name, isn't it?'

'Not it isn't, old boy. That's your nickname. A name that your friends address you by, not just a tag that anyone can use. So who would think to put that on your name badge? But also, what's the gist with name badges in the first place? I have suspicions, Bonzo, grave suspicions.'

Bonzo reached down and took a long hard look at his new costume accessory.

He couldn't deny that it didn't look snazzy, but then he also couldn't deny that he'd just taken the badge handed to him and acquiesced to a social norm.

'Yeah, well, we were all given name badges at the door. It seemed rude not to take one and follow the crowd. Apparently, or so the meet-n-greet geezer said anyway; it helps to break the ice and allow for more friendly and personal interactions. But to be honest, there ain't much here to get *me* going. I'm more of a rock-n-roll type chancer myself and, if I'm being honest with you, Monty, this all looks a little bit…Well, jazz.'

'Jazz?'

'Yes, jazz. A bit *plain trousers*, if you get my meaning.'

I did.

But I couldn't agree with him on the plain trousers remark, I've always found plain trousers the perfect attire for all occasions.

But I couldn't stand around here talking fashion all night.

As much as I'd like to.

'So how come you're here on your own? Surely you could get a date if you wanted.'

'Yeah, you know how it is, Montgomery. Everyone is allowed to have a dry patch. I'm sure it won't last, they never do. You here with the missus?'

'Yeah, Gertie is over there.'

'And looking rather splendid as always.'

'Yeah, well, I'd avoid her if I was you, Bonzo. She thinks you're a git.'

'And she's right. I am a git. That's why the ladies love me.'

And he looked around as if his statement was a matter of fact, which it probably was. But I sensed this was my big chance to get him on board for tonight's big fight.

'Well, I've heard that there's going to be a grand finale tonight, Bonzo. A big surprise. Something like a mystery guest-type situation. A very cool, mysterious guest. So if I were you, I'd lay off the booze and not eat too much. You wouldn't want to be slouchy for it. Not a gunslinger like you. There might be some big points to be clocked up tonight. Who knows what hits you could get.'

'Ooh, nice heads-up there. Ya, very much. A grand finale, you say?'

'Yep.'

'With a very cool mystery guest?'

'Yep.'

'And with the possibility of accruing some major point-age?'

'Absolutely.'

'Sounds fun, I might just stick around for it. Cheers. So, erm, do you know anyone else here? Anyone of the female variety.'

'Not really, only Lucy. She's in the back with her Ouija board trying to drum up a bit of trade. But other than—'

'Ahh, Lucy, that scrumptious little beauty. She still doing all that voodoo stuff then, is she?'

'Aye.'

'I might have to go and say hello. You know, after the food and stuff, wouldn't want to miss out on that, not even for Lucy.'

'Yeah, that's a good idea, she's trying to earn a few crowns. You know what she's like; never one to miss an opportunity. But yeah, you should go check her out, she might even do you a reading.'

'Yeah, thanks, I think I'll pop in.'

Then always the gentleman, I reached over and grabbed a couple of glasses of champagne.

'Cheers,' I toasted. 'So do *you* know anyone here? Me and Gertie, we haven't a clue who most of 'em are.'

'Erm, well, I know Salty. He's sat over there by the bar; the one with one shoe on. Oh, and one sock too it appears.'

'Salty? Why is he called Salty?'

'Oh, he has a propensity to drink too much tequila when in a melancholy mood. Which seems to be getting more and more regular these days so you might wanna steer clear of him. It's not good getting too up close and personal with someone who could kill themselves at any minute. You tend to end up with blood and brains all over your being. Yep, he's a real space cadet, but at least he gets noticed. And it's much better to be talked about than not, that's what I always say; even if the things they say revolve around the crazy shit you got up to on the weekend. And then there's Jobe, another loner, but really good at boggle. Not that that's ever served him as any use in his life. Another one destined for the obituary's column in the next few years, I'd say. But other than that, no one. All complete strangers. And all just fresh meat for the Bonzo.'

Whatever that meant.

The conversation appeared to be coming to a logical conclusion.

You know how they do.

'Cool, well, keep your wits about you, Bonzo, old plum,' I offered generously. 'And hopefully I'll get to see you at the end of the night, should all go well.'

Now, Bonzo was many things.

Mainly depraved.

And Bonzo wasn't the brightest lightbulb off the production line.

Barely a flicker of a candle.

But if there was one thing you could say about Bonzo; it was that he could always sense when something was fishy.

Like when a fish that looks like a fish should smell like a fish, but it actually smells of something much more pungent that I can't quite think of at this precise moment. It will come to me.

And tonight, apparently, I'd overplayed my cards a tad and was acting rather too fishy for his liking.

You see, I'd already alluded to a grand finale with a mysterious guest.

And I'd already mentioned the possibility of scoring some big points.

But when I said I'd *hopefully* see him at the end of the night.

He suspected a great big fat juicy rat in the room.

Or maybe a fish.

'And why wouldn't I be seeing you at the end of the night? Do you know something menacing? Is there something going down here tonight other than the option of clocking up some points for the Bonzo? If there is then I'm in, don't you worry about that. Is there? Is there something going to kick off?'

I'd been found out.

Me and my big mouth.

'Well, actually, yes,' I answered, now thinking I'd best come clean now I'd let the cat out the bag, so to speak.

And I laid bare the assumptive facts and guesswork to Bonzo in their purest of forms.

This took some considerable time as Bonzo had questions and wasn't bothered about asking them while I was in full flow.

Eventually, this irked me to such a point that I stopped before I punched him on the mazzard, and concluded with:

'But it's probably best you don't tell anyone. It'll just scare them away.'

'What!' shrieked Bonzo. 'Don't tell anyone they're about to get skewered? Seriously, P, how is that right? They'll be like lambs to the slaughter. How is that right, dude, seriously, how is that right?'

'Well, it probably isn't, Bonzo, old buddy. But you know what Dinglewits are like—they panic. They don't like this sort of thing. And if they find out what's going to happen, they'll probably hightail it to another Halloween party leaving us all on our Jolly Rodger. And you see, if Satan doesn't get her kicks, then who knows what will happen. All Hell could freeze over. And anyway, we don't know for sure anything will happen. All we have to go on are the ramblings of a madman and some bones being chucked randomly onto a table. That's not exactly conclusive evidence of anything, I'd say. So I say, let's just be ready if it kicks off, and give it our best labours if it does. So you in or what?'

'In? In? Of course I'm in. I couldn't be more in if I tried. I'm about as in as in can be. I've never been more in…in anything in my life. Bring it on, Montgomery, bring it on.'

To which I applauded the fellow.

Perhaps he was a tremendously decent chap after all.

Chapter 15

So, with a final splash of smelly stuff, and a temperamental flicker of the brushy thing, Satan had finally finished her preparations for the last ever Halloween party.

Tonight, she was going gothique.

Nothing else would do. This was going to be the last time she did it, so it needed to be done suitably.

No quick slap-n-dash here.

After all, a grand finale is a grand finale, and she was to look her best.

Earlier in the day, she'd bought herself a new frock in dark red so the blood stains from all the innocent Dinglewits she was about to butcher didn't show up as had happened before, and Satan was always one to learn from prior wardrobe malfunctions; like the time with the translucent ball gown…lesson learnt.

And she'd even splashed out and got herself a new cloak.

It was red.

To match the frock.

She'd even decorated her new flame thrower which, she stated, "Would only be used on the worthy, as death by fire was a privilege only a select few deserved."

She was looking forward to this like nothing before.

Biscuit, on the other hand, would rather be inserting a red-hot poker into his eyeballs for entertainment, although rather coincidentally, this is probably what he'll be doing to others later, and not all of it under duress, it must be said, he was in Hell for good reasons, after all.

But for Biscuit, it was going to be a long night.

Because every weapon that Satan had brought along for the slaughter, well, it would be he who'd be carrying them.

And they were all heavy.

And whenever she found herself in the soup with no means of escape, it would be him fishing her out.

And the soup would be hot.

And if she didn't get to dismember at least a good dozen Dinglewits tonight, no doubt it would be entirely his fault.

And he'd be paying a heavy price.

So it wouldn't be unfair to say he was slightly apprehensive on the matter.

Uneasy, you may wish to add.

And with the mood that Satan was in, his fears were likely befitting.

Earlier that day, she'd decided to get the ball rolling by releasing a few of the more, minor and mischievous occupants, from the depths of Hell.

This would dampen the loins, so to speak, and lubricate the joints in time for the big show.

The minions always did enjoy the occasional outing from the fiery pit, and it had a secondary consequence of keeping them in check for the bigger stuff required of them at a later date, something else she learnt from prior experience.

'This,' as she quite elegantly put it, 'would nicely set the tone, early doors, and build up the temperature slowly.'

A slow boil, you might say.

The only way to cook.

And to achieve this simmering of malice, Satan had released a flesh-eating book that had engorged itself on some fresh flesh until it could eat no more. Some mini-imps…likewise, a curious form of exotic berry which—if the reports are to be believed, and why wouldn't they be—is doing a pretty good job of warming up the audience, and a certain bog monster.

But it was now time for the main event.

The coup de grace.

The magnam finalem.

But first…food.

One must eat if one is to perform to one's best.

And that is true for both sides of the sketch.

One should never go around committing acts of grievous murder on an empty stomach.

And Satan couldn't think of anything worse than being killed on an empty stomach, either.

'Going down into the quandary of Hell without any breakfast. It's positively uncouth.'

And on that point, we agree.

'Biscuit,' she announced. 'Let the feast begin. Let them eat before they die.'

Biscuit turned and gave the nod to the caterers who'd been waiting patiently in the kitchen.

The first course was tomato soup.

An old classic that no one ever objects to.

Everyone loves tomato soup.

It's the soup of gods.

Nice, rich, tomato soup with a touch of basil on top, and served in a piping hot cauldron with the soup over-spewing to look like blood was dripping onto the floor.

'Perfect,' said Satan. 'Let's get them used to seeing the red stuff. It won't be such a shock later.'

'What? When it's gushing from their necks?'

'Exactly, Biscuit. Now you're thinking along my lines.'

'God, I bloody hope not,' mumbled Biscuit, but he gave the order anyway.

The waiters rushed out from the kitchen and threw a bowl full of piping hot, blood-red soup onto everyone's table.

This was accompanied by a roll of bread, also piping hot, and tabasco sauce, really piping hot.

This served as a much-needed wake-up call for Bonzo. Fuelled by a familiar case of the munchies, he dived into his meal, only to quickly realise that dumping the entire bottle of tabasco sauce into the soup was a grave mistake. Now, he found himself in urgent need of water.

And a lot of it.

Gertie was sat more on the suspicious side of the fence.

'Please, tell me that's tomato soup,' she said, while looking scornfully into the bowl as though someone had just placed in front of her a bowl of how the night was going to unfold.

'Looks like it to me, old bird,' I replied. 'I was hoping to start with pea soup, but I guess tomato is an old classic that no one will object to.'

'Well I object to it.'

'How so, my sweet little treacle pudding. How can you object to tomato soup? It's the soup of gods. No one has ever objected to tomato soup in the whole history of, well, soup.'

Lucy looked over and shook her head. 'I'll tell you why, shall I? It's because this has been set up. That's why. It's been set up so that we get used to seeing dripping red fluid all night coming from the mouths of Dinglewits. I would bet the main course has dripping red stuff too. That way, when the real stuff starts to flow later, we won't be so surprised. We'll all just think it's all a part of the festivities and carry on.'

'Oh, honestly, chaps,' was my riposte. 'It's tomato soup. Nothing bad can ever come from tomato soup.'

Lucy didn't agree. 'Well you mark my words, I've seen it in the cards. And the bones. This is where it all begins. And Gertie agrees with me, don't you, Gertie?'

'Oh Gertie always agrees with you. Ya like two peas in a pod, you two. Just like Cleese always agrees with me. Here, watch. Cleese! Nice soup, eh?'

Cleese replied by offering a thumbs-up.

But he didn't speak.

He couldn't speak, too much tabasco sauce, you see.

'There you go. That's two-two. Shall we get someone to cast the deciding vote?'

'No, let's not,' interrupted Gertie. 'I think the less the Dinglewits know about the shit-show that's about to erupt, the better.'

'Now ya talking, Gertie, old fruit. We wouldn't wanna ruin their fun. Or Satan's.'

'Ruin their fun!' yelled Gertie, who then realised that shouting probably wasn't the best course of action and immediately took to whispering. Albeit aggressively. 'They're about to get brutally murdered. Where's the fun in that?'

'They've come to a Halloween party, old fruit. What do they think is going to happen, tiddlywinks and dominoes?'

'They think they're going to have some pumpkin pie and play parlour games. That's what. Not spend their last few moments of breathing getting chopped up by Satan.'

'Well then, they've forgotten what Halloween is all about, that's what I say. They've become too casual and languid. That's the problem with folk nowadays, no sense of history and tradition. We all know the origins of Halloween. And so should they. Halloween is all about blood and gore. Slashing and stabbing. Perhaps a little asphyxiation. Not party hats and poppers. So lame. So maybe Satan has a point. And if I may say, I sort of admire her for what she's trying to do. You know, bring back some authenticity to the proceedings.'

'No, you may not say it,' snapped Gertie. 'And don't ever say it again. Innocent Dinglewits will perish tonight. And for what? Just so some old hag gets a good night's entertainment ripping someone's intestines out. Or so you get to use your magic coin and maybe take out a few demons from Hell. No, I'm starting to think coming was a bad idea, this is going to be dreadful.'

'Au contrare, old pigeon. This is going to be spectacular! And I *will* take a few of 'em out, that's for sure. Bring it on. The knight of Halloween is armed and ready.'

'Knight of Halloween, my arse. You're a buffoon. And put your sword back, will you, I'm trying to eat.'

Following on from the soup, the bread, and the tabasco sauce, all of which slivered past the old larynx with delightful wonder and curious astonishment, the main course was, as predicted, pumpkin pie.

But what was served up, could only best be described as pumpkin pie surprise.

The surprise being that what was inside the crusty pastry still appeared to be alive.

However, they weren't exactly talking or showing much ambition to escape from the fate of being devoured.

But nevertheless, definitely functioning on a cognitive level.

Now ordinarily, I hope, this would have been enough to arouse the suspicions amongst the locals, or at the very least, prompted something resembling a walk-out.

But not tonight, it seems.

Tonight, anything and everything looks to be *fair game* in the cold town of Glint Tae.

'Gertie,' I enquired, squinting an implausible eye at my dinner. 'My food appears to be moving. Is yours moving? Because mine is definitely moving. Or am I going mad? Do I need to go to bed? Or is yours the same?'

'Nope, mine's the same,' she answered.

'And mine,' came a voice from the chair next to me. 'But don't be worrying yourselves, they're called Sweet Slugs. They're a delicacy in certain parts of the Universe. And very hard to catch.'

I turned to see an unusually clad individual—who appeared to be very content with his lot in life—sitting next to me.

'Oh, hello. Really? These? A delicacy?'

'Oh yes. An expensive one too. So the real mystery is how come they're being served at a random Halloween party in an old chapel in Glint Tae? That's what I want to know. The committee that put this gig on must really have spent some considerable time and crowns.'

'Oh, really?'

'Yes. Oh, forgive me, I'm being rude. I haven't introduced myself. My name is Barmy, but everyone calls me Barmy. And you're Montgomery Plum, aren't you?'

'That's the chap. Have you heard of me, then?'

'Heard of you, I know you. We're good friends, you and I.'

'Are we?'

'Yes, very good friends. Just not just yet. But sometime in the future. Or maybe it is *just yet*. Because we've met now, haven't we? Maybe our friendship starts now. Maybe now is the future, and we become friends now. Confusing, eh?'

'Very confusing, Barmy. I know I'm confused, but that doesn't take much, just ask Gertie.'

'It's true, it doesn't take much,' Gertie responded.

'But, hey, maybe it's best not to think about it, eh?' I continued. 'Or we'll end up having an aneurysm, or something. Perhaps we should just enjoy the food and not get too confused or what strangeness is coming next.'

'Not a fan of strangeness, then?'

'Absolutely I am. Strangeness is a dear old friend that I cuddle up to on most days for a heart-warming snuggle. It's *confusing* I know, even I get confused by it. But I get confused a lot. Don't I, Gertie?'

'It's true, Barmy, he does get confused a lot.' Gertie answered..

'Yes, so meeting a stranger claiming to be my friend from the future isn't about to offer any disruption to my own mental homeostasis, I'm afraid.' I added. 'Or my grip on the Universe, for that matter. But moving food…this is starting to test the limits. I don't like moving food, Barmy. It gives me the impression that the meal isn't ready to be eaten.'

'Oh I wouldn't worry too much about that,' responded Barmy. 'Sweet Slugs don't worry about being eaten. In fact, I hear they prefer to be eaten before they begin to turn sour. So we're actually doing them a favour.'

'Really?'

'Yep, a big fat old favour.'

'Well I guess that's okay then. But anyway, aren't you the chap who met Lucy this morning?'

'Indeed I am. She's a delightful spirit, don't you think?'

'A delightful spirit? Well, yes.'

'And exceptionally well proportioned.'

'Well proportioned?' I answered, hoping that the conversation wasn't about to get creepy.

'Yes, all of her spirit pieces are just in the right places. I prefer my life-forms like that, don't you? I get so muddled when someone doesn't know their soul from their reason. Or their heart from their instinct. But not with Lucy, she's all there, just as she should be.'

This prompted me to take a closer look at this, Barmy chap.

He was definitely an interesting-looking fellow—being as he was—adorning a hospital gown with the back open.

And also, that he seems to have found himself a top hat with a red feather sticking out the top.

Surely this wouldn't have been a part of his normal hospital attire.

Someone of the likes of Barmy would've been sitting around with a colander on his head blowing bubbles through a sieve, or something.

But here he is, looking all dashing with a top hat and feather, while all the time prancing around with his bum on show.

A most unusual outfit for a party.

'Are you from the loony bin on the other side of town then, Barmy?'

'Yep, that's me. Number one Waldorf Gardens, GT11 1TQ. Room number seven. I share it with a fellow inmate called Cedric. Do you know him?'

'Er, no. Sorry.'

'Oh, don't be sorry. He's a frightfully boring old boiler. As dull as dishwater with all the trimmings. Do you know how many times he's tried to escape?'

'Er, no.'

'None. Not one single time. Can you believe that? He hasn't scaled the walls, dug a tunnel, or bribed a guard one single time. I don't know how I get along with him, to be honest. But you know, you must make the best of these things. Now remind me, you live with—'

'Gertie, over there.'

'Hello, Gertie, nice to meet you again.'

Gertie frowned.

'And that's Lucy, whom you've already met.'

'Yes, hello again, Lucy. You're looking well.'

Lucy didn't respond.

'And that stoner down there is Cleese. He is my friend.'

'Oh yes, I know Cleese. Just not yet.'

'In the future?'

'Yes.'

'Hmm, and that's pretty much it. Oh, this chap here is Bonzo, not his real name of course, just some goofery that he thought up to sound cool. It doesn't work.'

'Hello, Bonzo. Sorry, how it all ends for you.'

'Eh?' countered Bonzo.

'And that's pretty much everyone I know here,' I concluded.

Barmy clapped his hands, then gave them a rub.

'Well that's all I need to know. Or should I say, *we* need to know. And I'd say we've got ourselves a nice little posse together tonight, don't you think? I like the dynamics. I think we're in good shape.'

'In good shape?'

'For the scrap with Satan and her lot.'

'Oh, you know about that then?' I asked.

'Of course I know, that's why I'm here. Why else would I have attended this godforsaken over-commercialised event for the lame? This is happening, Mr Plum. This is a reckoning. And I know all about it. I've been hearing voices you see. And the voices say to come here and give the old ice queen a good seeing to.'

Bonzo's eyes lit up.

'Not like that, you dirty old rogue,' I intervened. 'Crack on with your pumpkin pie. I'll let you know when your services are needed. Now, Barmy, you have me intrigued. On tenterhooks, if you will. You've been hearing voices. That's what you said, right?'

'Correct.'

'Well, at the risk of sounding like an old musical from the human era…Tell me more.'

Barmy grinned and waved a knowing index finger at his eagle-eyed, hairy-eared friend.

'He said you'd be quizzing me on this. He warned me—he did.'

'Did he now? And I presume we're talking about the same individual from another dimension, I take it?'

'The very same. And he was quite complimentary about you. More than is normal, if I'm being honest. He thinks you are the saviour of the Earth. In fact, even more than that, he thinks you might very well be the saviour of the Universe.'

'High praise indeed, eh? Shame he didn't tell me himself, rather than having to go through a receptacle.'

'He couldn't tell you, your ears are too hairy, he said. He suggests you trim them.'

'Yes, yes, yes, I've heard all about my hairy ears. But I really don't get the hindrance. I seem to cope well enough in day-to-day matters. And yet, it appears, others struggle in this regard. Especially others from other dimensions.'

'But it's not just your hairy ears. You see, he needs me here tonight as well. So he thought, why not kill two birds with one stone, so to speak. He's quite a clever chap, this voice—he seems to know much.'

'Hence why he's a professor.'

'Yes, I suppose so.'

Barmy paused for thought.

'So you really do know him then? That's good, saves me having to explain the whole shizzle to you. I was fearing you didn't really know him at all and that you wouldn't believe me when I had to tell you. Folk tend to do that when I tell them something incredible. It might be something to do with me being off my rocker, I suppose. And that's true. I am. I'm completely off my rocker. But being off my rocker affords me insight and a free mind that the sane simply don't have the pleasure to enjoy. So I guess you must be a little cuckoo yourself. You know, seeing as you believe me and all. So I guess that sorts that out.'

'Barmy, a Dinglewit speaking from another dimension isn't gonna touch the sides with me, old buddy. I've experienced a lot more bizarre than that. So whatever Crump has to say, he can just bally get on and say it. And maybe ya right about me being a tad loony. I've always thought the same if I'm honest. And Gertie.'

'True,' chipped in the aforementioned.

'But that's why he should've come to me.'

'And he also said you'd be miffed that he contacted me and not you, as well. He seems to have got that right too. But anyway, let's not get bogged down with dissension. I fear it will get us nowhere.'

'Oh, hang on a minute. Did you just say that Crump needed you here as well?'

'Yes.'

'To save the Earth?'

'Yes.'

'Why?'

'Ah yes, hubris. Crump did say that hubris would rear its ugly head at some point. I didn't think it would be quite so soon though. I thought it would at least wait until Satan made an appearance. But there you go. But yes, I'm needed here too. I have a superpower to offer, you see.'

'Like?'

'I'm completely mad.'

'And that's a superpower?'

'Oh yes, and an important one at that. Probably the most important of all superpowers. Well, maybe except for juggling, because that's good for all occasions. But when you're fighting Satan herself, being completely mad is definitely a requirement. And I have insanity in spades.'

'Yes, I imagine you do.'

Now, in lieu of all this *going around the twist* talk, it could be observed that, perhaps, the Universe had decided to get involved in tonight's melee of wanton killing and butchery.

For if one were to take a step back and look, it was pretty obvious that it'd evened up the odds somewhat.

The Universe, you see, is many things, many unconventional things, and not all of it good, but it does like a fair fight.

It really can't tolerate is one-sidedness (except when it benefits from it).

So while Satan and her happy gang of killer hell hounds were heading towards the surface on the preface of ending Halloween with a right old slasher-fest, you may have noticed that the Universe had levelled things up a tad.

Firstly, I, the magnificent Montgomery Plum and my magic coin would be in attendance, and it knew I was always up for a scrap.

The Universe had used my reliable services on many occasions before, and it seems that it'd enjoyed my interactions so much that it'd decided to use me once again.

Also, this Barmy chap and his superpower of being completely bonkers would be there.

Why this was important has yet to be established, if it ever will.

But the Universe felt it an apt form of leveller, and I guess we should trust it on this matter.

And one thing was for sure, it will definitely be offering some humour to the battle.

As would Bonzo, although no one is actually quite sure why he was chosen, except for his ability to eventually get eaten by his own socks.

Which is sort of funny in its own right, I suppose.

And maybe that was the whole idea all along.

And then we have Lucy, the queen of tarot and throwing bones; she was to be front and centre of this whole murderous event.

Lucy had also been used before, and it would appear that she'd also made a good enough impression during her last outing.

Plus, she's a survivor, which was always a bonus, the Universe doesn't have much use for those who die at the first chance they get,

All good so far.

Behind the scenes, Professor Crump had been drafted into the fight.

He currently resides in another dimension and presumably, he'd be operating in an advisory role; offering some sort of strange wisdom from beyond the realms of reality, whatever that means these days.

While at the same time not classed as adding a body to the actual fight.

The numbers do need to match up, this isn't a handicap.

And all this would be facilitated by Biffin the Peddler, who'd just rocked up with a cart full of weapons.

Excellent.

All the ingredients are in place.

But what this fight really needs is jeopardy.

Anything that pretends to call itself exciting must have jeopardy.

And just a few random characters killing each other can't really be classed as jeopardy.

Not in today's market.

So sat in the corner, minding its own business, was a cuddly Marsh Boomer.

Mine and Gertie's cuddly pet Marsh Boomer.

A fluffy and playful thing of happiness with a large tongue, and a kind soul.

Just like all other Marsh Boomers.

The Earth's favourite pet.

And Marsh Boomers were Satan's favourite snack.

So should all go the way of Satan and her merry gang of killers, we will see one of them getting eaten.

There—jeopardy.

So, with all that in mind, let's crack on, shall we?

Chapter 16

Just as in comedy, timing is everything in life, and it's not always easy to get the blooming thing right.

I mean to say, it just isn't a good look to appear too intrusive, premature, or even keen, at a time like this; just ask anyone who's ever had the misfortune of being in the company of Satan and you'll see where I'm going here.

Etiquette, I believe it's called.

So that being said, Satan in her infinite wisdom, had decided that now was probably the right time to make her entrance and commence forth with the night's festivities and main event; that being, kill everyone in the room, and feast upon their pain.

She pushed open the double doors of the chapel and, without a care in the Universe, skipped youthfully into the main hall, waving her arms, smiling a jolly smile, and dancing a merry dance as she did.

Behind her, and under duress, her faithful servant, Biscuit, struggled on with the task of carrying her heavy bag of killing tools.

He certainly wasn't skipping.

Not waving his arms.

And definitely not youthful.

'So the tomato soup went down well, Biscuit,' said Satan happily. 'But the main course of Sweet Slug pumpkin pie didn't. What strange creatures these Dinglewits really are. And ungrateful too. You go to all that effort to put some decent grub on the table, and they shun it out of hand.'

'Can't say I blame 'em,' responded Biscuit, his face looking somewhat like a slapped bum after a large night out. 'I wouldn't be eating that stuff either.'

'Oh nonsense, you grumpy old sod, pumpkin pie is the king of the trough, as far as I'm concerned. I love a bit of the old pumpkin pie on Halloween. It's not Halloween until I've had some. And do cheer up, won't you? The girls will be here in a bit, and I don't want you bringing the mood down with your negative vibes. I want this to be a night of boisterous, good old-fashioned carnage, just like the good old days. And so will the girls. So be on your best behaviour, will you? And when they ask you to get them an axe or a hammer or whatever they want, you just be ready to deliver. Got it?'

'Got it, M'lady.'

'Good, and while you're at it, turn that frown upside down before I turn you into ashes and kick you into the wind, got that too?'

'Yes, M'lady.'

And then she got to thinking.

'Or actually...I could have you roasting on a spit for all eternity. Yes, that might be fun, you know, different. Yes, I might just do that anyway. Let's see what happens tonight, eh? We could have you as an ornament, just there in a corner, roasting away for all eternity. Yes, I like the sound of that, roasted Biscuit. I'll tell you what, I'll ask Mummy when I get home.'

'Yes, M'lady.'

'Oh you are a bore sometimes, Biscuit, can't you tell when I'm winding you up? Yes M'lady, no M'lady, do you actually know any other words? Because from where I'm standing you've become quite the yawn these days. It's most unbecoming. Constantly agreeing with everything I say and do. Do you actually have an opinion of your own?'

'Yes, M'lady.'

'Well it doesn't sound like it to me. And you're beginning to drag me down. And believe me, you don't want to drag me down, do you? You do know what happened to the last butler, don't you? I did tell you, didn't I?'

'Yes, M'lady. Most days.'

'Right, so let's see some teeth then. And for Hell's sake, show some grit, will you? No more of this sulking around.'

Biscuit feigned a fake smile as he fidgeted the bag of weapons further over his shoulder while he staggered into the main hall behind the dancing Satan.

It was all he could muster at present.

But *his* night was yet to begin.

That would come later.

'Good evening, one and all!' Satan announced, as if everyone had been waiting with bated breath for her to show up and kill them.

'How was the soup? Was it good? I see the pumpkin pie died on its arse. But never mind. I'm here now, so let the fun begin.'

This, in the view of Satan, should have stirred an excited response from her audience and caused for much merriment.

Lots of singing and dancing, I believe was the expected response.

But instead, it was met with a stunned silence trickled with the occasional gasp, some old lady fainting where she stood and needing her undergarment loosening, Bonzo undressing her with his eyes and giving her a satisfactory seven out of ten, and someone dropping an empty plastic beaker.

Underwhelming.

And a big mystery to Satan.

She was, after all, the life and soul of the party and worthy of applause wherever she went.

'Oh, please, don't be overawed by my beauty,' she offered with a smile. 'I am but a girl on a night out with my friends. Pretend I'm not here. I'll tell you what, I'll just merge into the background until we're ready to begin, how does that sound?'

It sounded like stunned silence.

'I know, I know, you're all star-struck, this always happens whenever I enter a room full of glitter and pluck and looking fabulous. But please, eat, drink, and be merry, you never know, it might be your last night alive, which is the most likely option I would say. Or perhaps you've heard of my plans and are so thrilled to be getting the chop by Satan herself that you've been rendered speechless. And if that's the case, then I'm very honoured. But please, it's much more fun for me if you put up a bit of a fight. How does that sound?'

Still stunned silence.

And one that was starting to try Satan's patience.

'Or perhaps you're all just ignorant fun-thieves who deserve everything you're about to get. Yes, that's probably it. Oops, sorry, I got a bit angry then, just ignore that bit. Anyway, is there anyone here I know?'

Satan looked around inquisitively.

'No? Are you sure? Okay then, I'll re-phrase it, is there anyone here I will get to know in the future? The very near future!'

But still nothing came from the lips of the terrified congregation.

And this she couldn't believe.

'Oh come now, surely they'll be someone who's been bad enough to justify an existence of pain and suffering for all eternity. In fact, I know there is, I have a knack of seeing these things, you see. I can see into your souls. Deep into your souls. I can see everything you've said and done. I can spot a potential new customer in the making from a hundred paces.'

Which, of course, there always was.

'You!' she shouted, pointing at a surprised, if surprisingly well-dressed, lady who'd taken perch on an end table. 'Now I'll get to know *you* in the next life, you naughty little minx. Now what have you been up to?'

The lady in question was a rather fetching-looking example of Dinglewit who'd decided that tonight would be a good time to wear her new blue frock; complete with matching blue shoes and blue hat.

For narrative purposes, and seeing that she won't be in the story for long, we'll just call her Blue Dress.

'Nothing,' came the surprised response from Blue Dress.

'At least, not yet,' responded Satan. 'But you will. Give it time.'

Blue Dress looked round at her husband, whose eyes gave away the tip-off that he knew he'd end up dead at the hand of his wife, but to hear it confirmed by Satan herself, well, that was the last straw.

'I knew you were slowly poisoning me!' he yelled. 'Someone help me! Get this psycho bitch away from me!'

'Oh, do shut up, Humphrey,' Blue Dress retaliated. 'All you do is whine, whine…whine and whine. You're like a big baby. God knows what I saw in you in the first place. I must've been insane.'

'I'll tell you what you saw in me, shall I? You saw crowns, lots and lots of crowns. 'Cus that's all you're good for…spending my crowns. Well, no more. From now on, the gravy train has come to the end of the track and is permanently stationed at the no-more-crowns-for-you ville-station. So you can forget about my wallet being open from now on…it is well and truly stitched up.'

'Yeah, well stitch this.'

Blue Dress reached up her frock and pulled out a silver dagger from her stockings and stabbed him right between the eyeballs.

The Old Chapel, previously filled with stunned silence, was now filled with streams of *gosh* and *oh dears*, as Blue Dress pulled the dagger out from her recently deceased husband's forehead and wiped it on his new evening jacket.

'There,' she announced, looking straight at Satan. 'Does that get me a pass into Hell?'

'Oh yes,' Satan answered. 'And if you carry on with good work like that, you can sit next to me at the big table.'

But the arrival of Blue Dress into Hell came quicker than she'd expected.

For no longer had she wiped her dagger clean and placed it back into her stockings, was her severed head rolling along the old chapel floor; only coming to a stop at the foot of the tyrant queen herself.

Satan looked displeased.

'Who did that?' she screamed.

'Oh, that would be me, old fruit…sorry, and all that, rush of blood to the old bean. It happens from time to time. I can't seem to control it. It's like, I know I shouldn't throw the first punch, and all that, but then I think to myself, oh sod it, it's going to happen anyway so let's just get stuck in. Sorry again.'

'And who are you, exactly?' Satan enquired.

'Me, Satan? Oh, I'm Montgomery Plum,' I announced. 'A big fan of your work. Big fan. And I'll be your worthy adversary tonight, If you will.'

Satan was obviously intrigued by my introduction.

Why wouldn't she be? I mean, I'd just lobbed the head off a cold-blooded killer and watched it roll along the chapel floor without a care in the world.

Impulsive.

Reckless.

Hot-headed.

And I've often been called worse.

And I'm happy to accept that to those unacquainted with my work I might seem rather rash.

And true, it's got me into some deep and very hot water from time to time.

But I find it always pays off in the end.

Plus, it keeps 'em thinking.

Satan turned to Biscuit.

'Who is this killer? He has a natural fervour about him. I like him. He's ruthless. He's a go-getter. He wears a funny beard. But he's also declared himself for the other team, so that means he'll be dying too. Although that was my intention all along, so it doesn't really matter, does it? Well, Mr Plum. My name is Satan. And this is Biscuit. Biscuit, come here and say hello.'

Biscuit chose not to approach, instead opting to offer his greetings from afar.

'Fair enough, he's a bit shy,' Satan continued. 'I will deal with him later. But I do have a few friends coming along. They should be here anytime soon.'

'Excellent, I do like a fair fight,' I answered, giving it the big 'un, seeing as I was *in for a penny*. 'It's makes for a more pleasant victory party, I always find.

There's nothing worse than getting all dressed up for a bit of a do, only to find it over in two shakes of a lamb's tail, don't you agree?'

'Indeed.'

'So do you want to wait until they arrive?' I asked. 'I don't mind watering the old gullet for a few minutes until ya all ready.'

This was insolence, considered Satan.

And certainly not the scared stiff and screaming for mercy act that she'd been expecting.

Or indeed hoped for.

But life gives you what life gives you.

And if life gives you Montgomery Plums' on the last ever night of Halloween, then life is being an ass and should be indulged.

'Well, if you don't mind, Mr Plum, that would be swell. They've been looking forward to this for quite some time. I wouldn't want them to miss it.'

'Excellent. A good oiling first, then some gratuitous killing to finish off. I'll grab myself another glass of the good stuff then, if you don't mind?'

Still giving it the big 'un.

'Not at all, it's all paid for. And there are crates of the stuff in the back too. It would be a shame to waste it. For I sense once the fun begins, there won't be much sipping going on. I mean, I won't be drinking that much tonight, and I know you lot won't get much chance, and I don't think the girls will drink much that isn't blood, so you may as well get stuck in.'

Which, I have to say, came as music to my *supposedly* big fat hairy ears.

'Righty-ho,' I affirmed. 'See you in a bit then.'

'Yes, I'll see you in a bit, Montgomery Plum.'

'Fine.'

'Good.'

'Okay.'

'Cheerio.'

'Tinkety-tonk.'

Blah. Blah. Blah.

The niceties ended.

After which, we slowly moved away from each other in a mutual understanding that everything that needed to be said, had been said, and that saying anymore now might just unsay the unsaid, and cause the need for more unsaid said's to be said.

Need I say more?

Then I slid back towards a remarkably unimpressed Gertie, who did have something to say.

'What are you doing, you goof?' she snarled. 'You are taunting Satan, you absolute dimwit. This isn't going to end well.'

'Oh I'm just giving it some trash talk. You know, laying it low. Sticking a few in the ribs. It's generally considered to be the accepted practice in these types of gigs, wouldn't you know? It's all part of the fun.'

'Fun! Do you think this will be fun?'

'Well yes, why, don't you?'

'No, I bloody well don't,' Gertie sneered. 'And neither will the rest of the assembly when they figure out they're all going to die horribly in some bizarre act of terror purely for the amusement of the anti-Christ. There will be a lot of bemused folk around here.'

'Oh, you don't know that, old puffin? Why, they've come all this way to a Halloween party, haven't they? And they've all got dressed up for the occasion. And they're all eating the pie. So why wouldn't they expect to be meeting Satan? Isn't that what Halloween is all about?'

'Actually, no. They'd be thinking that they'll be playing some silly games, eating silly food, getting tipsy, then stagger home thanking the Lord that it's all over for another year, and then getting prepared for Christmas.'

I had to enlighten her.

'Well, my sweet little cherry pudding, if that's what they think, then they've massively misjudged the night's meaning, haven't they? Because it looks like Satan's mates have just turned up and, erm, well…they're definitely looking for a fight. Look, that one's taking a file to her teeth.'

Gertie looked on in revulsion at the prospect of having a fight with someone who felt it acceptable to file her teeth away.

For not only was it a sign that they were probably as mean as mustard, and would therefore win in a fair fight, but also, it made them look positively ghastly.

'So perhaps we should leave,' came Gertie's suggestion. 'This might be a job even too big for you, I'm afraid.'

'Leave, Gertie, old sponge? No, we can't leave,' I answered, taking it as an affront to my masculinity. 'That wouldn't be right. Wouldn't be right at all. My reputation would go right down the swanny. I mean to say, how would it look if

I ran away every time someone decided to perform a few homemade dental improvements?

'No, I can't do that. I'd be ruined. Besides, look at 'em. They ain't that scary. They might be filing away at their own teeth, but they do look a rag tag bunch of red bloods, don't they? I'm not even sure they'll have the required staying power mandatory for the job at hand.'

'Oh really, and what would that look like, can I ask? Because that one has big sharp teeth; that one looks like a werewolf; they all look like death warmed up, and as for that one, well, I'm not sure what we're dealing with there, but I sure as hell know I don't wanna get tangled up with it.'

I sensed choppy waters ahead, Gertie was clearly having second thoughts about the current state of play, and I felt it was my job to keep her away from crash landing on the rocks and foundering to the bottom of the ocean.

So I offered solace.

'Then, I shall explain,' I said. 'You see this is what's what.' And I pointed at Satan's friends one by one. 'Now that one with the big sharp teeth, she's a vampire. And by the looks of it, a very successful one.'

'How do you know?'

'How do I know what?'

'That she's a successful vampire.'

'Because she has superb skin. Nice and moist. All prosperous vampires have superb skin, you see. It comes from all the goodness they've ingested. I heard that it's something to do with all the oils. So anyway, that one is a vampire. Now, the one that looks like a werewolf, well, she is a werewolf, that's why she looks like one. But the big problem with werewolves is that they tend to charge headlong into the hunt without a pause for thought or a plan B, and that tends to get them done for. So I'd doubt if she'll be too much bother to a seasoned professional killer like me.'

'Like you?'

'Yes.'

'A seasoned professional killer?'

'Yes.'

'Do you know what any of that means?'

'No. But it sounds good, so I'm sticking with it. So, when you begin to break it down like that, the job becomes a lot less intimidating and easier to manage. Now, as for how we're going to actually take 'em out, that one is still a mystery.

But I tend to find that something will come up, it always does. And I don't mean come up from Hell. Like they have. And sure, they must be some badass bitches if they ended up in Hell in the first place, but they still ain't gonna last long when the proverbial goes down. That's what I say.'

'Provided you know how to kill 'em,' interrupted an intrusive voice with a peculiar northern accent, and one that had, until now, remained mute. 'Cus if you don't know how to kill 'em, then it's gonna be a whole lot harder than you think.'

Gertie about turned about one hundred and thirty degrees to the left, or for ease of purpose, let's say about 8 o'clock, and I followed suit.

'And you are?' enquired Gertie.

'I'm Biffin,' came the northern-accented response, and answering the question resoundingly. 'I'm a peddler.'

'A peddler! And what exactly does a peddler do?'

'I sell stuff, of course. Mainly knick-knacks. Odds and sods. That sort of thing. A bit like a mobile haberdashery. So if there's anything you want, I'm the one to get it for you.' And he handed a business card over and continued, 'I do the best prices in town and will match anyone else's price should they try to pull a fast one. I'll never be undercut. That's my motto, Biffin the Peddler, never been undercut on price.'

Gertie took a quick look at the business card and placed it on the table in the hope that a strong gust of wind would blow it into the night, never to be seen again.

'And is business good?' she asked.

'Ooh good enough. I can't complain. Well, I can, but who'd listen? No one ever thinks of the peddler, do they? We're invisible. Like a speck of dust in the wind. The life of a peddler, you see, is a lonely old game. Drifting from town to town. And from house to house. No one ever gives us a second thought. And we don't earn much either, just enough to keep the wolves from the door. And when it doesn't, and the wolves begin to close in…well, I leg it.'

'Is that also a motto?'

'No, but it should be. But you can have too many mottos, can't you? Bad for business. It's all about the punch. Anyway, rummy old business all this, yes?'

Gertie and I shared a confused glance.

'How do you mean?'

'The slaughter! Are you not aware? Surely, you're aware. You've just diss'd Satan and challenged her to a duel, so you must know.'

He'd made a valid point, so I relented.

'Yeah, I know. The question is, how do you?'

'Yes, well, I met this raver called Barmy earlier today, I guess the clue's in the name. And he told me all. I gave him a lift up here to the Old Chapel. He was on foot, you see. Didn't have any shoes on the poor chap. But he is interesting, if a little bit around the twist, but he seems to have his finger on the pulse on this one. Apparently, there's going to be a reckoning. This voice told him. And if that is Satan herself over there flirting with the bar staff, and not just some imposter, then I'd say he got it bang on.'

'Yes,' I added. 'I'd say you're right. But I have another question for you?'

'Go ahead.'

'If you knew what was about to happen, then why are you still here?'

Biffin the Peddler smirked.

'A business opportunity, that's why. A peddler should never turn down the chance to make a few crowns. And the best time to pull a few bob in is when there's chaos. Because wherever there's chaos, there's profit. That's what I've always found. And it just so happens that I have in my possession a large variety of weapons for sale. I've set up a stall over there. So feel free to come over and make a purchase. Oh, and spread the word too. I won't be beaten on price.'

'That's right, you have it as a motto.'

'Yep.'

'But you're the only one here selling weapons,' added Gertie. 'So you can charge what you like.'

'Exactly. A monopoly. My favourite type of market.'

'This is a setup,' Gertie snapped. 'Absolutely, not a doubt in my mind, a setup. And we're the pawns in this setup. And I don't like it.'

She picked up her glass of bubbling Venus Twinkle, admired its bubbles, placed it gently back on the table, and then looked for something else to be anxious about.

I, sensing that now would be a good time to be comforting, albeit in a socially awkward manner, offered kind words.

'Gertie, old lemon, chill,' I chipped in. 'You know the score by now, surely. Of course, it's a setup. Everything is. It's all just farce, that's all. A circus act, if you will. So the Universe wants to have a bit of fun on Halloween, so what? We all do. And I admire the fact that it's given us a fair fight. It doesn't have to, does it? It could easily have let Satan do whatever she wanted and sat back and enjoyed the evening. But no, it wants a contest.'

'But Dinglewits will die.'

'Yes, yes, yes, of course, they will. But they'll all die at some point anyway, so what does it matter? We'll all die, even me. Even you. Even the Universe itself. It will all end at some point in the future. So let's not get too bogged down with when we're going to die, but just enjoy it when we do.'

'But I don't want to die tonight, not inside this crappy old chapel at Blorkeney Knoll. I want to die in my home, surrounded by my family, at a ripe old age. Not at the claws of a psychopath on a night out.'

'Well, if that is what the Universe has in store for you, then that is what it has in store for you. Fate, Gertie, old crumble. Nothing can change it.'

'Well, I don't like it.'

'Maybe not, but that certainly doesn't warrant wasting expensive champagne now, does it? Look, why don't you take a seat and leave all this to me? I got this.'

And that seemed to do the trick, funnily enough.

If only everything else was as easy as that.

Offering Gertie alcohol.

And to which I joined her.

After all, if you can't get a gut full when you're about to fight Satan, then well, what's the point?

You see, when it comes to life and death, and everything else in between, I have a relaxed nature of it all.

I'm relaxed because I'm steadfast in my belief that everything is just one giant setup.

And I mean everything.

Nothing is just by chance.

It's all one big setup, organised by the Universe for its own amusement, and maybe to make a bit on the side, and that everything inside this Universe just has to play along and make the best of it.

And I'm fine with that.

Because I know.

I know it's all one big game.

One big, mesmerising, addictive, game, where the end goal is to enjoy as much of life as you possibly can.

What bothers me are the things that I don't know.

Chapter 17

Biffin the Peddler was doing brisk business, it must be said.

But then selling hope to the desperate was always brisk business.

And always had been.

It's a bit like selling reading glasses to a gullible blind chap—immoral, but very profitable if you can get the sales jib right.

But Biffin didn't need to get his sales jib right, Satan and her friends were doing that for job him.

ARGHH. CRUNCH. ARGHH. CRACK. *Even louder* ARGHH. *Followed by a more painful* OUCH.

Blood splatters up the wall.

A stampede of Dinglewits attempting to escape the carnage.

But failing miserably.

There would be no getting away tonight.

'Wolfie! How ya doing?' screamed Satan. 'You enjoying yourself?'

Wolfie was covered in blood.

'Of course I'm enjoying myself. I love the taste of fresh blood. How you doing?'

'Oh, I'm in the red. If you know what I mean? But where are they all running to?'

'They're heading over to that table. It looks like someone has set up a makeshift weapon shop.'

'A makeshift weapon shop?'

'Yes, a makeshift weapon shop. And it looks like he's got a good brain for commerce.'

'How much for a couple of knuckle dusters?' enquired a customer.

'A couple of knuckle dusters?' responded Biffin.

'Yes, one for each hand.'

'Ambitious…I like it. Two crowns.'

'Two crowns? That's a bit much innit?'

'Each.'

'Each! Jesus. You're a rip-off merchant, that's what you are, a rip-off merchant.'

'It's a buyer's market, my friend. A buyer's market,' hustled Biffin. 'And those beasts from Hell look quite tasty to me, so I'd be getting myself fully packed if I were you.'

And the words: barrel, had, over, and you, were also used.

'But two crowns each! Mate, it's life and death here. Surely we can cut a deal. If I don't get something to defend myself with, I'm done for.'

'In that case, three crowns.'

'Three crowns?'

'Yep, three crowns.'

'For them both?'

'Nope, each. And considering what you've just told me, I'm doing *you* a favour. So if you want them both, that'll be six crowns, please.'

And then the words: hell, rot, and in, were mentioned.

'But I haven't got six crowns.'

'Then you need to find it. And if I were you, I'd find it quick. Death is coming.'

Cue some interesting profanity and generally unpleasant remarks aimed at Biffin which—with hindsight—might not have been the best negotiating tactic the buyer could have employed.

'Seven crowns now, for all them unkindly gestures. I do have feelings, you know.'

'Seven! How can you charge seven? It started off at four!'

'You showed your hand, old boy. Sorry, and all that, but business is business, and I got school fees to pay for.' He didn't, of course, but what a line. 'So if I were you, I'd pay up the seven before it gets to eight.'

The buyer quickly reached deep into their pockets and pulled out seven crowns and handed them over.

'Here! And I hope you choke on it.'

'Why, thank you, it's been a pleasure. Be lucky.'

And that's pretty much how the next few minutes went.

The good folk of the Old Chapel at Blorkeney Knoll are being sold some wishful thinking.

And Biffin the Peddler making himself a nice bit of bunce.

'If only a reckoning would come about every week,' he muttered, 'I'd be a made man. Right, who's next.'

A sultry and slight female was next in line.

And if there was anything that might break the stone heart of Biffin, this could be it.

'How much for a sword?' came the request.

'To you, six crowns.'

'Six crowns, get the fuck outta here.'

'Okay, your choice. But I've just sold two knuckle dusters for seven crowns, so a sword for six is a bit of a bargain if you ask me.'

My mistake, Biffin was unrelenting.

And seemingly made of wood.

'But I'm begging you. I'm begging you to have a heart. I'm about to get mauled by that werewolf over there. Look! She's a savage. Where's your compassion?'

'Oh, that was sold a while ago. Along with all my empathy. I'm operating on margins here, sweetheart. Six crowns.'

'What, six crowns for a sword? That ain't margins, that's daylight robbery.'

'I didn't say the margins were small, did I? You gotta make hay while the sun shines, that's what I always say. And right now the sun is blistering. So if I were you, I'd be snapping up this sword while you still have arms to do so. That werewolf looks hungry.'

A good line, if he didn't say so himself.

'Oh bugger, well can I pay you some now, and the rest in the morning?' came the panicked response.

To which.

'You may not be here in the morning; then where would I be? Out of pocket, that's where I'd be. Nope, it's all on the button or not at all. I have other customers you know,' was the answer.

'What do you mean I may not be here in the morning? Of course I will. Well, I'll be here if you sell me the sword. Tell you what; I'll give you three crowns now, and another four in the morning. That makes seven crowns, a bit of interest there. What do you say?'

Biffin was not a fan of drip payments, not a fan.

'I'll tell you what I say, I say you are asking me to gamble on the quality of your swordsmanship, that's what I say.'

'How do you mean?'

'What I mean is; you are giving me three crowns now, yes?'

'Yes.'

'So that means I only have three crowns. I don't know what will happen to you, do I? You might be terrible at fighting demonic monsters from the depths of Hell. And if that's the case, and you get mangled to death, I'm three crowns out of pocket. Now I know that you said that you'll give me four in the morning, but that's only if you make it alive. So what you're asking me to do is to gamble on your swordsmanship. And I don't know if you're any good at wielding a sword or not, do I? And I certainly don't like to gamble, it's a mug's game. So, it's six crowns or nothing.'

Some would argue he had a fair point.

'You are one ruthless git. Do you know that?'

'Maybe, but a wealthy git. Six crowns.'

'You'll be going to Hell, that's what you'll be doing. Ripping off the desperate like this.'

'And that may be true as well, but I would guess that you'll be going there first. Especially without this sword. Now, what will it be? Six crowns or certain death.'

And with that, the trade was made, and the tidy sum of six crowns was handed over to the unscrupulous merchant.

He placed the crowns into his bulging pouch that hung proudly on his belt.

And sat patiently waiting for his next customer.

Meanwhile, the slaughter continued.

'Run for your life! Over there, we can hide under the table.'

'Won't Satan look under the table? Duck, watch out for that head.'

SWOOSH.

'And that torso.'

SWOOSH.

'Wait, is that Hilda?'

A limbless Hilda flew past.

'*Was*, I believe is the correct grammatical term. For Hilda is no more of the land of the living. She's now making her way slowly to the pearly gates to await her fate.'

'That's a shame, I liked Hilda. Hold on, she had a nice bracelet on tonight. Hey, if we can find her arms, we're in the money, that bracelet's worth a fortune.'

'Really? Nice. Let's go seek.'

Which was heartening to hear.

For even when the chips were down and certain doom lurked heavy on the horizon, nothing could temper the entrepreneurial spirit of the Dinglewits of Glint Tae.

And speaking of such matters, Biffin was still doing his thing.

Although now he was bartering with Lucy.

'How much for that spear?'

'Eight crowns to you, miss. Good price.'

'What do you mean eight crowns? That's not a good price. They're one crown for four down at the corner shop. And I think even that's expensive.'

'Then I suggest you pop down there and buy 'em then, because here at the Old Chapel at Blorkeney Knoll, when Satan has turned up and is turning the walls a pleasant shade of Dinglewit red, they're eight crowns each. And like I said, good price.'

'But I could buy…erm…10, 20—'

'32!' interrupted Biffin, after doing the maths for her.

'Really? Yes it is, isn't it? 32. Thirty bloody two. I could buy thirty bloody two spears for that price down at the corner shop.'

'Then it's a shame you didn't buy thirty bloody two spears, isn't it? Because if you had, you'd be pulling a profit right now, wouldn't you? Look, the spear is the weapon of choice if you ask me. You can poke with it, you can swing it round to scare everything off with it, it's an all-rounder. And good for all creatures from Hell. So I'd be snapping it up right now before some other desperado wants to buy it.'

Biffin was chuffed with that sales pitch too.

The spear was a good all-rounder, a weapon for the ages.

Something you could pass down from father to son.

And from son to—whatever.

A bit like a family heirloom.

Although the wood does tend to rot after a while, so quite how many generations it would last for is anyone's guess.

But the process of timber undergoing destructive dissolution wasn't helping Lucy achieve a decent price for this one.

She needed an edge.

'Erm…I know, how about I give you four crowns for a spear so that I can fight my way to the door? Then I'll run down to the corner shop and buy four spears for a single crown. And then when I get back, I'll give you your spear back along with the three other spears that I won't need, and then we can call it quits.'

Biffin pondered.

'A rental system?' he queried.

'Yeah, a good idea, yes? We'll do a rent on one. I'll pay you four crowns to loan it for a bit, then give you it back when I return along with three more. That way, you get four crowns and four spears. Everyone is a winner.'

'So I make four crowns as well as increase my stockpile at the same time?'

'Yep.'

'Intriguing, have you thought about going into business?'

'No. But I do need a spear. And right now, would be nice.'

Biffin pondered some more.

'I'll tell you what, you give me eight crowns now for this spear now, then I'll give you four crowns back when you return it with the three additional spears. We can call it a deposit system.'

'But I don't have eight crowns on me.'

'They all say that. But they all find a way of finding it.'

'Well I can't.'

'Then you'll have to make a run for the door.'

'But I won't make it to the door without a spear, will I? I'll get got.'

'Exactly, so you need this spear, nine crowns.'

'But you said eight.'

'I'm haggling.'

'Haggling! Haggling! I'll tell you what, how about you give me the spear and I'll let you live. How's that for haggling?'

'What do you mean, let me live?'

'I'll let you live. Give me that spear and I'll spare you your little, measly, ghastly, good for nothing, life. How about that for a deal?'

'That's not a deal, that's threatening behaviour. You can't just go around threatening peddlers because you don't like the price. Where would we be if folk just started threatening hard-working traders just like that? Anarchy, that's where we'd be. The system only works if a fair price is set, and the customer pays the set price. That's capitalism. Otherwise, we may as well just give the whole thing up as a bad job and go back to killing each other for a bowl of food.'

'Couldn't have put it better myself,' responded Lucy.

And with that, she grabbed the spear from Biffin the Peddler's hand and jammed it into his neck.

'I don't know about killing each other for a bowl of food, but I'd certainly do it for a spear.'

But the trade was yet to be completed.

For as Lucy pulled the spear from his neck, blood spurted all over her brand-new frock.

'Damn you, you useless cretin. Look at my new frock now. It's ruined. And it cost me two crowns as well.'

He couldn't look though, because he'd already breathed his last breath on this carousel of life and was lying lifeless on the floor.

So she reached into his pouch and took the two crowns from his night's profits.

'There, that'll cover it,' she said. 'You won't be needing these anyway now, you miserly old penny-pincher.'

Chapter 18

So, the Old Chapel at Blorkeney Knoll was now-a-rocking.

A steady trickle of blood ran through the ancient brick floor, forming a gloomy mini waterfall on the front steps before dripping into the street below.

But it was inside where all the fun was happening.

Lucy, having pierced Wolfie with her spear, found herself flying through the air and landing at my feet while I was busying myself eating a cheese and tomato sandwich that I'd prepared in advance, fearing the food would be a total washout.

Which, apart from the vol-au-vents, it was.

'I say, old flower, if you don't mind me mentioning it, but the problem you had there was that you attempted to kill a werewolf with the wrong sort of weapon. A spear is no good. You see, you need an axe for that kind of job. If you jab it with a spear, you'll just annoy it.'

'Yes, thank you,' answered Lucy. 'I've just found that one out for myself.'

Which she had.

'Now, if you don't have an axe, then a chainsaw will suffice. But that takes time to get started, and then you need to be careful not to chop yourself up as well, which is easily done in the heat of the moment. So, I would highly recommend an axe. Wouldn't you, Gertie?'

Gertie wasn't interested in playing a game of *matching the deadly weapon to the demon from Hell*, so she shook her head and helped Lucy off the floor.

'You okay, Lucy?' she asked.

'A bit grazed, but thanks for asking.'

'Good, you were lucky to get away from that one. That werewolf is tetchy, and you may wish to avoid her. And just ignore this biff too, you know what he's like at times like these, you won't get any sympathy.'

I was in agreement there—sympathy. I always say is, in the dictionary between shit and syphilis, and at this moment in time, we've no place for either.

So I commented, 'It's just a few bumps and bruises, Lucy, they'll go away, but the glory won't.' And I wasn't done yet. 'My suggestion is to go and see Biffin the Peddler, he has loads of weapons, just perfect for the job. He's set a stall up somewhere.'

'That won't be possible,' answered Lucy.

'Oh no, have you run out of money? Here, I've got some, here's 20 crowns, now go buy yourself a nice sharp axe and have another go.'

'He's dead.'

'Who?'

'Biffin the Peddler.'

'Is he? Oh, well, that's a bit of a floater, I must say. I wonder how that happened. But well, these things do happen, never mind. So, what you need to do now is pick your battles. If all you have is a spear, then have a go at the vampire one. I think they call her Blood. Not that it matters what her name is, mind. She could easily be called Thelma or Dotty, it really doesn't matter, I don't know why I said it, to be honest.'

'Oh, thanks very much for your sage advice on the matter,' came the sarcastic response. 'Any other nuggets of knowledge while you're at it?'

There wasn't.

But I just don't see why they have to use sarcasm all the time either.

It's the blunt end of a pencil if you ask me.

But, like any gentleman should do in a time like this, I overlooked their dependence on mockery and offered some outstanding counsel.

'Actually, yes. I've been looking around and taking notes. Mental notes, that is, not writing it down. But I think I've cracked it. In essence, there are six of 'em. Some are more important than others, of course. I sense that a few have sneaked up through the cracks and are here like limpets, making up the numbers, so to speak. But Satan has her close friends, now they're the ones we need to be careful of. So, there's Satan, of course, she's the hardest, we'll come back to her later. Then you've got the werewolf, Wolfie, you've already met her. She might be a bugger to kill, just poking her with a sharp instrument may not cut it. You need a chopping device to deal with that nuisance. An axe perhaps. Something to chop the old claws off and maybe a few teeth. That'll neutralise her while you have a go at the head. That's her sorted. Then you have the vampire, Blood, a stake through the heart apparently is the best way to deal with vampires. Quite how you're going to manage that might be the tricky part. But if you can get a stake through the heart, you're in business. Now them two, and Satan, they're the main gang. The girls, I believe they're calling themselves. If we take them out, we've cracked it. Then we have the others, they shouldn't be too much bother, but still need dealing with.'

'Oh God, you really have been giving it some thought, haven't you?' asked Gertie.

'Oh yes, been using the old noddle on this one.'

'Oh heaven help us.'

'No, no, no, Gert, not heaven, there's no room for heaven here. I'm on the job. And what we need is brute force. Brute force and as much gratuitous violence as you can possibly muster. So pay attention. Now, the blue-looking thing, that's a zombie. That one is a bit awkward, but not impossible. I think fire is the only way to get her. You really do need to burn zombies. It's the only way.'

'And how do you suppose we do that?'

'By using fire.'

'Brilliant!'

'Now the other one, the one with the eyeball hanging out, I presume that's a cannibal. Easy. You just kill it. But you need to be quick—mind—she's a live wire. But your spear is perfect for that. I reckon that's why the Universe had it put here.'

'The Universe put it here? Oh don't start with all that *this is just a game for the Universe* dinkum that you always drum up.'

'But it's true, Gertie, old crumble, this *is* all just a game. And when you realise it, then it becomes easier to deal with. Now, the other thing that's latched on to them, I'm not quite sure why she's here, she doesn't look like a killer to me. So she's a bit of a mystery, but I fancy she'd be the easiest to dispatch off though. A quick double-tap to the dome and she'd be history.'

'So that brings us to Satan.'

'Yep, that brings us to Satan. I'm not really sure about that one. It might just be a case of, let's have a go and see.'

'Let's have a go and see? And you think that's a master plan, eh?'

'It's always worked for me.'

'Yes, it has, and I don't want to disappoint you as I know that *let's just have a pop and find out* is your philosophy on life. But I don't think that'll work this time. She's a demon. *The* Demon. The mightiest of all demons.'

'Well, she is Satan, Gertie. You'd expect her to be a bit on the tasty side, wouldn't you? At least I hope so. It would be a bit of a let-down if she just crumbled into a pile on the floor and began crying. But I'm not worried, summat will come up. It always does.'

'Yeah, like my innards coming up through my chest when she yanks 'em out. That's what'll come up.'

'Oh, ya so negative at times, old pudding. Look, nothing good has ever come from being a negative nelly. It's positive vibes we need right now. It's the only way to beat the hopelessness of what life chucks at you. Tell you what, how about I go first and show you how it's done?'

'You go first what?'

'You know? Slashing 'em up and all that. I'll go first and show you how it's done, then you can follow my lead. How does that sound?'

'It sounds like you've taken leave of my senses,' said Gertie. 'And that I'd be better off putting my underpants on my head and mimicking the actions and sounds of a gobbled turkey, if that is such a thing.'

And that she was tempted to grab me by the collar and give my head a wobble, although through past experience, she'd learnt that doesn't actually change anything.

So on this occasion, she refrained from taking such drastic measures and opted for verbal insults.

I liked this new approach.

Less need for painkillers.

'Now look here, numb nuts,' she aggravated, if it's indeed possible to aggravate words. 'This isn't one of your little games. That's Satan over there. Not just some gangster or drunkard looking for a scrap. She'll be able to take you down without even flinching. She is the actual devil, you know. This whole *I'm the saviour of the Universe* impression that you have of yourself could get you killed tonight. Please, let's just make a run for it. I promise no one will think any less of you.'

This, as one might imagine, did not sit well with the saviour of the Universe, that being me, of course.

Nor did it do anything in my attempt to bring positive vibes to the proceedings.

And this was not what I aspired to when I suggested that she should stop being a negative nelly and smile more.

So, in the typical cowardly fashion that I adopt when it comes to confronting Gertie, I dismissed her remarks with humour.

'My dear girl, the only thing that'll be flinching tonight will be her anal sphincter when I stick my plimsole up her back passage. Okay, she might be the queen of the underworld. And okay, she's already slashed up a good many Dinglewits tonight without breaking a sweat. But she is mere flesh and blood, and she can be taken to task. Now, hold my glass while I demonstrate what I mean.'

I passed Gertie my half-full, or half-empty, depending on whether you're on the positive or negative end of the spectrum, glass of Halloween punch and pulled out my magic coin from around my neck.

This normally does the trick.

I gave it a good luck kiss and strode over to the nearest hell-dog, who just happened to be Wolfie.

Wolfie, it turned out, had just eaten, so he was in no mood for more food, but did quite like the idea of taking this chaps' long ginger beard and making a new scarf from it.

'Hello,' she announced. 'Do you want something?'

'Yes, I want you to fly across the room while screaming.'

I then kicked her in the shin, and when she bowed her head to look at the damage, I administered the biggest uppercut I could possibly muster.

And pleased with my work, I contemplated a dance of some sort.

But there was a snag.

For rather than watching the werewolf hurtle across the Old Chapel at Blorkeney Knoll—wondering what she'd got herself into and regretting leaving the depths of Hell at all—she looked up at the curiously handsome-looking chap wearing, what can only be described as, banging shorts, a really suave jacket, and a top hat from the gods, and punched me back.

Thus sending Montgomery Plum, the saviour of the Universe, hurtling across the room, and landing at the feet of Gertie and Lucy.

'You were saying?' asked Lucy.

'Oh, I think he said something about holding my drink and watching how it's done, Lucy,' Gertie smirked.

'Well, it looks like he did exactly what I did, Gertie.'

'What? Get his butt kicked and humiliated?'

'Yep.'

'Yeah, yeah, ya both very funny,' I mumbled, as I re-aligned my jaw. 'She caught me off guard, that's all. It won't happen again; I'll tell you that for nothing.'

And I got up from the dusty floor and patted myself down, somewhat lowered in morale.

'Sneaky little trick, and not what I expected from a werewolf,' I continued. 'Maybe it's right what they say about them.'

'What is?'

'That you can't trust 'em to play fair.'

'What, like they don't follow your expected rules of engagement?'

'Exactly. We all know that the only way to fight is to make a funny comment before doing something marvellous. I didn't hear a peep from her. Low-down and dirty, that's what I think.'

Now, if I was to be completely honest with myself, I wasn't sure what I was most annoyed about.

Was it the fact that I'd just been handed my arse by a werewolf and was now licking my wounds in front of the missus—the only Dinglewit whose impression actually mattered to me? Or, was it that I'd got my new shorts dusty, as I was hoping to wear them tomorrow night for the bingo and now they'll need washing.

Best not mention that to Gertie, I thought to myself, she hates washing mid-week.

Either way, this werewolf creature would pay for the insult.

I didn't quite know how.

Or when.

But she'd definitely pay.

Gertie, on the other hand, had bigger things on her mind than her mid-week laundry washing duties, or how embarrassed I was with getting whooped in front of her, for she was currently stuck inside an old chapel on the banks of the River Bog, and about to get eaten by the occupants of Hell.

'Well think of something fast, will you?' she requested. 'Because they're working their way through that lot at a considerable rate of knots, and it won't be long before we're the last ones standing.'

The sounds of screaming, and flesh being slashed, echoed from the main table of the chapel.

I glanced an annoyed glance at the state of affairs and couldn't help but agree with Gertie on this one.

This was a pickle and no mistake.

And if we were to get out of this one alive, I'd have to use all the cunning and magic powers of my magic coin, which further annoyed me because it was starting to become obvious that I could only perform these feats of magnificence because I had a magic coin.

And what I really craved was some small monocle of acknowledgement for being a superhero on my own merits.

But that might have to be a mission for another day, I mused.

Because if I didn't get my butt into gear and see to it that Satan and her shindig of hellhounds didn't get their way with the good folk of Glint Tae, then my remarkable story of adventure and heroism might very well end here.

No prologue.

No second series.

It'd just end here.

In this decrepit old chapel.

That doesn't even have running water or mains' sewerage.

And at the hands of six girls from Hell looking for a good night out.

This simply wouldn't do.

Especially as the party was now in full flow.

As was the blood.

And Satan, always grateful when the living part of the Universe died as they should—and in a manner that she wished for—was starting to enjoy her night out.

She'd been hoping that the whole bash would be a raging success with plenty of death and unpleasantness, and that was just how things were turning out.

They'd decided—the lot from Hell that is—to start a book on who could slaughter the most Dinglewits in one single night.

They'd assign one point for each soul skewered, skewered only being confirmed once pulseless, and five bonus points, to be judged at the end of the night, for the most spectacular of all kills.

At the moment, Blood, being a vampire who was able to transform into a bat, was winning the bonus point race. She metamorphosised into a bat and flew directly down the throat of Big Hank—a well-known eater in these parts. Then she turned herself back into her original vampire shape thus exploding Big Hank all over the old chapel hall.

Satan applauded this effort.

But never one to be outdone, Gnasher, a cannibal of the most gruesome kind who'd lagged on to Blood so she could get away for the night, made her pitch for the old five-pointer.

'Oi, Blood,' she shouted. 'Watch this.'

Gnasher had come across some of the innards of Big Hank and decided that they would make a complimentary filling for a Dinglewit and innards sandwich.

This was to be no mean feat.

For taking two Dinglewits—a distant member of the lizard family and famous for not lying still when about to be murdered—and spreading the intestines of Big Hank in the middle, was going to take some doing.

But do it she did, and thus got herself in contention for the big five-pointer debate that would definitely be had later.

But there was only one snag to Gnasher's plan.

And that was that while she was occupied in the act of sandwich making, her attention wouldn't exactly be on defence.

So once a bite from the sandwich had reached her gullet—and was making its way down to the stomach to be dissolved by some rather potent gastric acid with a long name or other—she was completely unaware of the fast-moving club that was ascending its way to the top of her head.

WALLOP.
Followed by.
SPLURT.
Followed by.
SLUMP.

'Woohoo! Take that you beast of death,' came the cry.

And the whole room stopped in its tracks.

What was this new development?

Was this supposed to be in the script?

Surely this wasn't the narrative given to the author upon commencement of the endeavour.

For the next few moments, the screaming and killing ceased as everyone looked around at the dead body of Gnasher, the crazed cannibal of Chichester. It was a title she was given following her execution at the hand of the hangman,

Sling 'em up Sledge. She sank to the floor and, well, for want of a better word…died.

Again.

And all at the working end of a wooden club held by Ol' Barmy himself.

He and many would concur, seemed to be very proud of his evening's work. It could be detailed from the huge grin across his face that extended from ear to ear.

And his proud-as-punch attitude was further enforced when he proceeded to perform some sort of victory dance.

And then followed by the warbling of a folk song or other.

It was quite the spectacle.

And more in line with what I expected a fight to be like.

'Look at me, chaps,' he announced. 'Now that's how you take down a cannibal from Hell. Hit 'em on the head with a big wooden stick. That'll sort it.'

And there was no doubting that.

Although some were easier to impress than others, it seemed.

'Easy target,' shouted Lucy, who seemingly had got herself quite peeved at the prospect of playing second fiddle to a self-proclaimed lunatic on unauthorised day-release from the local nut house. 'But I bet you can't do that to the werewolf or the vampire.'

Harsh words, thought Barmy.

Especially as, up to now, he'd been the only one to register a significant blow, so to speak.

And although his methods may be considered unconventional—if direct—they'd got results.

And perhaps if Lucy had spent more time whacking demons on the head with clubs rather than messing around with bits of bones and tarot cards, their situation might be moving faster towards the positive end of the ledger.

And he told her as much.

This then resulted in a small fracas that only got de-escalated when Gertie intervened and explained to both sides that "This wasn't helping the matter. And if we don't pull together, we'd all be dead come the morning.'

But I, on the other hand, was very complimentary of Barmy's nifty club work and the resulting end product.

'Good shot, old boy. That'll sting a bit in the morning. And what a cracking technique. You'll have to teach me that later.'

A request generously accepted by the great man himself.

Now it isn't common knowledge, but when devils from Hell get killed on the upper surface, they are instantly transported back down to Hell via the medium of flames and lightning; the flames being what happens to the body, and the other being a small electrical event that occurs directly above.

And it is often mistakenly portrayed, that it's the lightning that is responsible for the flames.

But it isn't.

The two are very different events and should be treated as such.

Anything else is giving undue credit to a thing that does not deserve it.

But Barmy's antics had not gone unnoticed, as is often the case when you smash someone's head in with a baseball bat.

'Noooo,' screamed Siren, the three-breasted nymphomaniac that had also managed to tag along to Satan's outing. 'What have you done? You've killed her.'

Which, although could be classed as stating the bloody obvious, was also a statement of fact.

And Barmy, sensing that a period of questioning was coming his way—with perhaps some form of retribution—held the club aloft.

'I've taken your friend to whoop-ass town,' he declared. 'And if there's anyone else that wants some action, well, they can join her. Any takers?'

This, of course was music to the ears of Satan.

For although she was keen on everyone getting their stockings full of goodies tonight—and when I say goodies, I mean the agony of innocent Dinglewits—she never wanted it all to be too easy.

Because that would take the fun out of it.

And what is killing without fun?

So for a bit of resistance to be initiated by this strange, and obviously deluded, loony was alright by her, said she.

Just as long as he didn't get too big for his britches.

Which it appeared he was beginning to do.

'I say, you there,' Satan enquired. 'What's your name? Do I know you? Or more importantly, will I get to know you?'

'Barmy's the name, Satan. And fighting devils like you is the game.'

And he put his club under his armpit and stuck his chest out like a freshly laid peacock.

Satan thought for a few painstaking seconds.

It felt longer, but these things always do.

Especially when it was Satan doing the thinking.

Because it usually *was* quite painful for all concerned.

'Ah, yes, Barmy. I've heard of you. But you're not for me, unfortunately. You're destined for the other place. Which is a shame because I think we'd have had some good times together. But you seem to have led a charmed life, rather disappointingly.'

'Good for you, Barmy,' I lauded. 'That'll show the old dragon. Plus, it looks like you've got away with that one.'

'Which one?'

'The one you've just bashed in with ya slugger.'

'Oh, you mean the bimbo on the floor with her brains leaking everywhere?'

'That's the badger.'

'Yes, I think when you brain a demon from Hell, you get a free pass,' Barmy replied. 'Or at least that's what I've been told. No Hell for anyone killing demons. That's the gossip.'

'By whom?' enquired Satan, looking all surprised, which no doubt you would be when you'd just found out that apparently killing your lot was fair game in the Universe.

And one thing was for sure, she wasn't overly keen for that kind of information to be getting out.

Suppression tactics will need to be adopted.

'Oh, it's just what I've heard. I'm surprised you're not aware of it—if I'm honest. You know, seeing as you're the one on the sharp end of the deal and all that.'

But Satan wasn't aware of it.

She was far from aware of it.

'Aware of it! Aware of it!' she yelled, somewhat proving my point on the matter. 'I'll be bloody well bringing it up with the Universe at the next meeting, that's for sure. The very cheek of it. Making me fair game like I'm some sort of mortal. I've never heard of such blasphemy.'

She clearly hadn't heard of it.

'That bloody Universe thinks it's untouchable,' she continued. 'I'll tell you, one day it will get its comeuppance.'

It was about this time that I felt it was my turn to join in with the gratuities—if gratuities is the word I want.

As since my own drubbing at the hands of a werewolf, I'd been chomping at the bit for the opportunity to give a bit more of the old trash talk, and letting Barmy have all the fun had given me the chirp.

So I stepped up. 'Well, Satan, if you don't mind me saying, but regarding all this massacre at Halloween malarky, it is, well, not to put too fine a point on it, well, it's playing with fire, somewhat. Don't you think? I mean, I know what you're thinking: this Montgomery Plum chap isn't exactly the most innocent of Dinglewits standing here tonight, is he? No, I'm not, that award goes to Gertie, but I do know a good tear-up when I see one. And all this killing and slashing on the night of Halloween—well, it draws attention, if you know what I mean. Let's just leave it at that.'

Satan didn't know what I meant, so she asked me.

To which I answered, 'It means that while you're out here with your girls, having some fun. Killing the living and drinking on their blood. There will be forces working against you. It has to, it's called equilibrium. The Universe must be in equilibrium. So if you thought that you'd just be able to smooch on up in here, up to the land of the living and do as you please, well, you're bang out of luck, I'm afraid. So if I were you, I'd turn around, find a mirror to sort your hair out, and skedaddle.'

Bang out of luck! That was a new one on Satan.

She'd always considered herself to be very lucky—in the sense that being born to rule over Hell could ever be considered lucky.

And being *bang out of it*, as I'd put it, well, that didn't quite cut the mustard.

Especially not tonight.

Her night.

Her own, very special night.

Her very own…very special night that she designed just for herself.

And her only guarantee of a good night out.

And as for mocking her hairstyle, well, she'd never been insulted like that before.

And she didn't much like it.

So she did what every other honest, vain, and dandy-looking demon from Hell would do in this situation: she hit back.

'My hair!' she hollered. 'My hair! How dare you mock the hair of Satan. No one mocks the hair of Satan, or anything of mine else for that matter. That's…that's…that's…Ooh, I don't know what it is, but you'll pay for it with eternal damnation. I'll have you scraping the mud from my boots for the rest of all eternity.'

'Sounds like a long time,' I responded, clearly working on the adage of in for a penny, in for a pound. 'But I'm sorry, old snowflake, but if you must wear your hair like that, then you really should take some volume out of your cheekbones.'

'Out of my cheekbones?'

'Yeah, they're too rounded for that mop on your head. Was your barber drunk when they chopped it?'

This was all too much as, apparently, Satan had put a lot of effort into tonight's look.

And especially the uppermost part, that being the hair, which she'd always prided herself on being immaculate, which of course it was. Hence, why I thought I'd use it to get at her.

'I mean to say, old girl, you look like a rambutan. And that's being generous.'

A good dig: I was chuffed with that one.

I turned and gave a covert thumbs-up to Gertie.

She didn't accept.

'A rambutan, what on Earth is a rambutan when it's at home?'

'Don't you know? Seeing as you've modelled your entire look on one, I thought you'd have known.'

'I don't.'

'Well…let's just say it's sort of a cross between the Beast of Blatherwycke and a troglodyte. Or…imagine if a lychee had sex with a sand squibbler, and the offspring was too hairy for them to love, so they sent it to live in a swamp. That sort of thing.'

Satan was apoplectic.

'Biscuit!' she screamed. 'What is going on here?'

'I beg your pardon, M'lady.'

'Don't be begging for pardons here, Biscuit. I want to know what is going on. This caveman has described me as a rambutan. A blooming rambutan. I don't even know what a rambutan is. He says it's something that comes from a swamp. And I'm presuming that's because of my hair.'

Biscuit held back the laughter, although the shoulders may have given it away.

'And I don't look like something from a swamp, I know that much. But a rambutan. What is a frigging rambutan?'

'A rambutan, M'lady, is an exotic fruit—'

'That doesn't sound so bad.'

'That is generally regarded as the funniest looking fruit ever evolved.'

'Oh…why you contemptuous little runt, Biscuit. We'll discuss this later after I've finished with these Earth slugs. And you'd better have a good explanation for such nasty words.'

'Yes, M'lady.'

'Yes. Good. Well, okay then. Now get lost before I chop *your* head off as well.'

'Yes, M'lady.'

Satan then turned back to me for, what most folk tend to call, seconds.

'And as for you, Mr silly beard and…Mr silly shorts, what exactly do you mean by calling me a horrible name, eh? Speak up.'

And seconds was something I was happy to serve up, especially now that she'd dug out my splendid-looking shorts.

'Look, Satan, all I'm saying is that you should've given more thought to the consequences of turning up here looking like that and thinking that you're going to just run all over us here in Glint Tae. We're a proud bunch, you see, we don't take to being slaughtered willy-nilly. So if you're going to be the grim reaper, or the prophet of doom, or whatever you wanna call yourself—'

'Satan—'

'Then you should've thought better of it, Satan. Because I don't take kindly to anybody coming round here and killing my acquaintances. And neither does anybody else.' And then I went for the jugular. 'And especially not by someone dressed up like a blancmange that's been dropped on the floor, scooped back up into a bowl and left to go off.'

Yes, that'll do it, trash talk accompanied by a victory grin.

But Satan, judging by the colour of her face, had heard enough.

'I'm going to enjoy making you suffer,' she announced. 'And not only that, but when you're lying on the ground begging for mercy, I'm going to make you sing it. And while you're singing for mercy, I'll be dancing.'

But as much as she'd like to rip my throat out and hand it back to me to eat, now would simply not be the right time for vengeance.

It's too early in the night, you see.

And everyone knows that your main adversary always needs to be left to die last.

That way you can kill them slowly and make them pay for their insolence.

Nice and slow.

Like a little cherry on top of a murderous after-dinner pudding.

Chapter 19

The Universe, it is often said, can be a vindictive old bugger at times.

And it is also often said that only the truly insane can make head or tail of its intentions.

Truly insane folk like Barmy, if one was to put a name to it.

I guess that's why no one truly understands him.

They can't; they're too lucid.

But it isn't that he doesn't try to help them understand.

If you spend any amount of time in his presence, he will harp on about the sky rambler; a tiny insect that's commonplace throughout the Universe, but one that no one understands.

Except him.

The sky rambler roams the air currents, seeking a nice home to rest its bones and enjoy the rest of its existence.

Swishing through the breeze and swaying with the wind.

Bobbling about and banging from rock after rock after rock.

Hoping that perhaps this would be the place where it can rest and grow roots, although they don't grow roots.

Until one day, it finally arrives at its destination.

And what happens next?

After many a distance travelled?

Well, it sheds its little wings.

Discards its little legs.

And eats its own little brain.

As if punishment for finding happiness.

Vindictive.

And designed to be such.

And this, as Satan was about to find out, was how the Universe works.

And it's the same for all of us.

Chapter 20

As with all good stories where there is a twist to the plot, foils, faints, and red herrings. It is sometimes appropriate, and indeed essential, to flit backwards in time to offer some substance to events that happened before the big event, if you catch my drift.

So with that in mind, let's discuss what Lucy had got up to.

Well, preparatory to leaving for the last ever night of Halloween at the Old Chapel at Blorkeney Knoll, Lucy sat at her dining room table for a good old spiritual chinwag.

She did that before leaving the house most of the time anyway, but considering the circumstances today, an essentially robust chat was on the cards—which, rather fittingly—takes us to the means by which she spoke with the spirits.

Ordinarily, if, for example, she was popping to the shops or taking the Marsh Boomer for a walk, then a bit of consultation with the tarot cards was all that would be required.

After all, there is no point in overdoing things; you can take up most of your day otherwise deconstructing upside-down hanged men and such like.

Something that Lucy knew all about.

And by all accounts, she was a bit of a whizz with the old *card deck of destiny*.

No one is better if the rumours are to be believed.

Today, Lucy sensed that she needed something more profound than her usual tarot card reading. With that in mind, she prepared herself for deeper exploration, knowing that simply shuffling her everyday pack wouldn't satisfy her craving for greater insight.

Something with a bit more ounce to the bounce is required.

She did have an authentic, and very old, tarot pack that she'd acquired from some boffin collector a few years ago, but she was saving those for a hen do next weekend.

For as you might all be aware, although saving the entire civilisation of Glint Tae might be a noble and laudable cause, it just doesn't pay the bills.

And the bills will need to be paid.

So today, it was to be a bit of Ouija board interaction.

It was the only thing that made sense.

So she turned the lights down, lit the big black candles that lined her dining room in all four corners and got herself comfy.

She'll be throwing some of the old bones as well, of course, you know, just to make doubly sure.

But, well, you know how it is when you're short on time and Satan is on her way to slaughter all and sundry, you just can't get a minute to yourself.

So at present, just the Ouija board will have to do.

But Lucy was under no illusion as to what the spirits would say, they always said the same thing when the chips were down, and the forecast was gloomy with spells of horrific.

They said, 'Knuckle up, it's going to be a rough one.'

Which was a fair point.

Not to say, honest.

If a little too honest.

And there had been occasions in the past when Lucy had begged for a little compassion with their commentaries.

But none ever came.

It wasn't in their nature, it seemed.

But when all was said and done, and whenever Lucy needed advice, Ouija had never let her down, for there always seemed to be someone out there willing to chip in their two-penneth to the discussion and offer solutions.

And who was Lucy to criticise the thoughts of a spirit?

She would never do that. Spirits are cool.

And she was hoping to be one someday.

But hopefully not tonight.

She set up her board, adorned her long purple hooded tunic with a green belt around the waist, and took some deep breaths.

Her long purple hooded tunic was what she called her *full-on* garb.

She wore it mainly when she was feeling nervous or edgy.

And today, she was feeling nervous and edgy.

Very nervous and edgy.

But then, she was always a little bit nervous and on edge when seeking out spirits with the Ouija board; especially (or wholly) after what had happened with King Viktor and the subsequent shit-show that followed.

So I suppose her nervousness and edginess were only to be expected.

She certainly didn't want a repeat of that.

But when considering that a comparable shit-show may occur tonight with Satan out on a bender with her girlfriends, her anxiety levels were at full throttle.

Thus, requiring her *full-on garb* of a long purple hooded tunic with a green belt around the waist.

She sat on a wobbly wooden three-legged stool that had seen better days a thousand years ago and prepared herself for the worst.

'O spirits of the dead,' she began. 'Grant me your words of wisdom. Offer me spiritual solace. And in return I will offer my soul.'

She'd written that opening line herself.

She thought it was chic.

Opening lines to a séance should be chic, if, at all possible, it starts the thing off well.

Then she placed the planchette onto the board and waited.

At first, as is often the case in times of turbulence, there may be more than one spirit willing to give counsel.

I don't know if you've ever come across this.

But the end result is always a mishmash of words which make no sense.

And that was what happened for the first few minutes today.

Everyone chipping in and Lucy getting nowhere fast.

But then, bingo.

A solitary voice emerged from the noise.

And Lucy was off.

WHAT IS THE PROBLEM?

'I need some instruction about tonight,' answered Lucy.

WHY, WHAT'S HAPPENING TONIGHT?

Lucy took a deep sigh.

'Well, apparently Satan is coming to the living world to kill everyone in the name of Halloween entertainment,' she answered.

AND?

'And I want to stop her.'

Which was a reply Lucy didn't think she would ever have to give when the situation was explained as it was.

But there you go.

SO, WHAT DO YOU WANT FROM ME?

'Err, well, just some advice on how to do it? If you don't mind.'

Lucy was beginning to ponder whether this whole conversation was worth her time.

Clearly this spirit was a bit preoccupied at the moment, or simply not interested in getting involved, and what she really needed right now was some razor-sharp logic and ideas on how to fight devils.

WELL I SUGGEST YOU DON'T GO, IF YOU WANT TO STAY WITH THE LIVING.

Good advice, thought Lucy.

Obvious.

And not something that, strangely, had crossed her mind.

But good.

This spirit was certainly thinking outside the box.

But then.

OH, DON'T LISTEN TO HIM, HE IS A USELESS OLD GRINCH, came another response from some other spirit. LISTEN TO ME. I'VE GOT A BETTER IDEA.

WHO ARE YOU?

NONE OF YOUR BUSINESS, YOU USELESS OLD GRINCH. GET BACK TO YOUR DARK CORNER AND CARRY ON HAUNTING THE OLD FOLK. THIS PROBLEM IS WAY TOO BIG FOR YOU.

Lucy stepped in, 'Hang on a minute. And who are you? Have you crossed into our conversation? I say, It's a rum old do when you can't even have a chat with an un-homed spirit without being interrupted. What is the Universe coming to!'

I'LL TELL YOU WHAT IT'S COMING TO—AN END. THAT'S WHAT. AND IT'LL COME TO AN END EVEN SOONER IF YOU DON'T GET HOLD OF SATAN TONIGHT AND SORT HER OUT. SHE'S BANG OUT OF CONTROL. SO YOU NEED TO GET YOUR ACT TOGETHER AND DEFEAT HER OR EVERYONE'S FOR IT. THAT'S WHAT.

Lucy quickly swapped allegiance.

'Good point, new spirit. So, erm, sorry to you, old spirit, whoever you are, but I think I'll listen to this new spirit from now on. It seems more on the ball than you. Sorry. I think you should go back to your dark corner and maybe we'll speak another time, yeah?'

CHARMING.

'Sorry.'

OH DON'T WORRY ABOUT HIM. HE DOESN'T KNOW HIS ARSE FROM HIS ELBOW.

'And you do?'

OH GOD, YES.

'And who exactly are you?' Lucy enquired, now feeling that perhaps they should be on first-name terms considering the stakes.

CRUMP, replied the spirit. I'M AN OLD FRIEND OF MONTGOMERY PLUM. YOU'VE HEARD OF HIM, YES?

'You damn straight I've heard of him. He's my mate.'

OH GOOD, THAT'LL SAVE US A LOT OF TIME. I'VE NOTICED THAT WHEN I HAVE TO EXPLAIN WHO I AM, IT TAKES UP SOME CONSIDERABLE TIME. BUT WHERE MR PLUM IS CONCERNED, WELL, THAT TAKES AN ETERNITY. HE'S A COMPLEX FISH AND NOT ONE THAT CAN BE READILY UNDERSTOOD.

'Tell me about it. It took me ages to figure him out too. And even now I don't think I've quite grasped him fully. He's like a complicated jigsaw puzzle where the bits don't fit together properly, and with some bits missing.'

AND NO PICTURE TO GO OFF.

'So you do know him then?'

OH YES.

'Good, then perhaps we should cut to the chase. Satan is on her way, and I'm up to the lugholes in worry.'

BUT THERE'S NO NEED TO WORRY, LUCY. ALL YOU NEED TO DO IS KEEP MONTGOMERY ALIVE. FOR WHILE HE'S STILL IN THE FIGHT, SATAN WILL EVENTUALLY SUCCUMB.

Now Lucy was well and truly in the dark.

'And how, precisely, am I expected to do that?' she asked.

Of course, she knew that her mate—that being me—was up to the mark when it came to tackling the undead, I'd never let her down before, but Satan—she thought—surely that was a step too far.

Even for the ginger-bearded, short-wearing, demon-fighting legend that I am.

I DON'T HAVE THE ANSWERS FOR EVERYTHING. BUT WHAT I DO KNOW IS THAT SATAN HAS A WEAKNESS. AND IF YOU USE THIS WEAKNESS AT THE RIGHT TIME, YOU'LL BE ON TO A WINNER.

'And what is that weakness?'

DON'T WORRY, I'VE SORTED IT. IT'S ALL IN HAND. ALL YOU NEED TO DO IS MAKE SURE HE STAYS ALIVE LONG ENOUGH FOR EVERYTHING TO WORK THROUGH.

'Work through?'

YES.

This wasn't helping Lucy with her anxiety.

As far as she was concerned, the outlook was gloomy.

Really gloomy.

And just because this Crump fella can speak out from another dimension; it doesn't make him a match for the devil herself.

'I need more information, Crump. I'm fighting Satan here. And just saying "Keep Mr Plum alive", doesn't quite cut the mustard.'

OKAY, OKAY, SETTLE DOWN THEN AND I'LL EXPLAIN ALL.

And that is what he did.

And the next five minutes could soundly be described as interesting.

That is to say, if an entity from another dimension in space communicating through an Ouija board to a medium who was about to fight Satan and telling her all of Satan's darkest secrets and how to manipulate them—could ever be described in any other terms—then I'd like to know.

And if this wasn't such a lethal game of life and death, then maybe Lucy would have been fascinated by the whole situation.

But as it was, she could only take note of Crump's advice and cunning plans, and vow to give it her best shot.

But this was music to the ears of Crump, for he wasn't overly confident that his many conversations with Barmy, back at the asylum, were the sort of conversations that would bear fruit.

Not that Barmy wasn't capable of carrying out his instructions when operating with a clear head, that is.

It was just he didn't have a clear head often enough.

Or ever.

So, having Lucy on board was a much better idea, thought Crump.

NOW, he finished. JUST REMEMBER THE INSTRUCTIONS. IT WILL ALL BECOME CLEAR WHEN THE TIME COMES. I PROMISE.

And with that, he was gone.

Very gone.

And Lucy was still anxious and edgy.

So there was only one thing for it—throw some bones.

Chapter 21

So let's get back to the Old Chapel at Blorkeney Knoll on Halloween night for some more action.

Satan was hard at it, doing what she'd come here to do—namely kill Dinglewits in the name of Halloween fun.

But there was just one minor snag with this.

For as Satan was partial to killing in the name of Halloween fun—something she seemed very good at—I was also partial to getting *my* hands dirty in the name of fun, and that was something I am very good at.

And I was determined to get me a Satan at all costs.

But that meant I was first going to have to get through her friends.

And first on that list was Blood.

The vampire.

The most famous of all vampires.

So famous, in fact, that a few of tonight's guests were happy to get murdered by her just so that they could say that they'd met her.

But I wasn't quite so forthcoming.

And on top of which, I had no intention of being next on the slab and staring up at the lights while my soul was being dished up as the next helping.

I pulled my sword, Excalibur, from its scabbard and took flight in her general direction.

This was a tactic that had always served me well, so far, at least.

But vampires—as I was soon to find out—are cunning little blighters, and Blood was generally considered the top of her class in vampire cunningness.

And this, I found out the hard way.

'Now where did she bloody well go to?' I mumbled, seeing as I was expecting a quick fight and then back home for tea and medals.

For no sooner had I swung my sword swiftly towards her neck, did she turn herself into a bat and swoon off.

'Remarkable! I've never seen the likes.'

Blood was proving to be quicker than even I had envisaged.

But I liked it, as much as anyone could like that sort of thing.

It gave her a certain something that is probably French in origin.

'I wish I could do that,' I shouted to Gertie, as she watched on in shame.

'You probably could if you put the time into practice, you lazy git,' she answered.

To which, again, I chose to ignore, as has been the story of my day.

But Blood wasn't having any of it.

'I'm here, you scuzzball,' she goaded. 'Fancy another try?'

I did, of course, and took another swipe.

And missed.

Again.

Which only provoked another insult.

'You can do better than that! Try harder. I have others to kill, you know. I can't be waiting here all night for you to get your act together.'

I was bemused, I certainly didn't want this to become habit-forming.

So I took another swipe.

Same result.

'Bugger.'

Harsh words were needed, and justifiably so.

'Now look here,' I moaned. 'If you want a fight, then bloody well stand still and let's have a fight. All this zipping around is making me dizzy.'

Blood had perched smugly on top of a piano.

'And be careful on there,' I said. 'It needs to go back in the morning or we'll lose the deposit.'

She had that smile that showed that she too was just a little too pleased for my liking.

And I couldn't wait to wipe it from her face.

'I'm a vampire, that's what we do. We drink blood, we turn into bats, and we live forever. It's not a bad job, is it? But you know, it's not every day that one gets the chance to turn themselves into a bat to avoid a swinging sword. So thank you, whoever you are. And despite your failed attempts, you're really doing your species proud.'

'You're welcome,' I answered. 'But I'm afraid you won't be thanking me by the end of the night when you find yourself skewered on the end of my sword, my dear vampire. For although that was a good move, and one you should be proud of—'

'I am.'

'It will, unfortunately for you, be the highlight of your night.'

'Oh really?'

'I'm afraid so. Oh, and by the way, the name's Plum. Montgomery Plum. And I'll be the one who takes you down tonight.'

Blood smirked and planted both feet firmly on the tiled floor, avoiding the blood, of course.

Then she pulled a whip from her belt and, if I may add, rather skilfully snapped Excalibur from my hands.

'Oh dear,' she laughed, as the cracking sound of metal on tile echoed around the walls. 'It appears you've lost your long pointy thing, it looked good as well. Does that make you feel a bit inadequate?'

I looked at my empty hands and found it hard to disagree with her.

I did feel inadequate.

Quite rudely inadequate, in fact.

But, as it turned out, I needn't have been concerned.

Because Barmy was on the job.

And seeing me in the soup that I was in, he jumped into action.

'Huzzah!' he yelled. 'Cop some of this.'

And a balloon filled with water came flying through the air and plonked itself fortuitously in the palm of my hands.

'Err, cheers, Barmy. Erm, what should I do with this?'

'Chuck it at her, you oaf,' he responded.

'Chuck it at her?'

'Yes, chuck it at her. And chuck it hard. The balloon needs to break.'

It would be fair to say that I was sceptical at this point.

Not because I didn't like chucking water bombs.

Of course, I did.

Who doesn't? Chucking water bombs is the greatest thing that any kid has ever done.

Ever.

But I always feel that when confronted by a killer demon from Hell, something a bit more substantial might be in order.

Like a spear or a chainsaw, perhaps.

Or even a baseball bat.

But certainly not a water bomb.

'Really, Barmy,' I questioned. 'Water bombs? I mean, I know they're fun and all that. But this is hardly the time. Perhaps in the morning we could meet in the park and indulge, but maybe right now isn't quite the right time.'

But Blood had heard enough.

She'd come here to get her fix of fresh Dinglewit blood.

Hot, fresh, and dripping from the veins of screaming Dinglewits.

Not stand around listening while a couple of klutzes make plans for an early morning water bomb fight.

So she took a lunge.

To which, I'm ashamed to say, made me panic and throw the water bomb straight at her forehead.

'Ow,' she muttered. 'That really hurts.'

I looked astonished at Barmy.

Then, I looked astounded at Blood.

Which isn't easy to do in the middle of a fight.

'Well bugger off then, you blood-sucking parasite,' I responded. 'Go suck someone else's blood.'

And after a second to think about it, she duly accepted my invitation, and buggered off.

'Ha, ha, it worked! It worked!' Barmy yelled. 'It worked, it worked. I wasn't sure it would work. But it did. It worked, it worked.'

At this point, I had a few questions.

'You mean to tell me that you didn't know it would work?' This being my first, and very obvious question.

'No. No clue whatsoever. But I'm glad it did, you know. I'm glad it did.'

'Yes, me too. Which leads me to my second enquiry, Barmy. How did you know?'

'The voice, Montgomery. The voice.'

'The voice?'

'Yes, the voice.'

'Oh, the voice, yes, I'd completely forgotten about that. You mean Crump?'

'Yes, Crump. That's him. Crump. And he told me to do it.'

'So, Crump told you to get a water bomb and have it thrown at the vampire?'

'Exactly. It's holy water, you see. From the bowl over there.'

'You mean the font,' interrupted Gertie.

'Yes, that's it. The font,' answered Barmy. 'The voice told me to fill up the balloon with holy water from the font, as you say, and throw it at the vampire. And it worked. It blooming well worked. That's stupendous.'

'So is it dead?' I asked.

'Oh no, it doesn't kill 'em. Gosh, no, it's not that powerful. No, it just sort of puts 'em off a bit. You know, gives 'em the hump. They don't like it, you see. Apparently it stings.'

'It stings?' I repeated.

'Yes, stings. You know, smarms a bit, tickles, burns, you get the gist. They don't like it. The voice told me that. It said, "Barmy, fill the balloon with holy water and get Montgomery to chuck it at the vampire." And that's what I did. And it worked. The voice was right. For once in my life, the voice was right.'

'Erm, you seem surprised, Barmy.'

'Well, yes, the voices in my head have never been right before. Not until now. They've always just got me into trouble. That's why I'm locked up in the loony bin. But not tonight, eh? Tonight it was right. The voice was right.'

'So now what?' I asked.

Barmy shrugged his shoulders. 'No idea.'

'No?'

'Nope. The voice talks to me when he wants to. I don't get a say in it. He just turns up in my head and starts talking. No invitation. No warning. Nothing. He just turns up and starts talking away. I don't know when he'll show up next. Or if he ever intends to. And to be honest, I wasn't sure if he was ever being truthful. You have to admit, it does sound a little bit far-fetched. You know, Satan and Halloween murders, and all that. But boy was he right on that one.'

At that point, it was safe to say, that both Barmy and myself were somewhat lacking in ideas about where to go from here.

We'd had a good run so far, and I've always felt that good runs don't last forever.

But then again, I've also always felt that momentum is key, and you should always strike when the irons' hot.

So we were at an impasse, so to speak.

'How about we try and get somewhere safe?' Gertie suggested, sensing the impasse for herself.

'Good idea,' I answered, knowing that when Gertie uses a tone that implies we should all do as we're told, then we should all do as we're told. 'I suggest we go upstairs.'

'Is there an upstairs?'

'Yes, up that spiral staircase. And I suggest we get up there before that vampire changes her mind and comes back for seconds. We need time to think.'

Others, however, weren't being quite so lucky.

Satan, now seemingly back on song—following a comfort break—was now starting to enjoy her Halloween bash again.

She hadn't taken my advice and visited a mirror, but she was up to her kneecaps in guts and severed heads, which were her intentions all along.

'Woohoo,' she hollered, as another victim fell to her killer fingernails, and laid on the floor writhing in agony while clutching their abdomens in the hope of keeping the innards in. 'This is more like it. Finally, a Halloween party just like the old days. If only Mummy could see me now. This is so much fun. You! Come here and get yourself sliced open.'

SLICE.

'Yes, that'll do for you. Maybe I'll see you in Hell. Biscuit, bring me another.'

Her ever-faithful servant, Biscuit—it must be said—wasn't quite as enthralled in all the carnage as one would have expected from the devil's errand boy.

He'd never been one for blood.

He didn't like the colour.

Perhaps if it was a nice shade of blue or mauve, then maybe he'd be able to get on board a bit more.

But the red that the Universe had opted for, really turned his stomach.

And on top of that, he didn't like screaming.

It was way too darn loud and made of all the wrong tones.

'If you don't mind,' he asked. 'But is it okay if I go and take a quiet seat in the corner and forego the slaughter?'

'No it bloody well isn't,' Satan screamed. 'I need more victims. I don't want to keep walking around to find them. Plus, I need you here to mop my eyebrows. They're getting covered in blood and sweat. It's most uncivilised. Do the honours, will you?'

Biscuit duly obliged.

Because he was many things when he was alive.

A git.

Sure.

And a scoundrel.

Definitely.

But he wasn't uncivilised.

So when confronted with the issue of keeping a pair of eyebrows free from perspiration and blood product, well, he considered that an obligation.

So he moseyed on over to his mistress, and with an undertaking worthy of any serf that had ever had the unfortunate task of serving the queen from Hell, and he wiped.

'That's better. And let there be no more talk of shifting off and sitting in quiet corners either. This isn't a traipse around the park on a Sunday morning, you know. You can't just pull out a book and admire the scenery. This is a slaughter. And slaughters need to be loud and bloody. Capisce?'

Biscuit answered in the affirmative.

'Good, now pass me something sharp. I can't keep using my fingernails, they'll get ruined. I've spent a fortune getting them ready for tonight. And this lot have thick skin.'

Biscuit reached into the bag of tools and pulled out something that looked sharp and deadly.

'Will this do?'

'Do you have anything longer?'

He went back into the bag.

'I have this.'

'Well it's longer, but it's not sharp. Try again.'

More fumbling.

'What about this?'

'Nope. Too shiny. I don't like shiny.'

'Right.'

Yet more fumbling.

'What about this, then? It's sharp and long and not very shiny. Will this do?'

'It's a bit on the dull side. Do you have anything with glitter on?'

'No, M'lady. I have nothing with glitter on. They don't tend to make instruments of death that are glittery. There's no market for it. So this is the best I have. Do you want it?'

'Oh very well. Pass it here.'

Biscuit passed the weapon to Satan and cursed his luck for getting such a gig. She gave the weapon a quick once over.

'It'll do, I suppose. Not much use for the delicate stuff though, is it?'

'What did you have in mind, M'lady?'

'Oh, I don't know, Biscuit. How would I know what I have in mind? And do stop asking me so many questions, can't you see I'm under a lot of pressure at work? Here, hold this,' and she passed him a severed head. 'Now, you tell me how I can use this thing to gauge the eyeballs out, 'cus I'm phaffed if I know. That's what I'm talking about, Biscuit. I want something with a bit of dexterity to it. Something subtle.'

'How about your own fingernails, M'lady.'

Satan gazed at her bloodied fingernails.

'Yes, they're perfect. Here, have this back, you useless grunt, I'll stick with the old and trusted.'

And then she got back to work; slashing, ripping, severing, and every other way of tearing flesh apart.

And that should have been that.

The Universe's most deadly killer, using her favourite weapon to kill folk.

It should have been a formality from this point on.

But this was where the Universe's alternative ending became clear.

Just not to Satan.

Not yet, anyway.

Chapter 22

And so, as the numbers dwindled, and with Satan and friends becoming weary but content with their evening, all the fun and games of the last night of Halloween were starting to come to a close.

The Old Chapel at Blorkeney Knoll was well and truly awash with blood and dismembered bodies. Its walls dripping with blood from every orifice.

The floor completely covered with limbs and heads.

Dead souls making a run for the hills in fear of being sent to Hell.

And the notion that a chapel is a place of safety now well and truly a thing of the past.

It had taken a good few hours to get this far, but now that it had, all that remained were for us two remaining cliques of venerable misfits, currently staring at each other from either end of the chapel, eager to get stuck in for a jolly old dust-up.

It was pretty obvious from the start that this was how the evening was going to end. So the Universe may as well have not bothered with the rest of it and just jumped straight in.

But then, what would be the point of that?

A climax is only a climax when it has a build-up, I suppose.

And, more often than not, the build-up is more enjoyable than the climax itself, I always find.

So, there we were. Satan and her lot, made up of Wolfie, Blood, and a couple of inconsequential groupies guarding the door, while Gertie, Cleese, Lucy, Bonzo, Barmy, and myself, deciding that we'd rather protect the buffet, which we'd all agreed had been the best part of the night so far.

Especially the prawn vol-au-vents, they were delicious.

And if I may also add, the tension in the old place could only best be described as *jittery*.

Next to me, Barmy was doing some peculiar stretching exercise, while at the same time complimenting Bonzo on his choice of socks.

Bonzo was accepting the compliments about his choice of socks and had pulled his trousers up to the knees to show everyone.

Cleese was pouring himself another glass of homemade brain dissolvent and had entrenched himself onto a sturdy chair.

Gertie and Lucy were talking about hairstyles.

And I cracked a few knuckles in an attempt to appear menacing.

So all looked good on our side.

No problems here.

On the other side of the chapel, Satan and her gang grimaced and smirked as they paced to and fro. They were eyeing their next, and quite possibly, final victims of the night.

But to be frank, I was simply having none of it.

In fact, I was starting to get a bit bored of the whole charade.

'I don't know about you, Gertie, old puffin,' I announced. 'But this is all starting to wear a bit thin, don't you think? I mean, it started out okay. I mean, it seemed like good sport at first. And the early exchanges were humorous. Not to say somewhat entertaining. But look at the mess they've made. Who's going to clean all this up? Not me, that's for sure. And the cleaner is laid over there with all her arms and legs pulled off. So what say we put a stop to all this nuisance so we can demolish the buffet and get ourselves to bed.'

Gertie—as one would no doubt feel appropriate at this junction—was confused by the suggestion that I could just *put a stop to all this nuisance* whenever I wanted to and was not backwards in airing this opinion.

'And just how are you proposing to *put a stop to all this nuisance*, can I ask?' she responded.

Just as I said.

And not for the first time tonight, I found myself stating the obvious.

'I think it's time for the magic coin, I reckon.'

'And about bloody time too,' added Lucy. 'Perhaps if you'd done that a few hours ago, all these folk would still be alive, and we wouldn't be up to our shins in blood.'

'But where would be the fun in that? It's Halloween,' I responded. 'No, I think right now is exactly the right time to call it a night. It's the only sensible conclusion one can make. So who's with me?'

They all answered in the affirmative.

With only one downside.

Now that they almost felt like equal partners in the jaunt, they had opinions and questions.

Something I instantly regretted instigating.

'Yes,' I responded after Lucy put her hand up.

'Just a quick one, if you don't mind before we get ourselves killed. But how are we actually going to kill the devils from Hell? Please, don't think I'm at all being a doubting Thomas. After all, I've actually spoken with this Crump chap myself, and he seems reasonably on the ball, all things considered. But, well, he has left us a little light in the way of a plan. That's all I'm saying.'

'Oh, nonsense, old sport,' interrupted Barmy. 'He knows exactly what we have to do.'

'Throw insults at Satan!' chipped in Gertie.

'Exactly.'

'Well that's great advice, but I've just one thing to add.' Gertie had the audience agog. 'But that just ain't gonna work. Now I will openly admit to being on the cynical side on this one. Because I actually want to get out of this alive. And call me a glass-half-full type of girl, but we're about to get in a fight with a werewolf, a vampire, a zombie, Satan, and whatever that other thing is.'

'She's a three-breasted nymphomaniac,' answered Bonzo.

'Fine, but she still needs killing. And that might take more than a few choice words.'

'Good point, Gertie,' agreed Lucy.

And if I was being honest with myself, I agreed too.

'Well, if only that peddler guy was still alive, we could've bought some weapons from him.'

'Who, Biffin?' chipped in Barmy.

'That's the chap. He seemed like a sound sort of bloke. With a positive outlook too. Shame he died so abruptly. His weapons would've come in handy right now.'

Gertie had heard enough.

'Are you for real?' she yelled. 'His stall is just over there. We can take what we want. It's not like he'll be needing 'em now, is it?'

'What, without paying for them?'

'He doesn't exactly need the money either, does he? He's dead. Finished. Extinct. No more. Money is no good to him where he is. So let's grab some weapons and send these bitches back to la la land.'

Lucy gave a high five.

Barmy was also in.

As was Bonzo.

And away they went to get tooled up.

But I chose not to get involved in the outright larceny on a corpse, instead opting to use my magic coin and sword that I'd been carrying all night to do all my killing.

It somehow felt more gentlemanly.

But not until I'd worked my way through some more of the buffet.

Which was probably going to take me some considerable time considering most of the food had been left untouched on account that all of the guests were now hanging from the ceiling or splattered up against the wall.

But when a man's gotta eat, a man's gotta eat.

And those vol-au-vents won't be eating themselves.

So I grabbed myself a plate and a chair and tucked in.

Now, aside from my dietary needs, Satan was also beginning to re-evaluate her evening.

So far, she'd been enjoying her evening jaunt of butchering the living folk of Glint Tae and feasting on their flesh. But as the night grew on, a certain amount of tedium was beginning to set in on her side too.

For although a decent amount of pleasure can be had from skewering the living, and hearing their bones crack as they turn into dust, occasionally a bit more of a challenge was needed.

She was needy like that.

And far be it from me to ascertain the level of indulgence that a beast from Hell would wish to load upon themselves when on a night out with the girls, as I have no knowledge on this matter, but I sort of got the impression that Satan was getting a bit uninterested also.

'Well girls, we're down to the last half dozen,' she said. 'This shouldn't take long, and then we can get back to Hell for the midnight bellringing.'

Her posse, now covered from head to toe in gore and guts, agreed.

At least in principle.

'Yeah, this shouldn't take us much longer,' stated Wolfie. 'I like the look of the weird one with the long ginger beard, I think he'll taste nice. I think I'll eat him next.'

'That's if you can get him away from the buffet table,' responded Satan. 'He looks hungry, the poor chap. But if you don't mind, Wolfie, could you possibly go out of your way and leave him for me? He insulted me earlier, and I've a score to settle. Plus, he looks strong-willed and should put up a good fight. I'm fed up with butchering the weak and feeble without a struggle. It started off okay, but now it's just a bit dull. How about that old codger in the hospital gown, there's plenty of meat on him to get ya big choppers around. How about you start with him and see how it goes.'

'Oh absolutely, Satan, whatever you wish, of course. Besides, I've my eye on the girl with the long dress on, she looks spiritual. There's nothing like eating the spiritual, they taste like almonds, I find. I once ate a witch while she was cooking up a broth; she tasted divine. And tasted like almonds, that's how I know. And since then, I just can't seem to get enough of 'em. It's like an addiction.'

'Have you tried cyanide?'

'Why, is that nice?'

'I don't know, but apparently it tastes like almonds too. It certainly smells of them. Perhaps you should give that a go. And it's probably safer than eating the spiritual because they cast spells and hexes, and one day they'll get you with one.'

'Ahh, so what if they do,' answered Wolfie. 'This can't last forever anyway. Nothing does. So I may as well go out doing the things I love.'

'What, eating witches?'

'Eating anything that lives. No self-respecting werewolf would do any other. So if you don't mind, I'm off for some nibbles. Ta-da.'

Wolfie brushed back her hair with both hands and enjoyed a slow meander over to Barmy who was standing with his rear end half hanging out of his hospital gown.

'You okay there?' she asked.

'Oh fine,' answered Barmy. 'You?'

'Yes, I'm fine too. Just looking for some lunch.'

'Any luck?'

'I think I might just have stumbled upon it.'

Barmy looked around confused, because even he wasn't impressed with what remained of the buffet.

That is to say, what remained of the buffet wasn't covered in blood and guts. But then he got it.

'Oh me! Gosh, that's very good. I thought maybe you'd seen something tasty on the table besides rotten old egg sandwiches and someone's eyeballs. I know I'm struggling a bit.'

'No, no, no, I prefer my food to have a bit more life about it.'

'As in…actually being alive?'

'Correct.'

'Well, then, I'm sorry, but I must disappoint you on that one because I have it on good authority that if I chop your head off with an axe-type thingy, then you'll burn up and be dead. Is that right?'

'Correct again. Spot on. But I've detected a flaw in your plan.'

'And what's that?'

'You don't have an axe-type thingy.'

Then a voice from behind yelled, 'He hasn't…but I have.'

And with a swing of an actual *axe-type thingy*, Lucy chopped Wolfie's head in two and watched her fall to the ground, lifeless and pathetic, except for the occasional muscle spasm.

Which they all found quite amusing.

'Oh that's excellent, Lucy,' expressed Barmy. 'You see, I told you it would work. The voice knows his onions, doesn't he? And that was *his* plan, provide a diversion, then whack her from behind with an axe. And it worked, just as he said it would.'

Lucy and Barmy high-fived and, knowing their work was done for a few minutes, took a smug stance near the drinks table and opened up a bottle of plonk.

'Prost.'

'Prost.'

Clunking sound of glasses.

And then a big slurp.

But Gertie—even though she'd just witnessed the magnificent slaughter—wasn't in such a victorious mood, and felt it her job to, at the very least, offer inquiries on the matter.

'This whole taking the piss theory,' she asked, sort of already knowing the answer as I wasn't one for questioning myself. 'Do you really believe it will work?'

'How do you mean?' I replied, rather predictively.

'What I mean is, shouting abuse at Satan, is that really a good idea? I mean, I understand that you are totally convinced it is, because this Crump fella is telling Barmy it is. But all I'm saying is, shouldn't we at least consider other options.'

'What, apart from the calling her names, or as well as?'

Gertie took a deep breath.

This was going to be painful.

As, apparently, reasoning with me always is.

'All I'm saying is that we should perhaps think whether taunting Satan to the point where she wants to rip you limb from limb is the best course of action here. She is mean, you know.'

'And?'

'And, you numpty, if you're wrong on this, then we're all dead. Got it. Dead. D.E.A.D, dead. And I know you don't care because of this belief you've convinced yourself of that you'll just be reincarnated back into another Dinglewits body. But what if you're wrong? What if Satan hands you your arse and you come back as a dung beetle, or worse?'

I sniggered.

'A dung beetle. The very suggestion, Gertie, old girl. But I do sense your concerns, and I've taken a mental note. When this is all said and done, and I've sent that vixen of death back to hell, I'll sit down and contemplate it further. Is that okay?'

It wasn't okay, but Gertie acquiesced.

'I guess it will have to be, won't it? But what about your friends, they may not be quite so lucky?'

'If the Universe wishes to end their mortal life tonight, then that is what it wants. Things are what they are, Gertie, you know this.'

'And you're happy throwing them to the wolves, are you?'

'The Wolf is dead, Gert. She's just had her head caved in. Didn't you see it? It was most glorious. Lucy crept up from behind and smashed it with an axe. It was awesome.'

Gertie sneered.

'But okay, I get your point,' I cowed, being the top bloke I am, and seeing that Gertie was uneasy by the whole thing. 'But you see, the Universe works in mysterious and wonderful ways, my plum pudding. And everything must be, how everything must be. I think that's been written somewhere.'

'No, it hasn't.'

'Well it should be because it's brilliant. Look, all I'm saying is we've got some inside info on the matter. And when you've got the goods, you've got the goods. That's all there is to it. So it will all work out in the end and be a raving success, I promise. And then we'll go home for tea and medals and have a jolly magnificent story to tell our offspring when we get old. How does that sound?'

Now, this may come as a surprise to no one, but it didn't sound very appealing to poor old Gertie.

And she told me as such.

Quite loudly too.

But then, after getting it off her chest, she left me to my permutations—if permutations is the word I want—and hid in the cupboard.

Just in time, as it turned out.

Because a certain vampire going by the name of Blood was getting hungry again.

And just like Satan, it appeared that she'd chosen her next meal.

'I'll choose the bloke that seems to be as high as a kite then,' shouted Blood. 'The world could do with one less stoner if you ask me. And I do like me some stoner blood.'

'Please be careful,' said Satan. 'We've already lost Gnasher and Wolfie. If you get toasted, then my afternoon tea parties will look quite the barren droll fest. And you wouldn't wish that upon me, would you, Blood?'

'Nope, absolutely not. You can count on me.'

Satan sighed. 'Oh well, if you must, you must. Go on then. Get yourself some fresh meat. But don't be long. I want some fun too.'

This was music to the ears of Blood.

As being quick to devour victims was something of a speciality for vampires.

They simply turn into a bat, fly over to a neck, turn back into a vampire, and get sucking.

And it's an efficiency that had taken many generations to perfect.

Blood, however, wasn't quite as—let's just say—adept as some.

Indeed, she'd already broken a few of her sharpest teeth in the blood lust thus far and really couldn't afford to lose anymore.

Not if she was to continue as a blood-sucking vampire, anyway.

After all, no one is getting scared of being gummed by a vampire, are they?

So, the hapless Blood turned herself into a bat and headed straight for Cleese, the aforementioned stoner who, up to now, had enjoyed a rather quiet night compared to his other fellow partygoers.

And he intended it to stay that way.

And he too had a special weapon.

Garlic.

Lots and lots of garlic.

Not the most obvious choice of ingredient for those who enjoy a drink.

And I can't recall it ever being used before.

But Cleese liked it.

He said it gave the final product a bit of a kick.

And it was probably just as well.

Because vampires don't like garlic.

They're practically famous for it.

So as Blood headed straight for the jugular vein of the spaced-out Dinglewit as he sat barely perched on the edge of a stool—and looking somewhat three sheets to the wind—the whiff of garlic knocked her for six.

'Euww,' she screamed. 'Is that garlic?'

'Oh, yes. Yes, it is,' he answered rather generously, and certainly giving no thought to her intentions. 'Would you like some? I've plenty to go around.'

'Who drinks garlic,' Blood responded. 'I've never heard of such a thing. I'm feeling quite woozy. I mean, I think I'm gonna be sick.'

Cleese laughed.

'They call that *throwing a whitey,* they do. It's very common, so there's no need to feel embarrassed. It happens to the best of us. Just ask my old friend, Monty. He's over there, about to pick a fight with Satan, it seems. He throws them all the time. He's not acquired like me, you see. So I won't judge, don't worry.'

But that was the final straw for Blood.

A vampire can take only so much.

Free-flowing blood, yes.

Especially when it's still warm and gooey.

And beautiful tender meat, yes.

That comes with the turf.

But garlic, well, that seems to be a deal-breaker.

She quickly turned tail and headed back to Satan, who was beginning to think that the night had taken a peculiar twist in a direction not in her favour.

'What's wrong with you?'

'Garlic, Satan. The half-wit is drinking garlic.'

'And?'

'And I can't bear it. It's atrocious. Just the very thought of it makes me want to pull my intestines through my nostrils and fry 'em with onions.'

'That bad, eh?'

'Yes. That bad.'

'Well then, it seems like your night is over. You can't very well kill anything in that state. But I have to say I'm very disappointed in the way things have gone. We seem to be getting picked off one by one here. The idea of this outing was to get myself some fresh meat for my own amusement, not get killed off for theirs. This was supposed to be my night. My very own night. My very own special night that I invented just for me. And look. They're loving it. The strange one with the beard is actually doing a jig. This wasn't supposed to happen.'

'Sorry Satan.'

'Oh. It's not your fault, I guess. You can't help how you're wired up. None of us can. It's just all so very frustrating. This should've been a magnificent swan song. A coup de grace for the miserable Dinglewits on planet Earth who are fed up with the back teeth of the commercialisation of Halloween. My Halloween. A night designed for misery and bloodlust. And what do we have? Those very same Dinglewits laughing and joking. Well, I tell you this, Blood. They won't be laughing for much longer, I'll tell you that much.'

Chapter 23

Sometimes, I find, when fighting an army of the undead, it helps to be a little on the brash side.

Not to say impetuous.

Because these things, you see, can be a bit awkward.

Some would say uncomfortable.

Especially at night.

Because the undead tends to be more uncooperative at night.

Downright obstinate, it's been said.

And worse still, it appears that the undead have an unfair advantage at night that the Universe felt worthy to bestow upon them.

Something that was probably justifiable when it was working out the algorithms, but now just seems unjust.

For as well as being bloody hard to kill in the first place, the undead also grow in strength when under the moonlight.

Something we were completely in the dark about.

But going back to the top of the chapter—when fighting an army of the undead—it helps to be a little on the brash side.

And perhaps, it might have been a little sporting of the Universe to have told me this because I'm not, what you would call, cerebral.

But I am keen.

'Well, if we're through with all the chit-chat, let's get on with it, shall we?' I announced. 'Because I, for one, am starting to get a bit sleepy and wish for my bed.'

'Past your bedtime, eh, Montgomery?' asked Bonzo.

'Oh, way past,' answered Gertie.

'And mine,' added Cleese. 'I like to be in the land of nod way before the sun passes the yardarm.'

'Not mine,' insisted Barmy. 'I like nothing more than to rock at a wrecking pace until the early hours. I'm like an owl.'

'Be that as it may,' I responded. 'But I think it's time we bring this ordeal to its logical conclusion. Those devils from Hell need to be sent back from whence they came, and I need to get me some shut-eye.'

And in true hero fashion, I made an advance towards Satan with my sword in one hand and my magic coin in the other.

For I too, as with Satan, had chosen my foe to fight.

And as with Satan, I'd chosen the one that would likely be the most fun.

And that was Satan.

The queen bitch from Hell.

Defeating her in pitched battle would be a feather in my cap.

A red feather, no doubt.

But she was an unusually formidable-looking old bird, even if I do say so myself.

And not one I could easily figure out.

Of course, I now knew she didn't like a bit of the old mickey-taking, but that would only go so far.

But after that…then what?

It was time to find out.

'So it appears that it's me and you then?' I declared, as I approached my nemesis for the night. 'This is it. The grand finale, so to speak. I hope you haven't wasted your time?'

'Not at all. It's been a blast. It's a shame all Halloween weren't like this, or I would probably have allowed them to continue.'

'Oh, you're ending Halloween, are you?'

'Yep, knocking it on the head. Calling it a day. Putting a sorry line under the whole event.'

'That is a shame.'

'Why? It's gone rubbish. Just a money-making exercise now, not like it used to be.'

'But it is fun though, and I sort of consider myself a knight of Halloween, if I'm being honest. And if this is to be the last ever Halloween, then I'm the last knight of Halloween. Yes, I quite like that title, the last knight of Halloween. In fact, I love the title, just like I love Halloween. Now, what do you say about that?'

'Well, if that's the case, then let's make it the last knightmare of Halloween.'

'Touché.'

'And anyway, you love this? Everyone wearing silly costumes and buying gifts for each other. Parties. Laughter. Rubbish films repeated over and over again. You call that fun?'

'God yeah, it really gets my juices flowing. Gets the old blood pumping through the veins. My favourite night of the year. I mean, surely you like it a little bit, after all, you did invent it.'

'Well thank you. I least I get some credit around here. Yes, I did invent it, didn't I? But I invented it for me. For my own pleasure. Not anyone else's. And as for blood pumping through veins, well, that stopped aeons ago. I just tend to do taxidermy now. That wastes a few hours when I'm bored. I've got quite a good collection now though, if you don't mind me saying. I've got most of the life-forms that have ever lived on planet Earth. The kalypohs, the dinosaurs, the humans, oh and some Dinglewits too, but not as many as I'd like. I think I'll take a few of these home thinking about it, that should pad out the collection a bit. In fact, I think I'll take you home and have you stuffed. That's if you don't mind.'

'Not at all,' I answered nonchalantly. 'But just one thing.'

'What's that?'

'You'll have to kill me first. And as many before you have found out to their own detriment, I'm not that easy to kill.'

'Oh, I do hope not. I've spent the whole evening playing around with the easily killed. Such a drag. I could do with something a bit more challenging. A worthy adversary, if you will. So please, don't disappoint, I've high hopes for you.'

'Well, Satan, I will certainly try my best.'

'Your damnedest even. If you pardon the pun.'

It took me a few seconds to get my head around that joke.

But eventually the penny did drop, and I sniggered in its simplicity.

'Oh, that's very good,' I responded. 'How about some of this for trying my damnedest.'

I grabbed my magic coin and punched her straight on the nose.

Now this, ordinarily, would've resulted in the receiver of such a sock flying across the room and landing in a heap on the floor.

But it was fair to say, that wasn't what happened this time around.

Instead, all that I experienced was a grinning opponent, Satan pulling back her arm, and me getting a punch on the nose sending me into low earth orbit.

I was going to need a better plan.

Or at the very least, a plan in the first place.

'Ah,' I acknowledged. 'I see how this is going. But fear not, Satan, I have more up my sleeve.'

Satan was yet to be convinced on this matter and feared that the imbecile promising so much would just end up offering the same bland and flat entertainment that she'd been enjoying all evening.

'Oh please do try harder,' she encouraged. 'Because if you don't, I'm going to have to kill you quickly and get on with someone else. And as we're running slightly low on Dinglewits here, I could do with you stepping up to the plate.'

Insulted, and marginally embarrassed, I took on board her constructive criticism, if indeed that's what it was, and promised myself that not only would I step up to the plate, but I'd wrap it around her head and ram it down her throat.

And not necessarily in that order.

'I'll give you *try harder*,' I mumbled.

I then fumbled around the pile of dinner plates and flung them, one at a time, straight at Satan's head.

All of which missed.

'Is that it?' she asked. 'Throwing stuff. It's like we're back at school. Don't you have anything else *up your sleeve*?'

I slowly looked up my sleeve.

Then, feeling rather embarrassed…stopped.

'Ha, ha, ha,' laughed Satan. 'You're right about one thing.'

'What's that?'

'You are providing me with entertainment. That was hilarious. I can't believe you actually looked up your sleeve. And it was you who suggested that you had more up your sleeve in the first place. So funny, who are you again?'

'I'm Montgomery Plum.'

'Well, Montgomery Plum. Do you have any other party tricks to cheer me up with? I could watch this all night.'

It was at this point that I had a decision to make.

I could: a) do as requested by Satan and think of other humorous ways in which to entertain her, or b) try again with extreme violence in the hope that, this time, I get to land a winning blow and walk away the victor.

But then a lightbulb appeared above my perfectly round head.

Some would say an epiphany.

Others might describe it as a brainwave.

Better still, it might best be explained as a neuronal innervation between two connecting neurones of the somatosensory cortex that had once fired together to form a weak relationship. But now, through sheer chance, had suddenly sparked to form a recollection of a former memory that, through another connection in a different part of the brain; and probably crossing the corpus callosum, spoke to Montgomery Plum and told me, *'Hey, remember what Clump said to you.'*

'Oh yeah,' I said out loud. 'Now, what did Clump say to me?'

'Eh?' questioned Satan.

'Eh, erm, oh, it's nothing really. Probably just piffle. But it's just that I have this friend, you see, and he lives in another dimension. It's a long story, so I won't bore you with it, but let's just say he's been giving a few of us a bit of friendly counsel on the matter. Sort of, how to go about things.'

'Go about things? Like what?' Satan asked.

'Defeating you.'

'Hmm, now that would be funny if it wasn't so tragic. You do know who I am, don't you?'

'Yeah, you're Satan, right? I think I've heard of you.'

'You think you've heard of me? Are you serious?' Satan squealed. 'Everyone's heard of me. I'm Satan. The baddest demon in the Universe. I'm famous, I am.'

'Are you?' I responded, thinking that if Clump was right, and he seemed to be so far, then I may as well go in with both feet. 'Well, you might be this Satan figure, as you say, but to proclaim yourself as the baddest, well, that's another thing entirely.'

'Are you insane? I'm Satan. The meanest and cruellest devil you'll ever see.'

'Hmm, well, if you say so, but, well, you ain't fooling me. Not with those ears. They're dreadful. And I know I'm not one to talk, but all I'm saying is I think the baddest devil around would have better lugholes than that.'

Satan put both hands over her ears and gave a shriek.

'What's wrong with my ears?'

'Well, it's not as if there's anything wrong with them, per se. A bit on the pointy side, yes. And a tad lob-sided. But I suppose they have a certain charm. In fact, they suit the rest of your face perfectly well. But that's the problem, you see, having those things suit the rest of your face isn't a great endorsement if you know what I mean.'

'No, I don't think I *know what you mean*. There is absolutely nothing wrong with my ears. Mummy tells me all the time how beautiful they are.'

'Well that's a mother's love for you. They just can't seem to see the woods for the trees half the time. What is it they say, unconditional love, yes that's it, unconditional love. It bypasses lots of obvious errors.'

'My ears are not an error.'

'Okay, I'm just putting it out there, that's all.'

'And what do you mean they suit the rest of my face? Surely that's an insult.'

'Well, if the shoe fits. Because I bet you can't get earmuffs to fit those, can you? And don't get me started on your feet.'

'Ooh, where are my friends? Blood! he's being nasty towards me, tell me he's wrong and say something nice.'

So, she did. 'Don't listen to him, Satan,' came the friendly words of support she was expecting. 'Your ears are impeccable.'

To which.

'And what would you know, Blood. Your ears are pointy and vulgar too. Anyone's ears are impeccable compared to yours, even hers.'

'Oh, charming,' Blood answered, not knowing that perhaps a moment of silence would have been far more preferable at that precise junction.

'Really? That's charming, is it? Well how about this for charming?'

Satan clicked her fingers, sending her vampire friend into an instant fireball, followed by a heap of ash.

'Blooming heck!' I shouted. 'You've just destroyed your friend. She's a heap of ash.'

'Oh, she was no friend of mine. Just a hanger-on. She bored me anyway. She can go join the rest of the Universe someplace else. There's plenty more where she came from. Biscuit, come here, I need you.'

Biscuit, Satan's faithful servant, and now her only ally, gave a big gulp and shimmered further into a darkened corner.

'I'm keeping me well out the way,' he muttered. 'You ain't turning me into ash.'

But, as it turned out, he had no choice in the matter.

'Biscuit,' she yelled. 'You're supposed to be here helping me, not cowering over there in a corner. Come here and help.'

'Yes, M'lady of course.'

And he moved slowly from the shadows.

'And what's with all this *I'm keeping me well out the way* business, eh? It's as if you don't want to me to have a good time, isn't it? Well? speak!'

But Biscuit didn't get the chance to speak.

Because I, the Last Knight of Halloween was in full flow.

'Perhaps he knows, Satan.'

'Eh, knows what?'

'He knows how all this ends.'

'What?'

'He knows how it all goes down.'

'Eh?'

'He knows how you end up getting descended back to the depths of Hell where you belong.'

'Rubbish.'

'Perhaps old Biscuit over there isn't quite as daft as you make out he is.'

'Oh yes he is. He is as daft as they come. In fact, you'd be hard pressed to find someone dafter. Ain't that right, Biscuit?'

'Well, erm.'

'Of course it is, you silly man. And you know it is. Now, be a good doggy and pass me something to destroy this cretin before he really annoys me.'

I sensed a glitch in the force.

And furthermore, sensed an opportunity.

And never one to pass an opportunity.

'Is that right, Biscuit? Are you as daft as a brush? Or have you had enough?'

Satan, now looking desperate reached her hand out.

'Pass me something lethal, I said.'

'Eh, Biscuit, are you a puppy dog,' I continued. 'Or are you a chap with pride?'

'He's my puppy dog, that's what he is. Now pass me something lethal, I said.'

'If so, then do it, Biscuit, be the chap you've always wanted to be and pass her something lethal.'

And Biscuit duly did.

He passed her the flamethrower.

That flamethrower.

That flamethrower that was prone to blowing up when it pleased.

'There you are, Ma'am. This should do the trick.'

'Yes, it should,' Satan responded. 'It will be perfect for what I need it for. Now go over there, little doggy, I'll deal with you later.'

'And what are you going to do with that?' I asked.

'I'm going to burn you alive, you wretch of a lifeform. I want to watch you squeal and scream like the slug you are. I want to watch you beg for mercy as the flames eat through your flesh and torment every nerve ending 'til you can bear no more and wither away. I want you to think about all the names you've called me in those final few seconds of life. In those very painful final few seconds of life. I might even go easy on you to make the torture last even longer. So when death does finally come, it will be a blessing that you've prayed for. Yes, that's it, death will be a blessing for you.'

And she held up the flamethrower as if to taunt me of my eventual demise.

'This'll teach you,' she continued, 'to make fun of Satan. To make fun of our family name. Our very proud family name. The name that has brought terror into countless generations before and will continue to terrorise long after you've gone. We're not to be messed with, you know. We're Satan. The gods of evil. The divine malice present throughout the Universe. The only evil that the Universe allows. That's right, we're the only ones that the Universe trusts to deliver the required amount of evil. So this little act of pain infliction will barely register. And you, my name-calling low-life scuzz-bucket, will have perished painfully for nothing.'

'Yeah, yeah, yeah,' I responded, now starting to get slightly non-plussed with the rantings of a deranged homicidal maniac hell-bent on destruction. 'If I had a crown for every time I'd heard that, I'd be a rich Dinglewit by now. So if I were you, I'd take my bony, wrinkled fingers with skin that doesn't want to be attached to them anymore, and just get on with it before you lose your audience.'

'You…You're insane,' Satan hollered.

'I don't believe in insanity, my dear. Insanity is just a state of mind. And my old lemon is too busy with the good stuff. So if you don't mind hurrying up, I've got a buffet to finish.'

Satan screamed the type of screech that can break a crystal glass at 20 paces and placed her finger on the trigger.

'This is what you get for meddling with my head,' she yelled.

Then pressed the trigger.

But alas, the flame intended for old Montgomery didn't materialise.

Not for me, anyway.

Because had had been previously made known to Satan; flamethrowers are just as dangerous for the user as they are for the recipient.

And when a flamethrower gets tampered with, as this one had, then the odds of it blowing up in your face were even greater still.

And the pain and scream that was intended for my good self, ended up being the pain and screams of Satan.

And instead of Montgomery Plum writhing on the floor in agony, it was Satan.

And instead of me wishing for death to come quickly, it was Satan.

And on today of all days as well.

Halloween…her special day.

The day that normally cheers up the old python above all other days.

Halloween—*her* day.

Her very own…very special day that she designed just for herself.

Her only guarantee of a good night out.

Her only guarantee of a good night out, full of plenty of blood and guts and a hatful of gruesome murders.

Perhaps a little bit of torture, if the mood allowed.

And maybe the odd bit of flaying.

Or even a decapitation or two.

But definitely something along those lines.

A night when she can carry out all of her vendettas in a civilised and bloodthirsty way that is socially acceptable, no questions asked.

It wasn't supposed to end like this.

It wasn't supposed to end with Satan herself burning to an ash pile, which then got kicked away by Biscuit as he made his way to the buffet.

But that's the Universe for you.

It can be a right vindictive bugger at times.

Encore

Oh yes, and there is one more thing to mention before I forget, and that's the matter of the chap who gets eaten by his own socks.

Do you remember?

His name was Bonzo.

Yes, that Bonzo.

The very same Bonzo who just survived Satan's last night of Halloween party.

The very same Bonzo who had managed to stay out of trouble all evening when all around him were losing their heads, quite literally.

And the very same Bonzo who was feeling quite smug about it too.

'You see, that's how you do it chaps,' he announced with a large degree of pride and self-assurance. 'Keep your head down, and all will end well. Just look at me, the Bonzo. Not a smidgen of blood on my threads. And not a hint of a bruise on my face. You lot should take note. This is how you survive a night fighting Satan without busting a sweat.'

Now, as mentioned before, Gertie wasn't Bonzo's biggest fan.

She thought he was creepy.

And not a little bit slimy.

Just the way he cavorts around the place like he owns the joint, riles her up something rotten.

But she had to admit that tonight, however, he might have a point.

'D'ya hear that?' she asked me. 'He's had the same experience as you, and yet he hasn't had to do a single thing. Perhaps, and that's all I'm saying but, perhaps, you should take note.'

'Of Bonzo?'

'Yep.'

'Take note of Bonzo?'

'Yep, you heard me.'

'Well that's a first. You can't stand the geezer. You think he's a charlatan.'

'No, I think he's a snake and a narcissist. And at some point in his pitiful life, all his indiscretions will come back to haunt him. But on this, I think he might have a point.'

'Explain further, my little pumpkin.'

'Do I need to? Take a look, he's dancing around the hall as if he'd single-handedly defeated Satan all by himself.'

I did look.

As did Cleese.

As did Lucy.

And Biscuit.

Then finally joined by Gertie.

Which meant that everyone who was still alive was now looking at Bonzo dancing.

But of course, he wasn't dancing.

And his delight at being present at such an event had also taken a twist.

His socks, as if I need to mention, had seemingly grown fangs and were now eating away at his legs.

'Should we help?' asked Gertie.

'I dunno,' I answered.

'Maybe we could give him some advice,' stated Lucy. 'Like *take your socks off*, or something along those lines.'

'You'd think he'd figure that out for himself, wouldn't you?' asked Gertie.

'Well, he was never the brightest spark in the pack, was old Bonzo,' I responded. 'Perhaps we should offer moral support. Because I don't much fancy his chances against them devil socks. They look tasty.'

'Yeah, good idea,' said Lucy. 'Go on, Bonzo, you can do it!' she shouted.

But it was all in vain.

Because Bonzo wasn't able to protect himself from being eaten alive by a pair of socks.

As silly as it sounds.

And as the seconds went by.

And as fewer and fewer limbs remained on the trunk of Bonzo.

The life that was once a cad and a gunslinger became just another carcass that'll need burying in the morning.

'Oh dear, a sad end to a sad life,' I suggested. 'He would've wanted a better death.'

'He *was* the centre of attention. He would've wanted that.'

'True, Gert, very true. That will be comforting to him in the next life.'

Then we all turned to look at Biscuit.

'Good job, sir,' I complimented, thinking that a good job well done was a good job well done. 'You are indeed a fellow of the highest order. So what plans do you have now?'

Biscuit held his head up high.

'I'm going to make amends for some things I did.' He answered. 'It may not be possible, but I'm going to try.'

'Good chap. But one question before you leave. The flamethrower, how did you know?'

'Oh, yeah, well, this may sound a bit crazy, but I've been hearing this voice for a while, and he told me what to do. Crazy, yeah?'

'Not at all, sir. Perfectly satisfactory. Especially, in my world. Now if you will forgive me, old Biscuit, my bed is calling, and I'm taking the missus home.'

I put my arm around Gertie's shoulders and headed for the door.

'You okay, Gertie, old sponge? Fun, yes?'

'Yes, I suppose that was fun, in a macabre kind of way.'

'Absolutely. And while we're on the matter of the macabre, I have a question. It's been playing on me all night.'

'Go on, ask.'

'Have you ever wondered what it would feel like to drill a hole into someone else's head?'

The End